*Look what people are saying about
these talented authors...*

Kimberly Raye

"Kimberly Raye is hot, hot, hot!"
—*New York Times* bestselling author
Vicki Lewis Thompson

"Amusing, erotic...Raye writes
a very naughty book!"
—*Romantic Times BOOKreviews*

Alison Kent

"For me Alison Kent's name on a book means that
I am guaranteed to have a story that is realistic,
entertaining, compelling and sexy as all get out."
—*ARomanceReview.com*

"Alison Kent delivers a knockout read."
—*Romantic Times BOOKreviews*

Cara Summers

"With exquisite flair, Ms. Summers thrills us
with her fresh, exciting voice, as well as rich
characterization and spicy adventure."
—*Romantic Times BOOKreviews*

"I can't wait to read more by Cara Summers."
—*The Best Reviews*

ABOUT THE AUTHORS

USA TODAY bestselling author **Kimberly Raye** has always been an incurable romantic. While she enjoys reading all types of fiction, her favorites, the books that touch her soul, are romance novels. From sexy to thrilling, sweet to humorous, she likes them all. But what she really loves is writing romance—the hotter the better! Kim lives deep in the heart of the Texas Hill Country with her very own cowboy, Curt, and their young children. Kim loves to hear from readers. You can visit her online at www.kimberlyraye.com or at www.myspace.com/kimberlyrayebooks.

Alison Kent is the author of a handful of sexy books for the Harlequin Temptation line, including *Call Me*, which she sold live on CBS *48 Hours*, a number of steamy books for the Harlequin Blaze line, including *The Sweetest Taboo* and *Kiss & Makeup*, both Waldenbooks bestsellers, as well as several stories for other imprints. She is also the author of *The Complete Idiot's Guide to Writing Erotic Romance*, and writes full-time from her home in Houston, Texas.

Cara Summers has written more than twenty-five books for Harlequin's Blaze, Temptation and Duets lines. Her stories have won several awards, most recently the 2007 Golden Quill Award for Best Hot, Sexy and Sensuous Romance. Cara loves writing for Harlequin Blaze because she can write so many different kinds of love stories—from Gothic thrillers to light romantic comedies, and last but not least, a romance about a Texas Ranger! Cara's new goal is to visit Austin and meet a Texas Ranger in person.

TEX APPEAL

Kimberly Raye
Alison Kent
Cara Summers

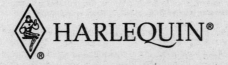

HARLEQUIN®

TORONTO • NEW YORK • LONDON
AMSTERDAM • PARIS • SYDNEY • HAMBURG
STOCKHOLM • ATHENS • TOKYO • MILAN • MADRID
PRAGUE • WARSAW • BUDAPEST • AUCKLAND

ISBN-13: 978-0-373-79379-2
ISBN-10: 0-373-79379-0

TEX APPEAL
Copyright © 2008 by Harlequin Books S.A.

The publisher acknowledges the copyright holders of the individual works as follows:

REAL GOOD MAN
Copyright © 2008 by Kimberly Raye Groff.

UNBROKEN
Copyright © 2008 by Mica Stone.

I CAN STILL FEEL YOU...
Copyright © 2008 by Carolyn Hanlon.

This edition published by arrangement with Harlequin Books S.A.

® and TM are trademarks of the publisher. Trademarks indicated with ® are registered in the United States Patent and Trademark Office, the Canadian Trade Marks Office and in other countries.

www.eHarlequin.com

Printed in U.S.A.

CONTENTS

REAL GOOD MAN

Kimberly Raye

To all my wonderful readers
Your support and encouragement
mean the world to me!

Prologue

New Year's Eve...

SHE WAS *not* going to kiss him.

Sophie Cameron closed her eyes and tried to ignore the strong, purposeful lips that nibbled and teased and begged her to open up. The smell of expensive cologne and rich champagne filled her nostrils. The heat coming off the six-foot-plus of powerful male drew her closer and she stiffened, determined not to lean in, to keep things strictly professional.

The way she'd been doing for the past four years since tall, delicious Jarrod Tucker had taken over the operations division for Deep in the Heart Communications. DITH owned almost every major newspaper in Texas, as well as several local community publications. Sophie had been the marketing director for the past eight years, a job she'd more than earned with a Master's degree in communications and a hellacious amount of overtime. But since she was the only daughter of newspaper guru and DITH president Jackson Cameron, there'd been several employees who'd resented her waltzing in and taking charge. She'd won them all over and earned their respect by keeping her mind on business and following a strict work ethic. One she was about to shoot to hell and back if she gave in to her desperate hormones, threw her arms around Jarrod and kissed him the way she wanted to. The way she'd dreamt of doing since he'd moved into the office next to hers. Much too close for her peace of mind.

Hell, forget kissing. She wanted to peel off his clothes and see the rest of the dragon tattoo she'd caught peeking over the top of his board shorts at the company pool party last year. She wanted to follow the intricate design all the way down the hard, muscular plane of his lower abdomen until she reached the substantial package pressed up against her.

He shifted, fitting himself more fully against the cradle of her thighs. A missile of heat rushed from her head to her toes and set off tiny explosions along the way. Her pulse throbbed. Her nipples tingled. Her thighs shook. Her knees trembled. Her toes quivered.

She leaned into him just a fraction—

Hello? her sanity prodded. *This is a very bad idea. You're coworkers. You know better than anyone what happens when you mix business with pleasure.*

She'd acted on a whim once before and ended up having a one-night stand with one of her father's interns. Not only had the guy told his buddies in the lunchroom, but he'd turned an hour of so-so sex into a wild, hot night that included a strip-tease, some S and M and a cat named Coco.

Sophie didn't even own a cat, much less a gallon of liquid latex.

The truth had meant little, however. It had been her word against the intern's, and his story had been ten times juicier. It had taken months for the rumors to die down. No way was she putting herself through *that* again.

But Jarrod wasn't a hormonal twenty-something with a fridge full of beer and a couple of frat buddies crashed on his couch. He was a thirty-three-year old *man*. Intelligent. Successful. Trustworthy.

She knew that firsthand. While she'd refrained from getting involved with him romantically, they'd become good friends. Sophie didn't just lust after him. She liked and respected him. Both as a man who spent every Saturday playing the loving uncle to five nieces, and as a colleague who'd helped double the company's overall circulation.

He'd been instrumental in ironing out a solid implementation plan for her latest marketing endeavor—a Valentine's Day contest that would run in the "Sex in the Saddle" column, a popular weekly installment for Lonestar singles that appeared in three of DITH's biggest newspapers—the *Houston Dispatch, San Antonio Star* and *Austin Herald*. Since each paper had its own "Sex in the Saddle" editor and ran its own content, the contests would vary from city to city. The only requirement? A sexy theme in honor of the holiday. Each city's paper would pick their own winner, and the contest that received the biggest number of entries would win a bonus to be distributed between the column's editor and staff.

Jarrod was pulling for San Antonio since it was his home town, while Sophie leaned toward the biggest city—Houston. Not that she really cared who won as long as the overall result meant more subscribers. Still, the planning had been fun. And stressful. She'd spent every day since Christmas brainstorming seductive themes with Jarrod to offer as suggestions to the three "Sex" editors.

They'd finalized all the details less than a few hours ago. Just two hours shy of the New Year. Much too late to make it to the company party being held downtown, but not too late to crack open a bottle of champagne and have a toast of their own.

A drink, her conscience reminded her. No touching. No kissing. Just *no!*

Her mouth tingled and her nerves buzzed. Her fingers itched to dive into the short dark hair that brushed the crisp white collar of his dress shirt.

"Aren't you tired of fighting?" he breathed a heartbeat later when he pulled away. They stood near a wall of windows that overlooked downtown Dallas. A frown tugged at his lips.

His deep-blue eyes were glazed with unspent passion. "You know *this*—you, me—it's going to happen. It's just a matter of when."

She fought for a deep breath and her control. "Does that line usually work?"

"Sometimes." He shrugged. "But if all else fails, I have to get creative."

"As in?"

"You must be a parking ticket because you've got *fine* written all over you."

A grin tugged at her mouth, dying a quick death as her gaze locked with his and she couldn't help but think that maybe, just maybe, he was right. Her heart gave a double thump. She definitely felt something for him. Something she'd never felt for any other man. Something that scared as much as it excited her.

"Out of all the newspapers in the world, I walked into yours," he told her. "I had a dozen offers, several better than this. But I came here."

"You were born and raised in Texas. You wanted to come home."

"Maybe. And maybe I had a gut feeling about this job. About you."

"And maybe you're just horny."

A smile played at the edge of his sensuous lips. "That, too." The expression faltered. "I mean it, Sophie. There's more here than just lust. I like you. You like me. It's fate."

She shook her head. "There's no such thing."

Not as far as Sophie was concerned. The daughter of a newspaperman, she'd been raised to reveal hard facts. She didn't put her money on intangibles. She left that to the tabloids.

His gaze caught hers. "Come home with me tonight."

"And what happens on Monday? I don't want an awkward morning-after."

"Who says it'll be awkward? I really like you, Sophie.

And I want you. I always have. Give it a chance. Give us a chance. It's meant to be."

Yeah, right. That's what she wanted to tell him. What she had every intention of telling him. But when she opened her mouth, her hormones slid into the driver's seat and she heard herself say, "Are you willing to bet on that?"

"What do you have in mind?"

"The Valentine's Day promo. Why not put more on the line than an employee bonus?" When he looked intrigued, she added, "You say it's fate. I say it's lust. Let's put it to the test. I'll take Houston. You take San Antonio. We'll leave Austin to chance. If you win, we spend the night together. If I win, we forget the attraction and keep our relationship strictly professional."

"And if Austin wins?"

"Then it's fate and we get together." She smiled. "I'm offering two out of three. You can't beat odds like that." She licked her lips and his gaze snagged on the motion.

"Okay." His eyes smoldered and he swallowed. "You're on."

1

*Skull Creek, Texas (forty-five miles north of San Antonio)
One week before Valentine's Day...*

IT WAS *just* a penis.

Cheryl Anne Cash drew a deep breath and tried to calm her frantic nerves. A sophisticated, worldly, do-anything city girl *did not* freak out at the sight of a guy's johnson. And she certainly didn't hesitate. Or blush. No, she simply tackled the situation with an interested gaze, a steady hand and an attitude that said *no biggee.*

Except that it was a biggee. A gargantuan monster, in fact, compared to the average male penis which was only five and a half inches long when erect—a little tidbit she'd picked up during her Internet research on the subject.

She eyed the specimen at her fingertips. This baby came in at a full twelve inches. Easy.

She drew a deep breath and gathered her composure. Reaching out, she touched the long, smooth shaft and eased her trembling fingers up and down in a quick slide.

There. That wasn't so bad. The thing didn't sprout horns. Or jump up and bite her. Even more, she didn't pass out from embarrassment. Nor did steam shoot out of her ears. A major coup since her cheeks felt as if they were on fire.

She shifted her attention to the forty-eight-inch plasma television her parents had bought her as a going away present six weeks ago. She studied the latest technique being demon-strated by a buxom blonde with bedroom eyes, bee-stung lips and crimson-tipped nails. After a few thoughtful seconds, Cheryl tackled the task with both hands.

"The key is to keep a firm grip," Buxom Blonde said, her tone bold and pronounced. While the appearance said *ditzy porn star,* the voice told a very different story. Smart. Educated. Knowledgeable. At least when it came to sex. "Despite male perception, the penis is far from invincible. It's very possible to cause serious bodily injury during an intri-cate hand technique, which would obviously undermine the overall objective—to increase the pleasure for both partners. Therefore make sure the fingers are touching at all points, but *do not* squeeze…"

Cheryl Anne fought down her reservations and followed along for the next few minutes, practicing the various move-ments on the sizeable member in her grasp. Her right hand did a twist and curl around the base of the shaft. Her left petted and stroked. She even practiced licking her lips and lowering her eyelids just enough to give her that hooded, bedroom look as she eyed the object of her attention.

Soon she moved with confidence, her grip just right, her technique smooth and polished, as if she'd been doing it for six years rather than a measly six weeks.

She could definitely do this.

In private, a voice reminded her. With the instructional video *Hand Jobs Made Easy* blazing in front of her.

But could she do it in front of a bunch of paying custom-ers eager to beef up their own sexual résumé?

Maybe. Maybe not.

In exactly five hours and forty-five minutes—at seven-thirty that very evening—she was going to find out.

She would have half the females in Skull Creek sitting in her sparse living room, looking to her for guidance.

Women who were sacrificing time with their significant other in the name of education. They would expect expert advice on how to jumpstart their relationships, and plenty of snacks to fuel the process.

Her gaze swept the small card table set up in her microscopic dining room. She had a half dozen bowls overflowing with everything from Chex Mix to Doritos, Cheez-Its to trail mix. She even had a vegetable tray that she'd sliced and diced herself.

The snacks she had covered.

As for the expert advice...

Eyeing the newly framed diploma from the UniversityofLove.com that hung on her wall, she tried to summon her courage. She'd completed every assignment of the online course *and* she'd made a perfect score on the final exam, and so she'd earned the title of Carnal Coach, as well as the Pleasure Chest of educational tools sitting on her coffee table and the phallic-shaped name tag pinned to her chest. She was more than ready to instruct her first group of paying customers.

Without getting embarrassed.

The thing is, when she'd signed up at the UniversityofLove, she'd expected to learn something about, well, *love*.

To have and to hold. 'Til death do us part. Forever and ever... That sort of thing. But other than a small section entitled "Revving up the romance"—which offered tips like writing daily love notes and starting the morning with a lingering kiss—the majority of what she'd learned revolved around the big S.

Not that being a sexpert was bad. It was great for a woman determined to do a complete one-eighty from boring, naive, sheltered country girl to exciting, knowledgeable, worldly woman.

Cheryl Anne drew a deep breath and went over her demonstration a few more times using the gonzo "penis"––also known as a banana.

Being the youngest and only daughter of overprotective parents, she'd lived her entire life being coddled. Her mother and father were both obsessive-compulsives who worried about *everything,* from allergies to natural disasters. There'd been a can of disinfectant in every room, a No Pets Allowed sign posted in the front yard and a half dozen weather alert radios scattered throughout the large farmhouse. They'd gone out of their way to keep their children safe, to the point that they'd isolated Cheryl and her older brother Dillon from the rest of the world.

Dillon had been a bookworm who'd spent most of his time indoors because of their mother's fear of pollen and insect bites. He'd never mowed the grass (dangerous machinery) or camped out with his friends (the woods at night? Shudder). He'd never even played sports. Not that their parents had forbidden anything, but they'd had a way of pushing their children in the "right" direction.

Other than one wild night when she'd turned eighteen and gone skinny-dipping down at Skull Creek, she'd spent her entire life playing it safe. Partly because she hadn't wanted to hurt her parents who, while extreme, had always meant well. And partly because, after leading such a sheltered life and being dubbed a geek, she'd actually *felt* like one.

She wasn't very pretty or overly charming or supermodel skinny. Rather, she had dirty-blond hair and an okay personality and a little too much junk in the trunk—and not enough in the chest. Sure, she had nice eyes and a cute smile, but she was still just average. Plain. Blah.

Ditto for her older brother.

Cheryl and Dillon had been the only twenty-somethings in Skull Creek still living at home. While Dillon had finally moved out six months ago, he'd still been the same geeky guy she'd grown up with.

Until last month, that is.

Just like that, he'd ditched his thick black glasses and pocket protector. He'd gone from bony to buff, traded in his slacks and button-downs for T-shirts and leather pants, and he'd even bought a custom-made motorcycle. He now spent his nights cruising around town. And—and this was the biggee—he had half the women in town panting after him.

Cheryl, on the other hand, had never had anyone panting after her.

Sure, there was Dayne Branson, her longtime steady boyfriend, but he didn't count. Dayne, a once-upon-a-time steer roper who now owned a local construction company, never panted, even when he faced off with a wily calf or picked up a nail gun to help out his crew. Rather, he smiled a lot. And winked. And oozed good ol' boy charm.

Enough to stir her hormones into a frenzy every Saturday night when they met for their weekly date aka roll in the hay. Despite their first wild night together (see the skinny-dipping above), Dayne had become just another part of her routine. While the sex itself was good, it was always the same.

Same time. Same place. Same position.

Predictable.

Safe.

No more.

She wasn't sure what had prompted her brother's about-face. She only knew that it had forced her to take a long, hard look at herself. If Dillon—known to the fine, upstanding citizens of their desperately small town as Dill Pickle thanks to the costume he'd worn as a kid in the Skull Creek Elementary health pageant—could declare his independence and go after his dreams, so could she.

Cheryl Anne was through with safe. She wanted to spread her wings, to take some chances, to shake things up.

Professionally and personally.

She'd left her parents' place and bought a small house near

the main square of town—hardly the bustling metropolis she envisioned herself living in, but still a step in the right direction. She'd sold her piano, packed away her chess set and adopted a puppy from the local SPCA. She'd ditched her old tennis shoes and sweats and spent an entire day shopping in San Antonio. *And* she'd left her job as a nail technician for an exciting career helping clueless women revive their stale relationships.

At least, that had been the job description listed online. In reality, however, it was more like a semi-embarrassing career giving verbal instruction and hands-on demonstrations for every sexual technique in the eighty-five-page course syllabus she'd recently memorized.

She ignored a niggle of regret. Sure, it wasn't exactly what she'd envisioned, but it was much more stimulating than listening to customers debate the merits of acrylic verses gel.

Bottom line, she'd said goodbye to her old routine, including Dayne.

She wasn't sure if he'd taken the news well or not—she'd broken up with him via voice mail—but he had left her a message agreeing to give her some space. She knew he thought she was just going through a phase and that she would change her mind.

She wouldn't, even if she did sort of miss him.

Not that it was Dayne she actually missed. It was the idea of having a steady boyfriend, even one whose idea of a romantic evening was a slap on the rump and a "Hop on, honey!" But steady was overrated. For ten years they had drifted along, never seriously discussing their future. She wasn't even sure if Dayne wanted to get married or have kids.

No more. She needed a new man. Someone romantic. Wild. Spontaneous.

Which was why she'd signed herself up for several online dating services. She'd also paid for a class at the local junior college—Mingling in the New Millennium. She'd become a faithful *Cosmo* magazine subscriber, and had started reading the weekly "Sex in the Saddle" column in the *San Antonio Star*. She'd even entered the Valentine's Day contest being sponsored by the newspaper. In honor of the holiday, the *Star* was offering a free sensual home makeover—Romancing the Room they were calling it—to the geekiest subscriber. To enter, she'd had to describe in fifty words or less why she deserved to win.

She'd done it in thirty.

Of course, she didn't *expect* to win. The contest was open to any and all readers—those who actually lived in the city as well as the surrounding areas—so the paper had undoubtedly been flooded with entries from equally clueless individuals.

Still, it was the principle of the thing. Writing the entry had been her way of saying goodbye to the old Cheryl Anne. She was taking every possible step in her life to ditch the *blah* and grab some *va-va-va-voom*.

She stared at her small living room lined with the folding metal chairs she'd borrowed from the seniors' center. Rather than take her mother's old gingham couch that was collecting dust in the attic, she'd made up her mind to buy all new furniture. She'd even invested in several decorating magazines and mapped out the perfect decor for her new home—lots of pale colors and clean accents. Something tasteful and modern—the opposite of the paisley-print room she'd had at home.

All the more reason to can her doubts and get her act together. She needed money and so, she had a job to do.

She finished up with the banana and added it to the overflowing stack that sat in a fruit bowl near her Pleasure Chest. The three dozen extra-large, passion purple vibrators she'd ordered hadn't come in yet and so she'd had to improvise. She'd wanted cucumbers because they had a wider girth and were, therefore, more challenging to women with smaller hands, but Mr. Presley at the Piggly Wiggly had been running a special on Chiquitas. Since she'd sunk most of her money into the vibrators, she'd gone the cheaper route.

A bad move, she decided as she eyed the long, slender fruit. This was her first workshop. It would set the stage for all others to come. The registrants would either tell all of their friends, who would tell all of *their* friends, who would tell all of *their* friends, or demand their money back. The last thing she needed was to cut corners, particularly with Old Lady Shubert signed up.

The woman was always the first picked for the tug-o-war team during the senior Olympics. And she'd been single-handedly responsible for cracking and shelling the twelve dozen pecans used in the pies featured at the last Senior Ladies' Bake Sale. Five seconds in the Widow Shubert's grip and the banana would be history.

"I need cucumbers," she announced to the ball of sleeping fluff parked under a nearby folding chair.

Taz, part doormat/part frantic puppy, lifted his head and started to wiggle his tail.

"Sorry, buddy. You can't come this time. But I promise to take you for a walk this evening if all goes well." She scooped up the dog and headed for the bathroom. She set him on the brand-new pet bed set up in one corner, rushed back to the kitchen and snatched up her purse. If she hurried, she could make it before the market closed—

"Congratulations!" the cry rang out as she hauled open the front door and found herself blinded by several camera flashes.

She blinked and tried to focus on the handful of strangers crowding her front porch. "Excuse me?"

"Cheryl Anne Cash?" asked a hunky, handsome man with the whitest teeth she'd ever seen. He wore slacks and a pullover Henley, and she knew right away that it wasn't the UPS guy.

"Yes." *Click.* She blinked frantically, trying to see as a

dozen red roses were thrust at her. "Wait—" *Click.* "What—"
Click. "I don't—" *Click, click, click!* "Who are you?"

"Randy Miles." A strong warm hand clasped her free one.
"I'm the marketing and promotions manager for the *San
Antonio Star.* And this is Darryl Boyd—" he pointed to the
man wielding the camera "—one of our photographers. And
Kimberly Jackson from Alamo City Interiors. And her assistant, Angela Stone. And Jimmy Powell from Powell Renova-
tions. And this—" he indicated the petite blonde next to him
"—is Lauren Nash, the editor for our weekly 'Sex in the
Saddle' column."

"Hey there, honey." The woman waved French-manicured
fingers while Cheryl's brain raced to process the smiling faces
and figure out what was happening.

The newspaper? Here? *Now?* But that could only mean—

"Your entry blew everybody away. Twenty-eight and still
living at home?" Randy went on. "With your parents *and* an
older brother? Definitely a first."

"I loved the part about the portable snake bite kit that you
carry in your purse," Lauren chimed in.

"Used to carry," Cheryl blurted. "I don't do that anymore."

"You're definitely our most sensually clueless subscriber,"
Randy went on, "which means that you, Cheryl Anne Cash,
are the winner of our Valentine's Day Romancing the Room
Makeover!"

The words registered. Shock bolted through her and her
mouth dropped open and—

Click!

2

DAYNE BRANSON liked sex.

Hell, he *loved* it.

As much as the next red-blooded cowboy with a weakness for great legs and an addiction to soft, sweet-smelling skin. And he certainly didn't have a problem with a woman trying to sex up her life.

Unless, of course, said woman was the one who'd dumped him a few weeks back.

"I *told* you it was Cheryl Anne's place."

Dayne tipped back the brim of his straw Resistol and stared at the cars that crowded the curb outside the small two-story traditional that sat on the corner of Main and Fifth in the heart of downtown Skull Creek. It was Cheryl Anne's new house, all right. His muscles stiffened and his gut twisted.

"I told you that was a five and not a seven," the man sitting next to him in the Chevy truck told him. "Margene's fives always look like sevens when she comes back from the beauty shop."

Dayne's gaze shifted to the work order taped to his dash. When he'd first glimpsed the address for his next job, he'd hoped like hell that it was wrong. It had to be because no way was *his* Cheryl Anne the one getting the romantic home makeover being sponsored by the *San Antonio Star.*

And so he'd convinced himself that Margene had made a mistake. The woman was sixty-four going on seventeen. She had an addiction to leopard-print pants and a weakness for manicures. She was also filling in for her granddaughter—Dayne's secretary—who was on maternity leave.

Margene had just come back from the local beauty salon, To Dye For, when she'd gotten the call that someone in town had won a makeover. The designer in charge—-a Randy something or other—wanted a local contractor to handle the remodeling crew. Margene had filled out the appropriate work order, but she'd been hampered by two inches of acrylic tipping each finger.

Dayne could hardly read the thing.

Enter Scotty "Hammer Toes" Hodges. Scotty was Dayne's electrical assistant. He was also Margene's grandson-in-law and the soon-to-be father of her first great-grandbaby. He and his wife lived with Margene and so he'd had plenty of practice deciphering her scribble. He wore a T-shirt, blue jeans, work boots and an expression that said *Yep, I was right.*

"See there?" Scotty pointed to the *San Antonio Star* emblem emblazoned on the side of the white van parked in Cheryl's driveway. "I told you it was the newspaper and not the bar association. Margene always does that funny little squiggle that makes everything look like a B when she gets rhinestone tips…"

Dayne's gaze swept the cluster of vehicles, from the newspaper van to a brand-spankin' new black BMW to another van that read Alamo City Interiors. Dayne shifted the truck into Reverse and angled himself between Herman Anderson's brown Pinto—Herman was a reporter for the local *Skull Creek Gazette*—and a sweet cherry red Corvette that belonged to Mayor Hallsey.

"I told you the mayor would be here," Hammer Toes said as they climbed out. "The man never misses a PR opportunity."

Dayne grabbed his clipboard and the pair of Costa Del Mars hanging from the rearview mirror. Sliding on the sunglasses, he tried to calm the churning in his gut. He had a bad feeling about all of this. A feeling that multiplied when he saw the UPS guy pull up across the street and climb out of his truck with a massive box that had *SEXTOYS.COM* stamped in big red letters across the side.

"Let me help you with that," Dayne said as he and Rich Boyd—aka the UPS guy—collided near Cheryl Anne's mailbox. Dayne and Rich had gone to school together and were old friends. "I'll make sure she gets it."

Rich took one look at his watch and another at the crowd milling about on Cheryl's front porch and handed over his handheld PDA. "Sign here," he told Dayne as he winked. "And have fun, buddy."

If only.

Cheryl Anne had told him to hit the trail. Get out of Dodge. Take a friggin' hike. She'd bucked him off way before the eight-second buzzer and so the *fun* she intended to have with this box of goodies did not include him.

Time, a voice whispered. The same voice that had urged him to keep his distance, play it cool and wait. She would eventually come crawling back. They were perfect for each other. He'd known it from the first kiss way back when. He'd felt pretty damned certain she'd known, too.

Obviously not.

"I told you Cheryl Anne was the one throwing the sex party," Hammer Toes said as he pointed to the box. "Connie Jackson down at the pharmacy said she saw Cheryl Anne passing out the flyers herself. I *told* you—"

"HT?" Dayne cut in.

"Uh, yeah, boss?"

"Shut up." Dayne adjusted his grip on the box, gathered his control and started up the front walk.

"WE'VE MADE arrangements for you at the Skull Creek Inn," Lauren the "Sex in the Saddle" columnist said as she hustled

Cheryl toward the front door. They'd given her all of ten minutes to pack her clothes, a few decorating magazines and her Pleasure Chest, and say goodbye to Taz, all the while briefing her on what was about to happen.

Four rooms. Seven days. Complete transformation.

"My assistant went on ahead to kennel your dog and make living arrangements for you," Lauren went on. "Before you know it, it will be Friday—Valentine's Day—and you'll have a home that oozes sensuality."

"I don't see why we can't both stay here."

"With the amount of construction that will be going on? Why, it's a lawsuit waiting to happen. We'll be ripping out everything. The flooring. A few walls. The kitchen cabinets—"

"But I sort of like those."

"No, you don't. Why, they're all but falling off the hinges. Trust me, you'll love *everything.* Once we're done, this place will see more action than a sports bar during the NBA play-offs."

"But I'm teaching a class tonight."

"You'll have to reschedule." Lauren hustled her closer to the door. "Order room service. Watch movies. Relax."

"I'm really not the room-service type." She tried to dig in her heels, but she kept moving forward. "In fact, I wasn't even aware that the Inn had room service. The last I heard, Winona delivered the occasional slice of cake and coffee. But that's only when she's in a good mood, which isn't very often— *humphf!*" She came up hard against a large cardboard box that had suddenly appeared in the doorway.

Her head snapped up and her gaze collided with a familiar pair of aqua-blue eyes.

Heat sizzled through the air between them and awareness zipped up and down her spine. For a split second, she forgot about the cameras and the newspaper crew and the interior decorators.

Instead, she found herself thinking about how transparent his eyes were and how she would really, really like to see him naked.

Again.

Dayne Branson set the box down near his booted feet and then there was nothing between them except warm, sizzling air. "Hey, there, stranger." His deep, rumbling acknowledgement sent a trembling down her spine. Her heart pounded faster and excitement bubbled inside of her.

A false sense of excitement, she reminded herself. While her reaction to Dayne was every bit as fierce as what she'd felt that night at the riverbank—the night of her eighteenth birthday—it wouldn't last. Once he peeled off his clothes and they hopped into bed, it would be the same old, same old. She would be disappointed and he would roll over and fall asleep, and that would be the end of it.

Like always.

Nod politely, turn and head for the back door. Now.

"Hey." So much for *now.* She smiled. Her eyes, the traitorous things, drank in the sight of him.

He was still as tall, as hunky, as hot as she remembered. With short, whiskey-blond hair, the faintest hint of stubble darkening his jaw and eyes so blue and translucent she could surely drown in them, he had the kind of rugged good looks that made women want to rip off their panties and scream "Ride 'em cowboy!"

And then there were the dimples. He had the most incredible indentations that sliced into his cheeks when he grinned the way he was doing right now.

She had the sudden urge to press the pad of her finger into one tiny crease.

She forced her gaze away from his face, down the smooth column of his throat, the frantic beat of his pulse and the bump of his Adam's apple, to the neckline of a clean white polo shirt that had Branson Construction embroidered in black letters across the left pocket. A pair of crisp, creased jeans clung to his muscular thighs and cupped his crotch. The hem bunched atop polished brown cowboy boots.

An image slid into her head of a pair of scuffed boots tossed on the river bank, worn, frayed denim piled in a nearby heap, a white Born to Raise Hell T-shirt puddled on the rich green grass…

"…is this?" Lauren's voice came from behind and yanked Cheryl back to reality, to the all-important fact that Dayne had tossed that T-shirt a long, long time ago, along with the bad-to-the-bone attitude and dangerous aura that had made him so damned appealing.

Cheryl's head snapped back and she gathered her composure.

"Dayne Branson." He tipped his hat in Lauren's direction, but his gaze never left Cheryl's. "At your service." His lips moved around the words so seductively that, for a few heart-pounding moments, her mouth went dry.

"Ahh, the local contractor," Lauren said. "Finally. We're already seven and a half minutes off schedule. Get her out of here," Lauren said to one of the assistants milling nearby. "And you—" she motioned to Dayne "—come with me."

Dayne didn't budge. "It's good to see you." His gaze never left Cheryl Anne's.

"I—I have to leave," she blurted, averting her eyes and sidestepping him before she gave in to the urge to press her body against his. "It was good to, um, see you, too." *Not.* Seeing him was anything but good. Because then her hormones started with their damned wishful thinking and she found herself forgetting—at least initially—that he'd morphed into Mr. Safe and Reliable. "Take care."

"Don't forget your penises." His deep, husky voice brought her whirling back around in time to see him heft the large cardboard box he'd toted inside.

She noticed the *SEXTOYS.COM* logo and heat shot from

the tips of her toes to her hair follicles. His eyes glittered with jealousy…and something else. Something dangerously close to passion, and her heart stalled.

Dayne? Passionate?

Yeah, right. The last time she'd seen him with that gleam in his eyes, he'd been standing on the riverbank, kicking off his boots.

"I think that's penii," she blurted, eager to do something with her mouth that didn't involve kissing him and breaking her self-made vow—out with the old and in with the new. She took the box he handed her. "It's plural."

"It's heavy." His gaze met hers. "I could give you a hand."

"Thanks, but no thanks. I can handle it on my own."

His deep voice followed her. "That, sugar, is what I'm afraid of."

IT WAS worse than he'd originally thought.

Dayne watched Cheryl Anne load the enormous box of penises—or penii—into the back of her beat-up Mustang.

A *Mustang,* of all things, instead of the economical, conservative *Kia* she'd always driven around town. She'd traded in the latter, just like she'd ditched her old clothes and cut her hair and exchanged her glasses for contact lenses.

His gaze swept the clean line of her bare legs, from a pair of high-heeled red shoes to the hem of her ultra-short miniskirt. The denim molded to her ass in the same way the cherry-red tank top clung to her breasts and he felt a stirring in his groin.

When she'd first told him she wanted to call it quits because their relationship was "stale," he'd figured she was just mad because he'd been putting in a lot of extra hours on a recent construction project. They hadn't been having dinner as often, or going to the movies, or playing bingo.

Truth be known, he wasn't really a bingo kind of guy.

Never had been, but he'd taken it up because of Cheryl Anne. Because he'd been eager for an activity that didn't involve kissing and touching and losing himself in her hot, lush body.

He'd been desperate not to screw things up with Cheryl the way his dad had screwed things up with his mom.

Bingo was nice. Safe. Boring. The perfect activity for a guy determined to keep his mind off sex.

He watched her shove the box into the backseat, toss in her suitcase and climb into the front seat. She gunned the engine and the V8 purred. A few years back, the sound would have been enough to give him a woody.

Not anymore. Dayne was older now. Mature. Controlled. *Stale.*

Christ, he hadn't thought for five seconds that she'd been talking about sex.

Aw, hell. Maybe five seconds. But then he'd let go of the crazy-ass notion. Doing the nasty ranked last on the list when it came to long-term relationship success. Real longevity depended on the little things—spending time together and talking and sharing and caring. He'd always thought Cheryl Anne knew that.

Obviously not.

She was now officially sex-crazed and Dayne was ancient history.

Good riddance.

That's what he told himself as he turned and followed the decorator from room to room, jotting down notes while some of the newspaper people packed up Cheryl's belongings to transfer to storage during the renovation.

"This wall will have to go. And these cabinets. And all the appliances…"

No sirree. Dayne sure as hell didn't need a woman with her priorities so screwed up. Sex was not the be all and end all of the universe.

"…I'm thinking we'll do a waterbed in the bedroom. She'll be rocking and rolling in no time."

An image pushed into his head and he saw the two of them "rocking and rolling," the bed moving beneath them, enhancing the pleasure as she rode him harder and he pushed deeper and…

Priorities, he reminded himself. It was better that they split now than later.

Before they got married and had a couple of kids.

While Dayne and his two younger brothers had turned out okay—the twins were now twenty-two and about to graduate from Texas A & M—they'd endured a hell of a lot of hurt in the process. Dayne wouldn't do that to his own kids.

Not no, but *hell no*.

3

A HALF HOUR later, Cheryl Anne found herself standing in the middle of room 24, the Skull Creek Inn equivalent of the presidential suite. Meaning, it had a king-size bed rather than a full and cable television. *And*—and this was the most important thing—a complete bathroom. While most of the rooms had a toilet and sink, none had an actual shower and tub.

The *Star* was obviously sparing no expense.

"If you want a wake-up call," said the elderly woman who'd shown her to the room, "just call Eldin at the front desk and he'll fix you up."

Winona Atkins was seventy-plus with pursed lips and thick bifocals. She wore beige orthopedic shoes, knee-high panty hose, a red-and-orange flower-print dress and a head full of pink sponge rollers. A ring of keys dangled from one hand, while her other clutched a *TV Guide*.

"There's maid service every day around noon time," the old woman added, "but not after two on account of I never miss *Dr. Phil* or *Oprah*."

Cheryl glanced at her watch and instantly she knew why Winona looked so cranky.

"The ice machine is in the lobby," Winona snapped, "and there's a vending machine right next to it. We also offer one of them there free cont'nental breakfasts at 7:00 a.m. But you have to get there right when the hour strikes if you want blueberry muffins. Those are Eldin's favorite and he likes 'em pipin' hot from the bakery. But if you like bran, then you're good to go until 9:00 a.m., on account of Eldin don't need no bran since he takes his daily dose of Metamucil."

Ugh. Way too much information. Cheryl forced a smile. "I'll remember that."

"There's no pool," Winona went on. "No mini-bar. No room service. And the TVs are on a timer that automatically turns off at midnight. Eldin needs his sleep and the slightest bit of noise keeps him up at night." The old woman peered over her bifocals and nailed Cheryl Anne with a stare. "And no funny business. This is a respectable place and we don't cotton to you celebrity types waltzing in at all hours, shaking things up with your wild parties and crazy antics."

Cheryl Anne glanced over her shoulder. "Wait a second," she eyed Winona. "Are you talking to *me?*"

"I don't see that there *San Antonio Star* making a fuss over anyone else. Smacks of celebrity to me."

But it wasn't the celebrity comment that had sent a burst of happy through Cheryl. "You really think I'm going to throw a wild party or do something crazy?"

"Never know with you people. I read the *Texas Tattler* like ever'body else. I know what sort of debauchery goes on and I can tell you—" she wagged a crooked finger "—I ain't puttin' up with it here." Winona gave the *SEXTOYS.COM* box a pointed stare. "I saw the flyers you were passing out earlier." She shook her head and made a *tsk, tsk* sound. "It's always the quiet ones you got to worry about. I can only imagine what your poor mother must be going through."

"Actually, she's not the least bit upset." Only because she was so fixated on Dillon who was sending her to an early grave with his outrageous antics—*a motorcycle!*—that she had only a few *Lord, help me*'s left over for Cheryl Anne.

Of course, she hadn't heard the round of gossip sure to result from her daughter's first official sex class.

Cheryl Anne ignored a niggle of anxiety and focused on the fact that Winona aka the CEO of blabbermouths thought she was right up there with Britney Spears and Paris Hilton. A smile curved her lips.

Winona's disapproving frown deepened. "A girl like you ought to be living at home with her parents. That's the way things were in my day. You lived at home until Mr. Right came along and then you lived with him."

"But I'm twenty-eight years old. It's time I started living my own life."

"Why, my Eldin still lives at home, smack dab in the same room he grew up in, and he's a good fourteen years older than you, and he's living his own life just fine."

"Refresh my memory, Ms. Atkins, but Eldin's never been married, has he?"

Winona bristled. "He's picky is all."

"And he doesn't have any children, does he?"

"He's only forty-two. There's plenty of time for that."

"And he doesn't have a girlfriend either?"

"Not at the moment."

"A boyfriend?"

Winona seemed to think before her mouth drew into a tight line. "Not that it's any of your business, but he's busy with the Inn. My daughter left him in charge of this place—with my supervision, of course—and he takes his responsibilities very seriously."

Translation: Eldin's parents had retired to Port Aransas and left him saddled with Winona and the family business.

"Eldin doesn't have time to date," Winona went on. "It's a choice. It certainly has nothing to do with the fact that he can't date on account of he's still living at home and no self-respecting woman would waste her time on a man who lives with his grammy." She pointed a bony finger at Cheryl Anne. "You just remember what I said and make sure you behave yourself. No loud music. No dancing around naked. And no men."

"What about women?"

Her eyes narrowed behind the bifocals. "Don't even think it—"

"It's not what you think." She turned and retrieved a pamphlet from her laptop bag. "It's my new job. I had my first class scheduled tonight at my place, but since that's off limits, I was hoping I might could do it here." It wasn't ideal, but it would be much better than cancelling. Particularly since she'd already spent the deposits to buy her supplies. She handed the colored flyer to Winona. "It's very educational."

"Humph," the old woman snorted. She pursed her lips as her gaze scanned the advertisement. "Looks awful scandalous to me."

"It's actually very educational and healthy. It's all about women taking the initiative and reviving their love lives."

"Looks like a bunch of hanky-panky stuff to me."

"Hanky-panky is a vital part of any relationship. But there's also a class that deals with how to reconnect emotionally with your spouse. I talk about finding common hobbies and taking walks in the park—that sort of thing."

Winona studied the information a few more seconds. "You're not going to play loud music, are you?"

"No, ma'am."

"Or dance around naked?"

"Actually, that *is* part of the course curriculum—the lesson entitled 'Pole Dancing to Passion'—but it's not on tonight's agenda."

"What about men?"

"It's female only."

"Humph." The old woman studied the information and color fused her cheeks. A light suddenly glimmered in her watery blue gaze. "I guess there'd be nothing wrong with it so long as you have everybody out of here by nine o'clock," she finally said. She folded the brochure and stuffed it into her pocket. "I'll have to sit in myself just to make sure there's no funny business going on. Not that I want to, mind you. I'm a good Christian woman and I certainly don't approve of the way you youngsters treat the sacred union between a man and woman like it's some new card game that that you gotta learn. Why, in my day there were only two things a woman needed to know before she did the deed. One, count to fifty and that'll pass the time quick. And two, act like you like it, which was hard to do when you barely made it past ten on the counting part."

She did *not* want to hear this. "Um, aren't you missing *Dr. Phil?*"

"It's a rerun." Winona waved a hand. "Not that my Harold, God rest his soul, was quick on the trigger. He was just anxious, was all. I *was* a handful back in the day." She snorted and glanced at the brochure again. "I'll be sitting in free of charge, of course. On account of I'm serving as a chaperone. It's not like I need to learn anything."

"Definitely."

"I guess I'd better light a fire under Eldin and send him to fetch the card table and some chairs. What about snacks? You got snacks? Because all that talk about hanky-panky is sure to make everyone hungry."

"I had snacks, but I got booted out of my place so fast that I barely had time to pack a bag, much less grab anything." She glanced around for a clock. "Maybe I can still make it to the Piggly Wiggly."

"They closed ages ago." Winona seemed to think. "It makes no nevermind. I've got Cheez Whiz and crackers in the office. I think I've even got a summer sausage left over from the Christmas party. It ain't Emeril, but it'll do in a pinch." She winked and disappeared, her *TV Guide* all but forgotten.

Cheryl Anne walked over to the small table with her computer bag and pulled out her laptop. She spent the next half hour calling students—all of whom already knew about the sensual home makeover—and giving them the new location.

"…at the Skull Creek Inn at seven o'clock."

"Will do," Geneva Peterson said. "Room 24, right?"

"How did you—" The words stumbled to a halt. Winona. Blabbermouths. Duh.

"Skull Creek Inn," Tara Gilbert said the moment Cheryl dialed the next number. "Tonight. Seven o'clock. And congratulations on the makeover." Winona strikes again.

And again.

And again.

By the time she finished the list, Eldin had delivered a card table and three stacks of folding chairs. Cheryl spent the next half hour setting up the room and unpacking her Pleasure Chest.

Her hands stalled when she turned to the *SEXTOYS.COM* box and her thoughts went to Dayne. Her nipples pebbled and she felt the sudden wetness between her legs.

Over, she reminded herself.

No more blah. It was all about revving things up.

The notion stirred a very vivid memory of a hormone-driven teen desperate to do something wild and crazy for once in her life. She'd peeled off her clothes, gone skinny-dipping for the first time and lost her virginity, all in the same night. With Dayne. And it had been phenomenal.

Then.

But things had changed.

He'd changed.

Back then, Dayne Branson had been everything she hadn't been—popular, attractive, sexy. He'd been the baddest, sexiest, most sought-after boy in town. She'd fallen for him the first time she'd seen him climb into the rodeo arena. Not that she'd actually seen him rope a calf that night. Her mother and father had been annoyed with all the dust and so they'd left early. But she'd imagined his strong hands wrestling with the calf, his powerful arms bulging as he slipped the rope around the animal's legs. His smile of triumph as he raised a hand in the air and took first place.

And on the night of her eighteenth birthday, she'd snuck out of her room and breathed life into her fantasy.

She'd watched him take first place in the county rodeo finals, and then she'd invited him out to the creek, where she peeled off her clothes. They'd gone skinny-dipping—she'd waded out into the water while he'd done a running leap off the dock with an overhanging rope. She'd meant to use the rope, too, but at the last minute she'd chickened out. Old habits were hard to break, after all, and she'd been playing it safe far too long to test fate that much. But then he'd swam over and she'd taken a chance and kissed him.

He'd taken the lead then, and what had followed had been even better than any fantasy. She could still feel the wild pump of her heart, her pulse racing and her lungs sucking for oxygen. A first that still lived and breathed in her mind. A feeling that had haunted her every night since.

While the sex in the years that had followed had been pretty fantastic, it had never come close to that one night. All night.

They'd grown up and while her life hadn't changed—she'd continued on as boring Cheryl Anne—his had. His mother had left and his father had been devastated, and so Dayne had stopped calf-roping altogether to help with the family's construction business. Over the years, he'd become the driving force behind Branson Construction, which meant he worked practically 24/7. No more hanging out with his friends. Or kicking up dust at the local honky-tonk. He'd taken on a world of responsibility and so he'd stopped skinny-dipping and swinging from ropes and started playing it safe.

He was now a member of the Chamber of Commerce, a

sponsor for the local Little League team, and he'd been voted Craftsman of the Year by the Skull Creek High School woodshop class. He made it a point to be in bed by ten and he'd even switched to decaf.

Not that she had anything against decaf. It's just that she'd spent her entire life following the rules and worrying about any- and everything. She wanted to cut loose. To drink the occasional cup of coffee without angst or guilt. To swing from the proverbial rope without worrying about breaking her neck.

She wanted to feel alive. To *live*.

She forced aside Dayne's image and the box, drew a deep breath and called the local kennel to check on Taz.

4

—————

"So what do you think?"

Dayne stared at the two DVDs that his father sat on his desk later that afternoon.

"I think you've been sniffing too much floor sealer. I asked for hardwood floor samples, not porn movies."

"It's not porn." Hal Branson grinned. "It's erotica. I'm meeting Abigail Gilmore at the Shade Tree for drinks and I can't decide which one to bring. *Captive Nights* or *Miss Pemburton and the Outlaw?*"

"What about the floor samples?"

"I seriously doubt she'll want to jump me over a piece of cedar."

"No, but she might want to whack you over the head. Whatever happened to flowers and candy for a first date?"

"I've got chocolate body paint out in the truck." Hal wiggled his eyebrows. "Margene likes *Captive Nights*. She said she's always had this fantasy about being abducted and held against her will."

Dayne's gaze pushed through the open doorway to glimpse the sixty-something redhead who stood in front of the file cabinet. She wore cat's-eye glasses that dangled from a chain around her neck, hot-pink lipstick and a pink camouflage jumpsuit and high heels. "That's more information than I need. What about the floors?"

"We're going with a natural cedar. At least that's what

Randy told me when I took them by the job site. I've already ordered enough to do the required rooms. It'll be here first thing tomorrow. So which DVD do you think she'll like? I can't show up empty-handed. I'm a man on a mission."

A man hellbent on sex.

Dayne's memory stirred and he remembered the last time he'd seen his mother. He'd been nineteen and still living at home. He'd come home late, as usual, to find his parents having another one of their fights. He hadn't thought much about it. They'd been fighting for years since Hal Branson had never been particularly good at keeping a job and providing for his family. He'd tried, but he'd simply never been the workhorse that Lorene Branson had wanted him to be. He'd been content with barely squeaking by and she'd wanted more for her three sons. And so they'd argued constantly. And then they'd made up. Both were noisy as hell—from the initial yelling to the make-up moaning—and Dayne usually bunked out in the barn until it was all over.

But that particular night he hadn't had the chance even to grab his sleeping bag. There'd been no heated words followed by passionate kisses. Rather, his mother had tossed the latest eviction notice at Hal, said her piece and then walked away for good.

"There's more to a marriage than sex," she'd said.

His dad was the classic good-time Charlie. He drank too much, laughed too loudly, and loved too fiercely. He'd been so busy doing all three that he hadn't had the time or energy to do right by his family. Even more, he'd been so caught up with "doing it" that he'd forgotten all the little things. He'd never given his wife a card for her birthday. No flowers on their anniversary. No candy on Valentine's Day. Nothing to make her feel special. Appreciated. Loved.

In his dad's opinion, sex was the glue that held a man and woman together. The bolt that kept the door hinged. The major factor when it came to long-term relationship success.

Dayne had wholeheartedly agreed. He'd been young. Wild. Horny. *Stupid.*

But he'd smartened up the night he'd seen his mother abandon twenty-two years of marriage despite the great sex. He'd stepped up, straightened up and he'd been holding his own ever since. Professionally, he'd taken his father's handyman service and built it into a bona fide construction and remodeling business. And personally, he'd learned to keep a tight leash on his libido.

Hal Branson hadn't been as quick to learn. The man had spent the past ten years making the same mistake over and over again, and so he was still alone. Lonely.

But while Hal still looked every bit the mature, confident womanizer, there was a gleam of desperation in his gaze that hadn't been there before.

"Did you read that book I picked up for you last week?" Dayne asked his father.

"That book about how to talk to women? Hell, boy." The old man shrugged and tried to look indifferent. "I don't need to talk. It's all about body language."

"And I've got some beachfront property in Montana you might be interested in. Plenty of sunshine. Warm temperatures. Great view of the islands."

"I may not have the most impressive track record, but I still know a thing or two about females. Namely, a gal likes a man who takes the initiative and isn't afraid to make his intentions clear."

Yeah, right. Dayne had made his intentions crystal-clear to Cheryl. He cared about her. About them. And he wanted a relationship. Not just sex, but the morning after. That's why he'd suppressed his wild and crazy urges—like the one where he tossed her over his shoulder, threw her on the nearest horizontal surface and screwed her silly. Or the one where he hauled her on top of him, tossed his cowboy hat on her head and gave her the ride of her life. Or the one where he slathered her with whipped cream and licked her clean.

She deserved more than just sex, and so he'd kept his outrageous fantasies to himself. He'd even bought a ring a while ago—it couldn't have been two years?—and had been waiting for just the right moment to propose. And he'd made it a point to remember the card for her birthday and the flowers on the anniversary of their first date, and the candy—a giant, heart-shaped box of Godiva truffles—every Valentine's Day.

Except last Valentine's Day, that is. He'd remembered the candy, but he'd also given her a gift. A keepsake box to hold all the cards he'd given her over the years.

If she kept them.

He'd always assumed so.

Now, he wasn't so sure.

She seemed so different.

And damned if he didn't like it.

"So what do you say?" Hal winked. "Which one should I go with?"

Neither. "The captive one," he heard himself blurt. Not because he'd seen the fuzzy handcuffs in Cheryl's pleasure bag and he'd been picturing her wearing them ever since. Hell, no. It was just that it was the first title that came to mind and he had to say something.

"Why don't you take this one—" Hal dropped the extra DVD on Dayne's desk "—over to the motel. Let Cheryl Anne know you're thinking about her. Maybe she'll change her mind and give you another chance." When he cast a sharp look at his dad, the old man shrugged. "Hazards of a small town, son. Everybody knows she drop-kicked you like an empty soda can."

"The visuals I can do without."

"Booted you out on your keister."

"Enough."

"Bitch-slapped you out of her life—"

"I get it, okay? She dumped me." He had to force the words past the sudden lump in his throat. Which sure as hell didn't make a lick of sense because he was better off without her.

She'd gone off the deep end. She was crazed. Obsessed. A sex maniac.

If only the notion turned him off half as much as it stirred the lust he'd spent ten years keeping in check.

"You CIRCLE the root of the penis with your thumb and index finger, twisting back and forth—"

"Would that be clockwise or counter-clockwise?" one of the women asked.

"Clockwise is usually good," Cheryl Anne told the room full of attentive women.

"I can only do counter-clockwise on account of my arthritis," Winona chimed in from her seat near the snack table. "It hurts when I turn to the right. Besides, if I do it like this, then I can do this little tap with my palm right there at the root."

"I've got carpal tunnel and can't do clockwise either," another woman chimed in. "But I'm willing to try if it's the only way to do it right. I'll do anything to make Lloyd happy. Maybe then he'll stop vegetating on the couch and start taking me out on Saturday nights."

"Do what feels comfortable," Cheryl told them. "But make sure…" Her words faded as her cell phone launched into an instrumental version of "Buttons" by the Pussycat Dolls. "I'm so sorry." She reached for the phone. "I should have turned it off." She powered the phone down and turned back to her demonstration. "Now, you can go either way with your technique as long as your wrist stays loose and you keep your fingers firm—" *Rrrrring!* The phone on the nightstand shrieked.

"I'm sorry—"

"Nonsense." Winona waved a hand. "You go on and answer it. We can just talk amongst ourselves in the meantime."

"But I—"

"Go on" another voice chimed in. And another. And another.

The phone kept ringing and Cheryl set her demo model on the small table that held her supplies. "I'll just be a minute," she vowed as she wobbled over to the nightstand, her feet crying with each step thanks to the stilettos she'd slipped on that morning, and picked up the phone. "Hello?" she said under her breath, putting her back to the group and shifting her weight just enough to wiggle the toes on her left foot.

"Your brother is sick," Dora Cash declared.

"Mom, I'm really busy right now—"

"I've gone by his place twice and it's locked up tight. I've been by the shop, but that's locked up, too. Mr. Davenport, his neighbor, said he comes and goes at all hours of the night now. But that can't be right. Your brother *never* stays up past nine. Mildred Donohue said he probably has a terminal illness. When her brother-in-law found out he had cancer, he went crazy. One minute he was recycling and the next, he's driving this gas-guzzling, atmosphere-destroying RV to every state park in the country."

"I'm sure Dillon doesn't have cancer," Cheryl Anne said under her breath. She shifted again to give her right toes a little wiggling room and chanced a glance behind her to see every gaze glued on Winona who was busy demonstrating her "tap" method. "I really have to go—"

"Have you talked to him?" her mother cut in.

"Not exactly. But Nikki said that she saw him and he was fine."

"Nikki? Nikki Braxton? The lady who owns the hair shop where you work?"

"Where I used to work, Mom. I'm self-employed now. Speaking of which, I'm right in the middle of—"

"When did Nikki see him?" Dora rushed on, oblivious to her daughter's predicament.

Thankfully her mother didn't seem to care what she was doing. It was hard enough ditching her old life. She didn't need her mother adding a megadose of guilt to make things that much more difficult.

At the same time, she was a Carnal Coach, for heaven's sake. *And* she was currently living in a hotel room while a major newspaper turned her nice, modest two-story colonial into a den of iniquity. While she didn't want all that mother-radar fixed on her, a few words of caution might be nice.

"When?" her mother pressed.

"Last week. He bought a motorcycle from Nikki's fiancé—Jake and his partner own that new custom chopper shop in town. Nikki said Dillon told her he was just having a few personal issues and that he needed some time to himself."

"Personal issues? Cancer is a personal issue. Or diabetes. Or heart disease. Or a prolapsed colon. I knew I should have made him eat more bran."

"Mom, I'm sure he's fine. Try to stop worrying so much. Now's the time for you and Dad to get to know each other again. Go places. *Do* something."

"We are. We're going to camp out in your brother's front yard until he comes home. Your father's already picked up a case of bug spray and some Benadryl in case a few of those little buggers gets through the tent netting. And he bought some spray for possums and skunks. He's even got this stuff that's guaranteed to ward off bears."

"You're going *camping?*"

"Desperate times call for desperate measures, dear. Your father and I don't see any way around it. Call me if you hear from Dillon."

Cheryl slid the receiver into place, gathered her composure

and turned back to her class to find Winona standing center stage, a purple penis in her hands.

"…all's I'm saying is, the tapping worked for me. Fifty-six years and I can count on my hands the number of times I stayed home on a Saturday night."

"I'm back," Cheryl announced.

"And I rarely cooked on Friday nights, either, on account of I've got this great little trick I used to do with my—"

"Winona?" Cheryl tapped the older woman on the shoulder.

"Yes, dear?"

"Thanks for filling in for me."

"My pleasure," the woman said. She looked oddly disappointed as she handed over the penis and hobbled back to her seat.

Cheryl Anne ignored her pinched toes—she wanted so much to slip off the high heels—pasted on a smile and went back to work.

5

LATER THAT NIGHT, Cheryl Anne stood in her kitchen and stared at the ceiling. Or what had once been the ceiling. The sheetrock had been demolished, the roof and shingles ripped away. A huge gaping hole stared down at her.

She drew a deep, shaky breath and tried not to panic as she picked her way past the chaos that filled the small room. The construction team had gutted the entire thing, including the cabinets.

And the problem is?

No problem, she told herself. The cabinets had been so old—eighty years to be exact—and old-fashioned. Peeling. Scarred. Ugly, even if they had been hand-carved and had the original glass knob handles. The newspaper was giving her a state-of-the-art kitchen. That meant lots of stainless steel and high-tech gadgets. Everything she'd ever dreamt of, including a cappuccino maker and an espresso machine. Not that she'd ever been fond of espresso. But that was the point—to ditch the old Cheryl Anne and embrace the new.

She blinked frantically against the moisture that burned her eyes and swallowed past the sudden tightness in her throat.

"The boys tore them down while I was going over plans for the bathroom." The deep, familiar voice came from behind and she whirled to find Dayne standing in the framed entrance where her kitchen door had once been.

He stood well over six feet, his hard muscled body filling up what suddenly seemed like a small space. He still wore the crisp, creased Wranglers and Branson Construction shirt he'd had on earlier.

"They really made a mess in here." He didn't sound any happier than she felt.

She shook away the crazy feeling and shrugged. "I hated those old cabinets anyway."

"Really?"

Yes. It was right there on the tip of her tongue, but for some reason she couldn't bring herself to say it. "Maybe *hate* is a little harsh. They weren't *that* bad. Nice even, *if* you like vintage."

He seemed to think about her words. "So do you?"

Once upon a time. "I'm going with a more modern, eclectic feel."

"So it's out with the old and in with the new?"

"That would be the plan."

"Seems a shame to throw something away just because it isn't as polished or as perfect as it used to be."

"Actually, it's a shame to hold on to something that's served its purpose and is no longer satisfying your needs."

"Is that why you dumped me?" He nailed her with a gaze. "Because I didn't satisfy you?"

"Listen, it's nothing personal. You're a great guy, but you're just not the guy for me."

"That's not what you said that night down by the creek."

"That was a long time ago. People change."

He eyed her, his gaze sweeping from her head to the tips of her stilettos and back up again. "Nice outfit."

A rush of warmth went through her and she forgot all about her aching feet. She glanced down at the button-up silk shell and matching skirt she'd changed into for tonight's class. It was bold, it was red and it made her feel more naked than clothed. A smile tugged at the corner of her mouth. "I figured it was about time that I bought something that didn't look like it had been featured in an episode of the *Golden Girls*."

It was his turn to smile. "You didn't dress that bad."

"I didn't dress that good." She shrugged. "But that's all behind me now. I'm turning over a new leaf. New job. New clothes."

"New man?"

She gathered her courage. "Eventually. Listen, I know this is hard for you to understand, but it's something I have to do. I'm so sick of living my life in a cocoon. I want to break out. To cut loose. I want some excitement."

"And I'm not exciting anymore."

"I'd still like to be friends."

"Friends, huh?" He looked ready to argue, but then his tight mouth eased into a grin. A strange glimmer danced in his gaze. "Why not?"

An awkward silence stretched between them for several long moments and she prayed for the floor to open up and swallow her. But at least it was done. She'd told him the truth and now she could truly move on. "So, um, what are you doing here this late?"

"Finishing up the demo on the bathroom. We've got a deadline. The bath and kitchen will take the longest, which means we have to be ready to start rebuilding first thing in the morning."

"I hope that includes my kitchen ceiling," she hedged, the curiosity that had pulled her out of bed in the middle of the night getting the best of her.

Okay, that and the need to pick up her *Hand Jobs Made Easy* DVD. Winona's "tap" move had looked oddly familiar and she was anxious to see if Buxom Blonde had mentioned something even remotely similar.

"So what's the plan?" she pressed. "Are you guys giving me a new roof?" She arched an eyebrow at him. "Or maybe a solar window?"

He grinned, his lips parting to reveal a row of straight white teeth. "I could tell you, sugar, but then I'd have to kiss you."

For a split second, she found herself pulled back to that night at Skull Creek when she and Dayne had had sex for the very first time. He'd smiled just like that and then he'd touched his lips to hers. He'd stroked and coaxed and seduced. Not that she'd needed to be seduced. She'd been ready, desperate to stop playing it safe and walk on the wild side. And Dayne had been wild with a capital *W.*

Then.

She focused her attention on the polo shirt that outlined his broad shoulders. "It's *kill*," she told him, eager to get them back on the professional track. The past was over and done with. He was a contractor. She was a homeowner. "You could tell me, but then you'd have to *kill* me."

"Says you." His eyes gleamed as he took a step toward her.

And just like that, she found herself neck-deep in the water, her heart pounding and her pulse racing as Wild Dayne Branson swam toward her.

Wait a second.

She blinked, but the gleam didn't disappear. She knew then that he was up to something. She could feel it. Even more, she could see it in the purposeful set of his stubbled jaw, the tense way he held his broad shoulders and heavily muscled arms.

Her pulse gave a wild *ka-thump* and her nipples tingled.

She tried to ignore the ripple of anticipation. She knew the first moment of contact would only be a letdown. Been there, done that. No more.

She took a step back but he matched her movements, his boots slowly gobbling up the bare concrete she tried to keep between them. "What's wrong, sugar?" he finally asked when she came up hard against the opposite wall. "You seem skittish."

"I'm not skittish." She debated ducking to the side, but realized that would only confirm his thought. "I'm standoffish."

He tipped back the brim of his hat before planting his

hands on the wall on either side of her shoulders. He leaned in and nailed her with an intense stare. His blue gaze pushed into hers. "Maybe it won't be as bad as you think."

If only.

"I thought you said we could be friends." She planted her palms against his chest to push him back a few safe inches. His heart thudded beneath her hand, a fast, furious rhythm that totally belied his cool, calm demeanor. Her own heartbeat kicked up a notch.

"I lied."

She stiffened, despite the enticing heat of his body that reached out and tried to lull her into submission. "I'm not going to bed with you again."

His gaze swept their surroundings. "Just for the record, sugar, we're in the kitchen." A slow, sensuous grin slid across his handsome face. "And there isn't a bed in sight." And then he leaned down and slanted his mouth over hers.

He tasted just as good as she remembered.

Sweet.

Rich.

Reckless.

Yeah, right.

This was *Dayne.* Responsible, grown-up—safe.

Denial rushed through her as he ate at her, nibbling at her bottom lip, urging her to open up.

Pull away.

She wanted to, but then he sucked her bottom lip into his mouth, drawing so hard that she felt the tug between her legs and suddenly she was eighteen all over again, and the only thing she could think of was getting closer.

Her lips parted and his tongue plunged deep to tangle with hers. Where her hands had meant to hold him back, they suddenly changed course, sliding up over the rippled expanse of his chest, his broad shoulders, to curl around the strong column of his neck. Her fingers dove into the silky hair at his nape and held on as heat sizzled through her. His body pressed into hers and he rocked his crotch against her. She felt him, huge and straining beneath his jeans. He rubbed against her and desire knifed through her.

Suddenly a kiss didn't seem like nearly enough. She needed to get closer. To feel his bare skin against her own.

As if he sensed the need that gripped her, he dropped one hand to her waist. His fingertips played over her rib cage and circled the underside of her breast before flicking her nipple through the fabric of her blouse.

She ached to feel his hands on her bare skin, the rough texture feathering over her flesh, stirring her senses. She wanted his hands on her body, his erection filling her and drenching her senses.

He slid one button free. Then another. And another. Until her blouse fell open. Her heart pounded faster and her ears started to ring as his fingertips went to the clasp of her bra.

"Shit," he murmured against her lips and she realized that it wasn't her fierce reaction making her ears ring. It was his cell phone.

"I have to get that. I'm on call with this project—"

"Of course," she blurted. Because he was Dayne Branson. Conscientious. Responsible. Safe. "I—I really need to get back to the Inn."

"Wait—" he started, but she'd already ducked past him.

She clutched the edges of her shirt together, and then walked away as fast as her aching feet could carry her.

FORGET UNLEASHING her wild side. She'd gone off the deep end. A straight plunge into full-fledged crazy.

That's what Dayne told himself as he climbed into his pickup and headed back to the office.

Sure, it sounded nice in theory. But the whole concept was

for shit. They could never be just friends. The kiss had proven as much.

He quickly covered the short distance to the two-story building that housed Branson Construction. Margene had packed up hours ago and so the place sat dark and quiet. Dayne unlocked the front door and walked inside, flipping lights as he went. He plopped down behind his desk and booted up his computer. He needed to go over the work orders to make sure he had everything for tomorrow. Cabinets. Bathroom fixtures. Flooring.

The screen came up and Dayne tried to focus on the spreadsheet in front of him. He succeeded, too. For about five seconds.

Christ, he hadn't meant to kiss her. Hell, he hadn't anticipated seeing her at all. He'd been working to finish up today's list and prepare for tomorrow's workload. He'd been busy, focused, driving himself physically so that he didn't have to think about the emotional crap going on his life.

The woman he'd loved, the one he'd planned to eventually marry, had chucked him like a pile of cow manure.

But then that very same woman had walked in and interrupted his work, and just like that, his focus had gone out the window. He'd meant to keep his mouth shut and hang back until she left, but then when she'd looked ready to cry at the sight of her roof—or lack of—he'd had the crazy urge to wrap his arms around her and tell her everything would be okay.

That they would be okay.

Desperation had rushed hot and potent through him, and he'd had to step up. To do something. To kiss her and prove to himself that it wasn't the sex.

That they still had the chemistry. That he still had it.

He'd tasted her initial shock—not because he'd kissed her, but because he'd done it so well—and his pride had prickled.

He'd held back all these years and kept a tight leash on his libido because he'd wanted to help their relationship. To build a solid foundation for a nice little house that wouldn't crumble during the first hailstorm. He hadn't meant to morph into a complete dud.

He'd just wanted to avoid wasting twenty years of his life only to have it end because of his damned greedy dick. He hadn't wanted to end up like his father. Alone. Lonely.

And all because of sex.

Yet here he was. Alone. Lonely.

And all because of sex.

Mediocre sex, a voice reminded him.

His pride burned and he turned from the computer. He hauled open the bottom drawer of his desk and rummaged inside for the small slip of paper that sat stashed behind the petty cash box and several ledger books.

He stared at the document. The edges were worn, the ink faded, but there was no mistaking the words *Eviction Notice* printed across the top. He'd kept the damned thing as a reminder. To keep himself from screwing up. From losing everything.

It had always served its purpose.

Until now.

He dropped the thing on the corner of his desk and glanced at the clock. It was almost midnight. Late by his standards.

Today's standards.

Once upon a time, he would have just been getting ready to go out. To boot-scoot his way across the Barnyard and have a good time. At one time, the local honky-tonk had been Dayne's favorite place in the world, second only to the local rodeo arena. It was the last place he wanted to be now.

He wanted to be with Cheryl Anne.

To be inside of her.

She'd wanted it too. She'd wanted him. But she'd obviously moved on to bigger and better things. Several of them to be exact, if the size of that *SEXTOYS.COM* box had been any indication.

You've been replaced, buddy.

"Like hell," he growled. If he wanted to get Cheryl Anne back, he needed to show her that there was no substitute for a real man.

A real *good* man.

He turned toward his computer and pulled up tomorrow's work schedule. Forget Romancing the Room. It was time to break ground on Project Sex.

Starting right now.

6

DAYNE BRANSON was nowhere in sight.

Cheryl reminded herself that she was thankful for that as she walked around the kitchen and noted the new cabinets and flooring. Even though the stainless-steel appliances had yet to be installed and still sat packaged in the far corner, the room looked a lot more put together than the last time she'd seen it.

Except for the roof, that is.

The overhead opening had been framed with two-by-fours, the edges taped and ready for the new solar window that sat propped against the far wall. She ran her hand over the granite countertop, the surface smooth and clean.

Hard. Cold.

She ditched the thoughts and walked into the living room. The walls had been painted a vibrant pink, so different from the crisp vanilla she'd seen in the latest issue of *House & Home*. But even so, it was nice. Sort of. The old hardwood floors had been polished to a fine gleam. She headed into the bedroom and saw more of the same. Freshly painted walls and polished floors, but nothing else. No furniture or wall decorations.

The bathroom, however, had been completely finished.

Shock bolted through her, along with a surge of delight as she stood in the doorway and stared at what had once been her dated powder room. The old tub and shower had been ripped out, along with the sink and countertops. A wall had been knocked out, turning the bathroom from moderate into gigantic. A whirlpool tub filled one corner and a gray marbled vanity occupied the full length of the opposite wall. Mirrored tiles ran from floor-to-ceiling, making the space seem even larger.

Her gaze went to the focal point of the room—a huge, triangular shower area in the far corner. It was one of those walk-in types with no shower door, just a small step down and lots of tile. There were two shower heads on either wall and a fancy swirl knob with a digital temperature read-out on the shiny handle.

Her sandals click-clicked on the tile and the sound bounced off the walls around her as she crossed the room. She stepped down into the shower and trailed a hand along the tiled wall. Her fingers played over the knob and a surge of excitement went through her. A vision pushed into her head and she saw herself standing under the warm stream of water.

One second she was alone, and the next, she saw large, strong hands reaching for her, trailing over her slick flesh. Dayne ducked his head beneath the spray and water sluiced over his deeply tanned skin. His body pressed against hers and—

Water blasted from the shower heads and killed the dangerous thought. She squealed and groped for the handle. Before she could twist, the water stopped and that's when she realized that the sudden spray hadn't been caused by the knob.

"What the hell?"

The drip, drip echoed in her head, along with a slow, warm rumble of laughter that slid into her ears and sent electricity skimming along her nerve endings.

She stiffened against the delicious sensation that rushed through her body, shoved the wet hair from her eyes and turned to find Dayne looking every bit as hot as he'd looked in her vision only seconds before. He wasn't naked, however, and he didn't look ready to gobble her whole.

Rather, he stood in the bathroom doorway, a grin on his

handsome face and a remote control in his hand. Excitement rushed through her and pumped her heart that much faster.

"Wh-what are you doing here?" she sputtered, wiping a hand over her face.

He held up the remote and amusement glittered in his aqua eyes. "Making you wet." The words were ripe with sexual innuendo and her stomach hollowed out.

A feeling she'd had many times where he was concerned. At the same time, there was something different…

She blinked and swept her gaze over him, and suddenly everything crystallized. Gone were his usual polo shirt and crisp Wranglers. His white T-shirt was soft and worn, the black lettering—Cowboys Do It Better—faded from too many washings. Soft, frayed denim jeans cupped his crotch and his strong, sinewy thighs. His boots were brown and comfortable, the toes scuffed from toeing the clutch on his motorcycle—

Wait a second.

He didn't *have* a motorcycle. He'd given up the bike just like he'd given up calf-roping and road trips and anything spontaneous. Even so, she couldn't deny the familiar boots.

Or the hat.

Her gaze shifted to the straw Resistol tipped low on his forehead, the brim worn and curved in the front. Familiar sponsor patches dotted the outside.

Surprise bolted through her, followed by a rush of *Oh, no*. Because the last thing, the very last thing she needed was to be reminded of the man he'd once been, and what they'd shared that night down by the river.

What they'd yet to share since.

She tried to keep her voice calm and indifferent. "What's up with you?" she asked as he stepped toward her.

"About eight inches thanks to the view." His voice was deep and teasing and her heartbeat kicked up a notch.

His gaze zeroed in on her chest and she glanced down to

see the transparent material of her pink tank top molded to her modest breasts. Her nipples were perfectly outlined, the tips hard and ripe and throbbing.

"If you peel that shirt off, we can make it nine," he added, closing the distance between them.

"Don't flatter yourself." She tried to cross her arms over her chest, but he reached out, one strong hand closing over her forearm.

"Don't." His smile faded and his eyes grew brighter. "I want to look at you."

"I don't…" she started, but suddenly, she couldn't seem to find any words. She swallowed and tried to ignore the heat of his fingertips that sank into her flesh, warming her chilled body from the inside out.

"You feel soft. And slick." His gaze darkened. "Do you remember the first time I touched you? You were wet like this."

The images rushed at her and just like that, she was standing on the river bank, the moonlight spilling down around her.

"And naked."

"I'm not naked now," she managed.

"Not yet." He reached for her and her heart pounded with uncontrollable excitement.

His hand went to the shower knob. The water sprayed from all angles, instantly warm and stirring as it rushed over her upper body.

"I don't think this is a good idea."

"This, darlin', is the best idea I've had in a long time." The water doused him, too, trailing in rivers over his head and down the handsome planes of his face, his corded neck, to soak his clothes. His T-shirt clung to his body, outlining the hard surface of his chest and his dark nipples. She swallowed against the sudden urge to dip her head and suckle him through the material.

As if he'd read her mind, he dropped his attention to her breasts. Before she could open her mouth to protest, he pulled her up against him.

His arms encircled her. His hands spanned her waist, then cupped her buttocks to pull her flush against his erection. He lifted her, urging her legs up on either side of him.

He slid her up the hard ridge of his groin until he was eye-level with her chest. Hot breath puffed against one throbbing nipple, then his tongue flicked out. Heat licked the tip of the sensitive peak and a burst of electricity sizzled to her brain. She grasped at his shoulders, holding on as he sucked her through the transparent material.

He drew on her and her legs quivered. The pressure of his mouth increased, his tongue stroking her, his lips suckling. Each pull on her nipple sent an echoing thrum between her legs. She clutched at his shoulders, wanting more.

He held her steady, his large hands scorching her through the denim of her jeans, nestling her crotch against his belly. Then he moved her, brushing her sex up and down the muscled ridges of his abdomen before he let her slide all the way to her feet. Her legs trembled as he pulled the jeans off her. Her lacy thong followed. Rough fingertips brushed here and there and her heart pounded that much faster. He urged her back against the smooth marble tile and dropped to his knees in front of her.

Before she knew what was happening, he dipped his head and placed a kiss on the sensitive crease where leg met thigh, and her body temperature went through the roof. Her memories stirred and she felt the cool grass at her back, the moon hanging full and bright overhead, the young man between her legs.

They were all grown up now, she tried to remind herself. But he felt so good and it had been so long. Too long.

He parted her legs, fingertips sliding over the soft skin of her thighs, up and around until his large hands cupped her buttocks. He drew her to him, lifting one of her legs and hooking it up over his shoulder. He rasped her clitoris with his thumb, just a casual flick, but it felt more like a lightning bolt. Her body zapped to awareness, her head fell back and her back arched.

He stroked her, sliding his rough fingers over the slick folds before plunging one deep inside her. The pleasure almost shattered her, and she fought to drag air into her lungs. He stroked and explored until she writhed and whimpered and then his lips replaced his hands.

He'd put his mouth on her many times over the years, but none had ever rivaled that first time down by the river.

Until now.

There was none of his usual tight restraint. No subtle kisses and careful nibbles. At the same time, there was just something about him...

He was still holding back. Still thinking.

She braced her hands on his shoulders to push him away, but then he sucked her clit into his mouth and her knees went weak. She clutched at his head. Her fingers threaded through the dark silk of his hair, holding him closer, urging him on all the while her mind screamed for him to stop.

For her to stop.

She was the culprit here. Weak. Gullible. She'd careened down this path many times before and the end result was always the same. Disappointment with a great big fat *D*. She *knew* that.

But it had been *ten* years. Ten long years spent wanting and fantasizing and hoping for a repeat of their first night together.

She spread her legs wider and held him closer.

He tasted and savored, his tongue stroking, plunging, driving her mindless until she came apart in his arms. Her orgasm was hot and fierce, slamming over her and sucking her down for a long, breathless moment.

When she finally managed to float back to reality, he stood in front of her, staring at her. Her heart drummed and her body ached and she longed for him to press her up against the wall and start kissing her. Wildly. Passionately.

No holding back. No second thoughts. Nothing but the two of them, feeling and touching and working each other into a frenzy.

His gaze gleamed hot and bright with passion, but he didn't act on it. Rather, he stared at her, into her, as if searching for something.

"So?" he finally said.

"So...?" She licked her lips again.

"Tell me that wasn't great." The words held a hint of challenge and she knew then and there that while he'd acted out of character, he hadn't been merely acting. He'd planned everything tonight. "That it was stale."

"It wasn't." She licked her lips again and fought for her voice. "It was..." She swallowed. "It was nice." Just as the surprise registered in his gaze, she eased from in front of him and bent to retrieve her sopping tank top.

"What?" He turned, his gaze following her as she struggled into her shirt and snatched up her jeans.

"You know." She struggled with the wet denim, pulling and tugging. *"Nice."* The material scraped up her calves. "As in pleasant." Over her knees. "Pleasurable." Her thighs and hips. "Enjoyable." She slid the button into place. *"Okay."* She turned and faced him. "It was pretty okay." She tamped down her disappointment, turned and walked away.

Because as much as Dayne had veered from his usual routine, he was still holding back. Still planning each and every move. Still playing it safe.

And Cheryl Anne Cash was through playing it safe.

No matter how delicious Dayne looked soaking wet.

DAYNE WATCHED Cheryl's taillights disappear before he walked back into the house and headed for the giant toolbox sitting in the kitchen. His hands shook as he reached inside for the change of clothes he'd packed away when he'd cooked up tonight's seductive surprise.

Okay? He'd worked his ass off all evening to finish the bathroom in time for tonight. And he'd rescheduled the nightly walk-through with the *Star* staff so there would be no danger of interruptions. And he'd turned off both his cell phone and pager and…

The tirade faded to an abrupt halt as his hand closed around the soft, fluffy towel he'd brought with him. The truth crystallized.

She was right.

In terms of spontaneity, tonight had been just *okay*. Not great. Not off-the-charts. Because it hadn't been spontaneous at all. He hadn't said to hell with anything and simply gone for it with no thought to the contrary. No, he'd worked and rescheduled and planned, desperate to keep that damned foundation solid for the nice little proverbial house. But if it wasn't solid enough after ten years, it would never be. Not as long as he let his fear of being hurt keep him from taking a chance with Cheryl Anne. That was why he'd yet to give her the engagement ring. Why it was still sitting in his office safe, and not in its rightful place on her finger.

Shit.

He peeled off his wet clothes and toweled off his skin. She was right. They were "stale." Hell, *he* was stale.

No more.

He no longer wanted the nice little house. Hell, no. He wanted a full twenty-acre spread. He wanted it *all*—a strong relationship *and* great sex. Wild sex.

His mind raced as he thought of all the wild and crazy things he'd wanted to do with Cheryl Anne. And then he stopped thinking completely, hauled on his clothes and headed for the door.

Because now was the time to act.

7

THEY WERE actually doing it.

Cheryl stared through the windshield at the sizeable tent perched in her brother's front yard. Lanterns gleamed inside, casting various shadows against the canvas. She made out her mother's shape as it leaned over and wrestled with a sleeping bag.

A sleeping bag. In a tent. At night. *Outside.*

She climbed out of the car, her wedges sinking into the soft grass as she started for the tent.

She was halfway across the yard when she heard her mother's voice.

"Get him, Harold!"

Before she could take another step, a large figure tackled her from behind and wrestled her to the ground.

"I hate to do this, son," Harold Cash grunted as he pressed her face into the ground and held her arms behind her back, "but you've been brainwashed."

"That's right, dear. You need an intervention. That's why we're here."

"Mom," she gasped at the woman who'd come barreling out of the tent.

"Cheryl?" Her mother leaned down and squinted through the darkness. "Harold, it's Cheryl Anne."

"Go away, dear," her dad said, adjusting his grip. "This might get ugly."

"She's not here," her mother said, motioning around them. "She's there." She pointed to the ground. "You tackled the wrong person."

"Cheryl?" Her father's grip loosened as he leaned down.

"Hi, Dad."

"I told you to wear the night-vision goggles we picked up at the camping store," Dora Cash said as Harold loosened his grasp.

"They don't fit over my glasses."

"But you're not wearing your glasses."

"I didn't want them to get broken during a struggle. The deprogrammer said no sharp objects."

"She wasn't talking about eye glasses. She meant no knives or forks or ball point pens. And only after we get Dillon in a holding pattern. It doesn't count during the actual take-down—"

"Excuse me," Cheryl Anne cut in. "I can't breathe."

"Oh, sorry, dear." Her father climbed off and helped her to her feet. "I thought you were Dillon. Your mother gave me the go-ahead."

"How was I supposed to know it was Cheryl Anne? That's not her car. Dear." Her mother nailed her with a stare. "That's not your car."

"It is now. I traded in my old one. I wanted something more sporty."

"A Mustang?" Her mother's mouth dropped open and a surge of victory went through Cheryl Anne.

"They're fast," she told her mother.

"Not half as fast as your brother's motorcycle. Why, we've come *this* close to nabbing him three times now. But then he sees us and poof, he's gone."

"He saw you," her father pointed out. "And it's no wonder what with the way you were waving that bug lantern at him trying to keep the mosquitos away during the take-down."

"It wasn't just for mosquitos. I told you I saw an armadillo early this morning."

"So?"

"So do you know how many diseases armadillos carry? The last thing we need is for you to tackle an armadillo."

"I think I know my own son, thank you very much."

"For your information, you just took down your daughter."

"At your call. You're the one who said to get him."

"You're the one—" her mother started to say, before Cheryl jumped in.

"So you haven't had a chance to talk to Dillon?" she asked her parents.

"Not talk, dear. Deprogram. See, we've come to realize that your brother isn't just going through a phase. There's something seriously wrong and the only thing we can figure is that he's fallen in with the wrong crowd." Her mother lowered her voice. "A cult."

"In Skull Creek? Don't you think that's a little far-fetched?"

"We've got Shriners."

Okay, so her mother did have a point. "Maybe Dillon's just tired of being bored," Cheryl Anne added. "Maybe he's trying to liven things up."

"And maybe I'm going to miss my flu shot this year." Her mother shook her head. "Who chucks their entire way of life just to liven things up?"

"Someone who eats dinner with his parents every Friday night while most other guys his age are dating."

"That's nonsense. He's welcome to bring a guest if he wants."

"Mom, you're missing the point. It's not about bringing a guest. It's about spicing things up."

"Things are plenty spicy. Why, I made spaghetti the last time, and I even used a double dose of paprika which has been clinically proven as an antioxidant—"

"I'm teaching sex techniques," Cheryl blurted.

"Excuse me?"

Yeah, excuse me? While she was trying to shake things up in her own boring life, she didn't want to give her parents a mutual heart attack. At the same time, she'd changed everything, swung to the opposite end of the pendulum. A little outrage wouldn't hurt.

"I'm teaching women how to have better sex with their partners." The words tumbled out, fueled by her pride and the sudden urge to prove to herself that she really was different now.

That Dayne Branson hadn't been holding back tonight because he lacked spontaneity and oomph, but because she did—because for all her determination to change, she was still every bit the same boring, predictable, *safe* Cheryl Anne.

"That's why I quit To Dye For and put away my manicure kit. I'm bored and I need a little oomph in my life, so I started my own business. I had my first class last night. I gave demonstrations and served Cheez Whiz, and I even sucked down some myself." If the sex demo didn't prove to them that she'd morphed into a wild child, ingesting a can of pure, processed fat would do the trick.

"So you think your brother is bored because he wants Cheez Whiz?"

So much for proving herself. She shrugged. "Anything's possible."

After swearing to call her parents if Dillon contacted her, Cheryl Anne climbed into her Mustang and headed back to her hotel room to get some much-needed sleep. It was late, a quarter past midnight, and she had a busy day ahead of her. Tomorrow night was lesson number two and she was determined not to let Winona show her up again.

But when she pulled into the parking lot, she couldn't make herself climb out of the car.

Her heart pounded and her blood rushed and she felt restless. Anxious. Unfulfilled. As spectacular as the orgasm had been, it hadn't been enough. She'd wanted all of Dayne. No hesitation. No holding back.

He'd done both.

Why?

Because he was the same old Dayne?

Or because, deep down, despite her best efforts, she was still the same old Cheryl and she simply didn't excite him as much as she once had?

Crazy. She'd changed. He hadn't.

It was that simple.

That complicated.

The notion stuck in her head as she turned down the dirt road that led to Skull Creek, determined to prove to herself once and for all that she wasn't the same naive scaredy cat she'd been years ago.

She didn't have a hidden agenda as she shoved the car into Park, climbed out and stripped off her clothes. She hadn't been desperate to lose her virginity and prove to Dayne that she was every bit as exciting as all of the other girls who clamored for his attention. No, tonight wasn't about proving anything to him. This was for herself.

She ignored a shiver of self-consciousness and walked out onto the dock. Grabbing the rope that hung from a towering oak, she clutched the nylon cord, ran a few feet and swung out over the water. Just like that, she was airborne, her body weightless, her heart hammering with excitement as she sailed through the air. Fear rushed through her, but she kicked it aside and forced her fingers to let go. A split-second later, she plunged into the cool water.

The creek closed over her head for several long moments before she managed to kick her way to the surface. She bobbed up, sputtering and gulping for air. Water burned her nostrils and her chest ached as she grappled for the dock. Soon, her hand closed around one cedar plank. She held tight to the wood and heaved herself onto the flat surface. She sat for a few seconds, her legs dangling in the water as she tried to catch her breath. Her panic quickly subsided and a smile tugged at the corner of her mouth.

And that's when she heard the steady *clap, clap, clap* of applause.

She twisted around to see Dayne standing a few feet away. "Not bad for a first-timer."

"Says you." She coughed, her throat still burning. "You didn't get a mouthful of water." She wiped at her eyes and climbed to her feet.

"You're supposed to yell before you take the plunge, not after."

His words registered and a jolt of awareness went through her. "How long have you been standing there?" She swept a gaze over him. He wore only a pair of blue jeans and a straw Resistol. His feet were bare, his muscled torso reflecting moonlight.

"Long enough."

Meaning he'd been an eyewitness to the stripping. The swinging. The near-drowning.

Embarrassment flooded her, but was quickly replaced by a rush of simmering heat as her gaze locked with his.

He tossed the cowboy hat next to the boots and T-shirt that sat discarded a few feet away. Just the shirt and boots, she noted. There wasn't a beeper or a cell phone in sight.

Panic niggled at her, along with excitement. "What are you doing here?"

"I was waiting for you at the Inn and followed you here." His hands went to his zipper. The teeth parted. He hooked his fingers in his waistband and shoved his jeans and underwear down in one quick motion. "We've got some unfinished business." Stepping out of the jeans, he chucked them to the side with the rest of his stuff and stood before her.

His shoulders were broad, his chest solid. His tanned skin gleamed in the moonlight. Dark hair sprinkled his torso, swirling down his abdomen. His penis, huge and hot and hungry for her, twitched beneath her stare, and an echoing tremor rippled through her.

He stroked himself, his long, strong fingers moving up and down his thick, rigid length. The sight of him, so bold and uninhibited, charged her own sense of wantonness.

Her heart pounded faster and blood rushed through her veins, warming her already dangerously hot body. Her nostrils flared, drinking in his scent—the intoxicating aroma of aroused male and barely checked lust.

"Come here." His voice was gruff, hoarse. Aqua eyes sizzled, gleaming with a predatory light that was unmistakable.

Instinctively, she knew that this wasn't the man who'd cornered her in the bathroom tonight.

No, this was the man who haunted her dreams.

Her fantasies.

Three steps and she reached him. Before she could decide what was happening, his lips covered hers. He thrust his tongue deep, plundering and stirring until she was breathless. Her ears buzzed and her heart raced and her hands trembled. His hands swept up and down her body, stroking and stirring until she wanted to scream from the sensation.

There was no holding back this time. She felt it in the way his hands slid between her legs and parted her slick folds. She heard it in the groan that rumbled from deep in his throat when he found her wet and ready. She tasted it in his deep, plunging kiss.

They clung to each other for a long moment, touching and kissing, until Dayne seemed to reach his limit. He scooped her up and walked toward the car. Easing her down his hard length, he turned her away from him and placed her hands on the still warm hood. The motion bent her forward and lifted her bottom. He stroked her, fingertips trailing over the wet heat between her legs, testing her, readying her.

She shivered and rotated her hips, as he moved away from her to retrieve a condom. He sheathed himself and answered her silent plea. She felt him straining in the cleft between her buttocks before he bent his knees and plunged deeply into her, one steel arm anchoring her in place.

He took her savagely, pushing deeper with each thrust, claiming and conquering and loving her in a way that no man ever had.

"Close your eyes," he whispered. "And remember how good it was between us."

But suddenly she didn't want a blast from the past. Because what she'd felt back then—however wild and wicked and wonderful—didn't begin to compare with the rush of sensation that whirled inside of her right now. At this moment. With this man.

She fixed her gaze on her own fingers splayed against the hood of her car, felt the damp dirt and leaves beneath her feet, heard the soft lap of the water against the bank, and smelled the musky fragrance of raw earth and hot sex.

Just sex.

There were no soft touches. No whispered words of tenderness. No staring deep into one another's eyes.

Regret niggled at her, but then Dayne slid deep enough to hit the spot that made her toes curl and her knees tremble, and all emotion faded in a rush of pure, intense pleasure.

EASY.

The command thundered through Dayne's head, pushing past the haze of sensation that overwhelmed him. The feel of her so hot and tight, pulsing around him, sucking at him,·

nearly made him spill himself then and there. But this was about more than sex. He didn't just want Cheryl Anne to remember how good it *had been* between them. He wanted her to know how good it *could be*.

Tonight.

Tomorrow.

Forever.

He withdrew and turned her in his arms. Grasping her sweet ass, he lifted her onto the hood of her car and urged her backward until she lay before him, her lush body bathed in moonlight. He trailed the head of his cock along the length of her slit for a quick shuddering moment before plunging back inside her. Her body tightened instinctively around his as if she never wanted to let him go.

He held tight to that hope and pumped harder. Faster. When her body arched and she climaxed, he caught her moan with his mouth. Every muscle in his body went tight and he plunged one last time. His mind went blank as he exploded, emptying himself inside her, his own groan rumbling past his lips as he tore his mouth from hers. He collapsed atop her, his heart thumping wildly as he tried to catch his breath.

When her hands slid up around his neck, it took every ounce of courage he had not to gather her close and savor the moment. But Dayne was determined not to mess this up. Cheryl Anne wanted wild and spontaneous.

And so Dayne fought down the urge to hold her close and did the last thing she would have expected—he snatched up his clothes, climbed into his truck and left her buck-naked and spread-eagled on her Mustang.

8

HE WAS gone.

The truth echoed in Cheryl's head as she clambered off the hood and did a frantic search for her clothes. No "Sorry, hon, I've got to get back to work." No lingering kiss. Not even a measly wave goodbye. He'd simply walked away.

And the problem is?

There wasn't a problem. Tonight had been perfect. He'd been perfect. Hot. Wild. Spontaneous. Her body still shook as she yanked on her clothes and climbed behind the wheel. She should be relieved. Excited. Victorious.

Instead, she had the insane urge to stop at the nearest Quick Stop and pick up a pint of Rocky Road. And maybe a box of Ding Dongs. And a few Snickers bars. And some Oreo cookies.

She definitely needed Oreos right now.

Because the hot, wild, spontaneous sex hadn't come close to satisfying the need that yawned inside of her.

Crazy. She was one-hundred-percent satisfied. She'd finally succeeded in changing every aspect of her life, both personally and professionally. Soon she would have the sexed-up house of her dreams. Life was complete.

It *was*.

At least that's what she told herself as she hit the city limits and turned down Main Street. The lights still blazed inside To Dye For and she caught a glimpse of Nikki, who stood at the counter and counted out the day's take. In the waiting area, her fiancé Jake McCann sprawled in a chair next to…Dillon?

She slowed the Mustang and stared as the car crept past the salon. Sure enough, her brother sat next to Nikki's hunky cowboy. Even more disturbing, her brother *was* a hunky cowboy. He wore faded jeans, a black T-shirt that read Save a Horse, Ride a Cowboy, black boots and a black Resistol. His hair had grown out over the past few months and now brushed the back of his collar. He didn't look brainwashed or sick with any of the number of things her mother had cooked up in her head. Rather, he looked relaxed and confident and happy.

A pang of envy shot through her and she barely ignored the urge to haul the car around, go back and beg his secret.

But she already knew.

He'd chucked everything about his past and truly *had* changed. He wasn't holding on to a box full of sappy cards or bemoaning a bunch of old cabinets or bitching about shoes that pinched his toes. He was embracing his new lifestyle. No regrets. No looking back. No *holding* back.

Because he truly liked the man he'd become.

Cheryl Anne couldn't say the same. While there were some things she liked about her new lifestyle—the miniskirts and tank tops, her dog, her own place—there were some things she missed, as well. She missed her old comfortable sneakers and her favorite An Apple a Day Keeps the Doctor Away mug and the occasional dinner with her parents and Dayne.

She missed snuggling with him on the sofa and playing Scrabble together, and watching television.

Because she wasn't a wild woman or a total scaredy cat. She was a little bit of both.

The realization made her that much more miserable.

Because Dayne wasn't riding the fence when it came to the old and the new—he'd climbed completely over to the opposite side of the pasture. He'd morphed back into his old self and she could only pray that she managed to lure him back. While there were a lot of things in her life that she was still unsure about, there was one thing she knew with dead certainty—she wanted the night before and the morning after, and she wanted them with Dayne Branson.

The trouble was, after seeing him walk away tonight, she wasn't so sure he still wanted her.

She tamped down her fears, ignored the lure of the Quick Stop and turned her Mustang around. There was only one way to find out.

"I WAS WRONG," she blurted when he hauled open his front door a half hour later.

His head emerged from the white towel he'd been rubbing his damp hair with. "Excuse me?"

"You heard me." She pushed past him and walked into his living room. "I was wrong." The words tumbled out and kept coming. "Not about our relationship being stale, but about breaking up with you. I shouldn't have called it quits, but I was so determined to change my life. I was stuck in a rut and I wanted out. I wanted to be different. But the thing is, nothing turned out to be quite what I expected. I wanted a more exciting job, but it's really just a more embarrassing job that I'm not nearly qualified to do. Even Winona showed me up. I wanted a better wardrobe with my own collection of killer high heels, but it turns out there's a reason they call them 'killer' and I wanted—"

The words died in her throat as she turned. He'd been partially hidden behind the door when he'd first answered her knock. He was completely visible now. Visible and nearly naked, with only a towel slung low on his lean hips and one draped around his neck.

He'd followed her back into the house and stood barely an

arm's length away, so close that she could feel the heat coming off him, smell the enticing aroma of clean soap and virile male that sent a bubble of excitement through her.

"You're naked."

"Most people are when they take a shower."

"Oh." She took a deep breath as her eyes drank in the sight of him. The white cotton wrapped around him stood in stark contrast to his tanned muscles. Broad shoulders framed a hard, sinewy chest sprinkled with dark hair that tapered to a slim line and disappeared beneath the towel's edge. The same hair covered the length of his powerful thighs and calves.

While she'd seen him naked plenty of times—less than an hour ago for one—for some reason this moment felt different. Because *he* was different?

As much as the notion turned her on, it also stirred a sense of dread.

"I want things to be the way they were between us," she told him.

The muscles in his forearms and chest bunched as he balled up the towel he'd been using on his hair and chucked it into a corner. "Stale?"

"Close." There. She'd said it. Now the ball was in his court.

She waited, but he didn't say anything. He kept staring at her, into her, and a wave of doubt crashed over her. "That is, if you do," she rushed on. "Maybe you don't. Maybe you liked the way things went tonight."

"Actually, I did."

Her heart sank and a lump jumped into her throat. "Oh."

"Up until I had to walk away, that is."

Her gaze collided with his and the gleam in his aqua-blue eyes made the breath catch in her throat. "Are you saying what I think you're saying?"

His jaw tightened. "I'm saying…you're a damned frustrating woman, but I love you anyway. I always have and I always

will and don't *ever* expect me to walk away from you again."
He stepped toward her and before she could absorb what he had
said, his lips covered hers. He held her face between his hands,
thrust his tongue deep and made love to her with his mouth.

"I guess this means we're ofricially back together," she said
when the kiss finally ended.

He grinned down at her, his eyes twinkling with hope and
love and promise. "Darlin', we never really broke up."

Epilogue

Two days later…Valentine's Day

"Forget about the size of the ship, ladies. If your man is driving a dinghy, a speed boat, a cruise ship—it makes no nevermind." Winona stood in Cheryl's brand-new living room, complete with red satin sofa and matching love seat, white faux-fur rug, and several mood lights—brass floor lamps topped with red fringed shades that responded to an automated keypad remote—and wiggled her bony hips in a clockwise motion. "It's all about the motion in the ocean."

Several *oohs* and *ahhs* and *yeah, babys* echoed through the group of women that filled the newly furnished room.

Cheryl Anne smiled. She stood in the back of the room near a glass divan topped with various bowls overflowing with snacks. She watched as Winona traded the wiggling for a swinging motion.

"Looks like she doesn't mind filling in for you," Dayne said as he came up next to Cheryl Anne. He had Taz in one hand and a box of Oreos in the other. He handed Cheryl the cookies and nuzzled the dog for a few seconds before setting him on the ground. The animal danced a few seconds before taking off for the kitchen. "She looks right at home up there."

"Let's hope she feels that way." Cheryl opened the cookies and dumped them on a platter. "I'm thinking of making the situation permanent."

"Winona's a nice old lady—most of the time—but I don't think this place is big enough for the both of you."

"I'm not talking about moving her in. I'm talking about handing over my Pleasure Chest."

He arched an eyebrow at her. "You thinking about going back to your old job?"

"Actually, I was thinking about helping you out at yours. I've done quite a bit of research on interior decorating and I was thinking—judging by the looks of things here—that you could use someone on your team with a little taste."

He wiggled his eyebrows. "I kind of like the mirrors on the bedroom ceiling."

"So do I. It's all the fur and velvet that I'm not too keen on."

"Hey, I did the construction, not the decorating. You can thank the 'Sex in the Saddle' people for the rest."

But Cheryl Anne had already done that. She'd smiled and posed for pictures and acted appropriately wowed at the unveiling that morning. A reaction that hadn't been that much of a stretch when it came to the kitchen and bathroom. Both were straight out of a dream. It was the living room and bedroom that looked as if they should be featured in an issue of *Hideous Bachelor Cribs*. She'd actually rolled up the fauxfur bedroom rugs as soon as everyone had cleared out and stuffed them in the closet. She planned on passing them to her brother when—if—he stopped avoiding everyone.

She knew something was up with Dillon. Something that went deeper than just a lifestyle change, but she'd yet to figure it out. Oh, well, time would tell. She was here if he needed her. And if he needed her parents, well, they were still camping out in his front yard.

"You *could* use someone on your team," she pressed. "Wouldn't it be great to offer a full-service business? Everything from pouring the foundation to actually decorating the finished product?"

He grinned. "I might be willing to work something out."

"I hear a big *if* coming."

"All of my people are licensed and trained. You'd have to have some credentials, babe."

"The junior college offers an Associate's degree in interior design. I'm registering on Monday. I can work in the office with Margene while I'm going to school. So am I hired?"

"*If* you'd be willing to do one more thing for me."

"I'm not playing bingo on Valentine's Day."

He grinned. "Actually, I was thinking we could play engagement." His expression faded into a look of serious intent and she noticed the ring box he held in one hand.

Shock bolted through her as the realization of what was happening hit her, followed by a rush of joy so intense that she wondered what alternate universe she'd been living in to ever think she could be happy without this man. "You want to marry me," she said, the words a breathless whisper.

"You're now living smack-dab in the lap of lust. Somebody has to keep you out of trouble."

A smile tugged at her lips. "Or help me get into it."

He winked. "That, too, sugar." And then he slid the ring onto her finger and kissed her.

* * * * *

Cheryl Anne is finally ready to settle down,
but her brother Dillon is as wild as ever.
But that's about to change...
Watch for Dillon's story,
DROP DEAD GORGEOUS,
in April

UNBROKEN
Alison Kent

To Taylor—my born and bred
Texan daughter-in-law.

1

DR. TESS AUTREY loved all things new.

The smell of new cars. The fit of new shoes. The dessert cart at a new restaurant. The first notes of a favorite artist's new song. The tight spine of a new paperback novel.

Then there were the patients new to her psychology practice, their personal issues testing her professional worth and often causing her to examine her own long-held beliefs about life and love, family and friends.

More than anything, however, she loved the new year.

There was something about the idea of a clean slate, a fresh start, another chance to ring in the changes she'd planned but never made during the year she'd just closed the books on. Or the one before that. Or, well, anytime during the last twenty-nine.

So far, 2008 wasn't going so well.

Her widowed mother—intent on seeing Tess marry into a family of status and means—had gone overboard arranging for eligible bachelors to escort her only child to their social set's charity functions.

Tess preferred to find her own dates, thank Georgina very much, and if not her own dates, then at least legitimate reasons to turn down the pity invitations her mother was sending her way more and more often these days.

The agreement she'd recently made with the Houston editor of the syndicated singles' column, "Sex in the Saddle," to write a piece examining the sex lives of rodeo cowboys and their groupies, was definitely legitimate.

Said editor, Judy Butler, was a very good friend and had suggested Tess tackle the project one night over margaritas, when she'd begged for ideas to get out of a fundraiser her mother was insisting she attend.

What made the piece in the *Houston Dispatch* more than just another psychology column—even though Tess would be in her professional element as she examined the culture of "buckle bunnies"—was the accompanying Valentine's Day competition being held between the *Dispatch*, the *Austin Herald* and the *San Antonio Star*.

The three publications, under the umbrella of their parent company, Deep in the Heart Communications, and the direction of its marketing head Sophie Cameron, were each running a sweepstakes celebrating Valentine's Day in order to increase readership. And the staff at the paper that received the most entries would win a bonus.

For its prize, the *Houston Dispatch* would be giving away a weekend for two at the Triple RC—a ranch southwest of Houston that supplied stock to event organizers around the country, and was worked by former rodeo cowboys and professional rodeo bullfighters.

Judy had arranged for Tess to go to the Triple RC to interview some of the riders for her "Sex in the Saddle" piece, hoping to stir up interest in the contest—especially among those buckle bunnies who would probably enter multiple times for the chance to be near their heroes.

The research for Tess's article had the side benefit of eating up any dating time she would have had during the month. She'd spent hours on the phone asking questions of the women to be profiled, as well as putting in a lot of face-to-face time gaining insight into the psyche of the female rodeo groupies.

Now she was on her way to the Triple RC to talk to the

rodeo cowboys who were the object of the women's obses-
sion. Missing the charity benefit and the company of any
number of Georgina-approved men couldn't be helped—
though Tess did promise her mother she'd make a donation.
Georgina was hardly amused.

With the first round of interviews transcribed on her laptop
and very vocal maternal displeasure still echoing in her ears,
Tess was more than ready for the four-day weekend at the
Triple RC. She'd finally be spending time with those whose
experience would tell the other side of the tale.

The cowboys.

Especially…*her* cowboy. The owner.

They'd only talked twice. The first had been a conference
call between the two of them and Judy during which the
Houston Dispatch editor had explained to the owner her
sweepstakes idea and her personal knowledge of the Triple
RC; being a long time rodeo buff, her husband was familiar
with the ranch and its accessibility from the Houston area. He
was also a good friend of the owner's and had been the one
to make the request that they offer the getaway package.

Judy had been absent from the second call—and a very
good thing she was, because that had been the one during
which Tess found herself lured by the anonymity of conversation with a stranger, spilling intimacies she couldn't bite
back, drowning in the words of a man she'd never met but
who'd listened, who'd said all the right things, whose voice
had vibrated along the curve of her ear and down her neck.

She would have been happy to have him read her a drive-
through menu. His voice was deep, steady, firm, as if he was
sure of who he was. He didn't question or think twice about
the answers he gave her. He was confident, self-assured and
his accent was pure perfect Texan, the drawl Hollywood
insisted on borrowing from Alabama absent from his slow
easy cadence.

She was from Texas, had been born in Houston in fact, but had never thought much about the cowboy way of life. Oh sure, she went to the rodeo each February, knew how to line dance, had three Country-and-Western stations programmed on her car radio and enjoyed much of the music they played.

Tess also knew how to waltz and tango and, depending on her mood, listened to an eclectic mix of classical, hip-hop and jazz. She drove an Audi. She lived in Houston's trendy midtown. She wore Nicole Miller and Marc Jacobs. She paid to have her hair straightened when she got tired of her natural curls, and to have the dark-blond strands highlighted more often than that.

Basically, she was a mutt. An incongruous mix of whatever tickled her fancy no matter the cultural significance. The women she'd talked to for her column were very similar except for the fact that they ditched their nine-to-five lives on Friday nights and hit the road for small-town rodeos where they were to bull riders what groupies were to rock stars.

They liked the excitement that zinged through the crowd, the risk and the danger of pitting man against beast, the status of being the one to sexually conquer the same man who'd emerged victorious in the arena. She'd even met a few who went so far as to schedule vacation time to attend the big shows in Houston and Calgary each year.

Most considered snagging themselves a cowboy just a way to have a good time, doing the same thing their counterparts in the city did—only they hunted their prey in the alleys behind the chutes or followed the men to their campers instead of hooking up in a nightclub.

Other women took their pursuit of the night's heroes a lot more seriously. They knew the names of the athletes, their rank in the standings, their income, even their vital stats. To those women, the conquests represented more…an escape from the drudgery of their day-in and day-out, the fantasy of finding a cowboy to take them away.

But the men of the Triple RC? They were the real deal, no doubt as married to their heritage as Tess's mother was to hers, filled with society's pomp and circumstance. They didn't have jobs they worked five days a week, or careers they left at the office at the end of the day.

They lived and breathed years' worth of Western tradition, followed in footsteps that had defined the Texas cowboy. Rough and tough they might be, but the thrill of the show that brought the bunnies hopping was a very small part of a much larger existence where no buckles were awarded for a job well done.

And speaking of cowboys and their jobs…Tess slowed her car, raised her hand to shield her eyes hidden behind a big pair of Dolce & Gabbana sunglasses. Then she slowed even more, bringing the car to a complete stop, shifting into Neutral and setting the brake.

There he was. Oh, there he was.

Sliding from the driver's seat, her heart in her throat, her stomach churning, she stood in the wedge of the open door smack dab in the middle of the ranch's main road, her hands curled over the frame above the window as she got her first glimpse of man and beast at work.

Her cowboy sat astride a big horse—chestnut, she thought the color was called—his back straight, the reins in one hand, a coil of rope in the other held against his thigh. He used those thighs to move the animal, cutting quickly to one side then back to the other before returning to where the two as a team had begun.

Tess pushed her sunglasses to the top of her head, feeling a smile spread across her face as she listened to his sharp whistles and the sounds—*oh, that voice*—that she guessed equated to words of praise and commands. She found herself captivated by the way the horse paid attention—ears flicking, head bobbing, nostrils flaring—and by the flex of the muscles in its massive hindquarters as it backed across the stretch of ground, snorting and huffing as it did.

The man giving the orders was equally impressive, his shoulders broad, his torso tapered, his biceps tight as he pulled back, left, right on the reins. Though it was late winter with spring hovering on the horizon, the damp fabric of his shirt clung to the small of his back above jeans that rode low on his hips and sat against his flat belly. And then there were those thighs.

She shook her head, slid her sunglasses back into place, and wrapped her tunic-length cardigan more tightly around her body even though she wasn't particularly chilled. The early February morning was surprisingly bright, the temperature mild. But this was the Texas Gulf Coast; there was no guarantee tomorrow wouldn't be stormy and dark.

She supposed the cowboy knew that, too, and was taking advantage of the day, though she imagined he spent plenty in the rain doing exactly what he was doing now, putting both himself and the horse through their paces. Whether the horse was his or part of the stock supplied for rodeos, Tess had no way of knowing from here.

What she did know was that *he* was the source of the shivers tickling her skin, and that just wasn't like her. She was more attracted to a man's brain than his brawn or the roman numeral after his name, and all she knew of this one was that he looked damn fine on a horse and could turn her to jelly with an almost inaudible word.

Except that wasn't all she knew, was it?

It took more than powerful thighs and a talented tongue to coax the horse beneath him to obey. He had to use the head on his shoulders in concert with the body which rolled fluidly with the animal's quick moves.

That's what Tess was responding to. That package. That combination. The skill he showed off with each order given, with the anticipation of each response.

She looked away, across the pasture that was on the verge

of being swept from winter brown to the green of spring, reminding herself that this was work, not pleasure, and that a
fling with a cowboy would not be worth what her mother
would put her through should she ever bring one home.

And then she looked back, feeling once again in control,
more centered, only to find him looking at her, his hat pulled
low on his forehead, just not low enough to hide what he was
thinking. Silly, the things going through her mind, this intense
reaction tightening her skin, tickling the hairs on her arms.

Was this what sent the women she'd interviewed into one
cowboy's bed after another? Was it this physical pleasure as
much as the thrill of bringing the arena's conquering hero to
his knees? Even if it wasn't her thing, she understood the
psychology of the latter, the power and confidence such a
triumph instilled.

But the former?

Pleasure she could get from a man wearing Armani as
easily as from a man in chaps, boots and jeans. For that matter,
she had no problem taking care of those needs herself—yet
even as she had the thought, she realized that the things his
look had her imagining went deeper than sex.

Okay…where had *that* come from? She could relate to
being physically itchy; the women she'd talked to held back
nothing when describing their sexual encounters—the
quickies with boots on in pickups, the blow jobs in country-
and-western dance halls, the hands inside clothing in broad
daylight offering sexual relief.

But none of those titillating depictions should have done
more than temporarily raise her temperature.

They should never have her thinking that this cowboy was
looking at her as though she had more to offer him than a stare,
or have her wanting to give him—this man she'd never seen
before, this man with dark and dreamy bedroom eyes—
anything he had on his mind.

2

THE MORNING had been cool, and for once Wyatt Crowe hadn't rolled out of bed to find more on his plate than his usual chores. Work lasted most of the day seven out of seven every week, but today he'd wrangled enough breathing room to take Fargo out for a ride before lunch.

He'd been just antsy enough about the rest of the day and the three to follow that he'd felt it best to get out from under the eagle eye of his ranch manager and foreman, Bertram "Buck" Donald. Doing so would save him a hell of a lot of ribbing when the other man put two and two together and came up with the answer to Wyatt's case of nerves.

He couldn't deny it.

He was itchin' with the wait.

He'd seen the dust kicked up by the silver sports car as the woman made her way down the road from the ranch's main gate. And, yeah, he was sure the driver was female. The psychologist-cum-newspaper columnist, Tess… She was due around noon, the only visitor on the schedule, and the only woman who'd had reason to come out to the Triple RC in a very long time—even if the reason was flimsy as hell.

Flimsy or not, he'd said yes when she and her editor had called and asked to talk to him and his men. He'd liked her voice. Liked it enough that he'd done a Google search to find out if her looks fit her voice. They were even better.

Though she came from high-society stock, he'd decided

then that having her at the ranch for a long weekend might be just the thing to put a spring in his step. Yeah, he was being shallow, but it would be nice to spend time with someone who didn't walk like she had a horse between her legs or smell like she slept with one most nights.

And then he'd realized the trouble he was courting.

Four days was too long for a quick hookup—not that he was expecting to get lucky, or knew if she had anything but work on her mind—but the more he thought about it, the more he wanted to go back to that phone call and say no. The first phone call, anyway. By the time they'd finished the second, he was ready to give her the moon. Still…

Four days gave a woman time to get ideas about sticking around even longer, maybe permanently—ideas that in his experience took on a life of their own once the truth of who he was came to light.

Dr. Autrey might not be at all interested in his celebrity or even understand the commodity of his name, but he'd just as soon not take the chance that, like most of the women he'd known in the past, she cottoned to the idea of bedding the legend more than bedding the man.

Four days. Lord love a cowboy and his horse, but he was inviting all kinds of trouble.

He'd collected a whole lot of buckles in his day—winning more Professional Bull Riders, Inc., regular season events and world championships than any cowboy in the organization's history—and had enjoyed the women who were part of the show. He'd been young and full of himself, and had loved having his pick of the bunnies every night to take for a long sweaty ride.

As the years had piled on along with the aches and pains, he'd given up the uncomplicated luxury of having a woman's body without asking and focused on making it out of the arena alive. He'd lasted a lot longer than he'd expected, and when he'd gone down, it had been in a very big way.

It had taken four surgeries to put him back together. He could sit a horse with no problem, though he still walked with a limp. Working from the back of Fargo was more for his own benefit than anything. The horse knew what he was doing. Wyatt was the one unable to make his muscles obey his mind's commands with the same precision as before.

Washed up at thirty-two.

It was a hell of a way to go.

He'd known bull riding wasn't a long-term career—it was too physically demanding, damaging, dangerous—and that when he finally did hang up his spurs, he'd be taking on the family business. His parents had groomed him to run the Triple RC eventually, knowing with Wyatt at the helm they could afford to take the early retirement they'd dreamed of and see the country from behind the wheel of their RV.

The Triple RC had been in the Crowe family for a whole lot of years as a working ranch raising grass-fed Angus for beef. Once Wyatt had been left with no choice but to quit the circuit, he'd returned home to take over the place.

It hadn't taken him long to realize that he didn't have it in him to fight both the market and mother nature. And since he had too much rodeo in him to quit the life altogether, raising stock had been a compromise that made perfect sense. He'd gone to his parents for their blessing, and then took a couple of years to plan, plot and make the change.

He'd been working Fargo, thinking about last week's shipment of steers, when Dr. Autrey had stopped on the road to watch him. He shouldn't have been bothered by having an audience. He'd performed in front of crowds as large as those drawn by Major League Baseball. Hell, the Professional Bull Riding World Finals in Las Vegas was no small thing.

He'd even had his ass handed to him a time or two by a big bad son of a bitch on national television. So, no. It wasn't being watched that had gotten to him. It was all about who was doing the watching and the way her watching had sent his itch traveling from his spine to his groin.

He'd let her come because he thought the exposure, the publicity, no matter how limited or obscure, might get his crew the kind of female attention they could use these days, the kind that was about sticking around for the long haul instead of following the boys from show to show, from town to town, which had been all they'd known in the past.

For the most part, Wyatt himself had found the women harmless and a whole lot of fun. They got what they wanted, and gave the cowboys a good time. Problems started when there was no respect for wedding vows on either side, or when the women thought they were signing on for more than a night or two of mutual satisfaction. And the more famous the cowboy, the more often that came to pass.

Life on the road, the injuries and competitions, the iffy income, the mental strain…none of it was conducive to permanency. But eventually the years began to stretch like a long straight road into the horizon, and not everyone—cowboy or otherwise—was cut out for making the trip alone.

Not a one of his men was married. None were in committed relationships. The companionship they did have was occasional and convenient, and, he knew, for some, paid. This article, this profile on the cowboys, if he could get the good doctor to slant it the right way, to hint at what the Triple RC had to offer besides rodeo stock, well, it seemed the least he could do to repay the years of loyalty Buck, Teddy, Skeeter and the others had given him.

As far as his own situation went, he couldn't remember the last time a woman had been interested in Wyatt Crowe and not the inimitable "Lawman"—the moniker he'd earned for laying down the law to the bulls he rode. High school, maybe? When he'd started competing professionally?

His time on the circuit also had put a big kink in his college plans. He'd eventually made up the lost time and had a degree in land management he wasn't sure did him a bit of good. He relied on experience—his own and his father's—as well as the business sense of his ranch manager and the common sense of his crew to keep the place going strong.

All of that kept him too busy to worry much about being thirty-five and alone, though it was funny how that very thing had been weighing on him of late. It shouldn't have been. His days were busy. He kept them that way so when his nights rolled around he was too tired for anything but sleep.

Still, with his men bunking in their quarters—for all intents and purposes, a frat house—his own two-story place had a lot of empty space and echoes. And his talking to Dr. Autrey, to Tess, had brought all of that home.

He couldn't get her out of his mind, the way she looked, her voice. How putting the two together and knowing what he did of the way she thought, the success she'd made of herself…how all of that intensified not so much his loneliness, but the fact that he was alone.

Why her? He couldn't have answered had Buck roped him to Fargo's belly and slapped the horse down the road. Right place, right time? Chemistry? The fact that she talked to him as if he was a regular Joe, not a legend or a celebrity or a commodity, and it had been way too long since he'd had a woman beneath him in bed?

So what had he done? Why, smart guy that he was, he'd set up Dr. Autrey in the room down the hall from his for the weekend, wanting her to be comfortable in the guest space that was rarely used but offered more privacy than the suite on the first floor. Stupid, because as quiet as the house was at night, he'd probably be able to hear her breathing.

He sure as hell would rouse any time she turned over. That particular bed frame creaked worse than his bones, which were held together with pins, and his joints, which had seen too much rough-and-tumble abuse over the years.

And the shower…no, he couldn't think about her in the shower, with steamy mirrors and slick white-and-yellow tiles and air too sweaty and hard to breathe, smelling as it would, of her. He wouldn't have anyone but himself to blame for the sleepless nights ahead.

He wondered how she liked her eggs, if she drank real coffee or needed all those extras that turned a cup of joe into a five-dollar affair. He wondered if she'd ever sat the back of a horse, if she'd be willing, or if a foreign sports car was the only way she liked her rides.

Thinking about her riding had him wondering what she wore to bed, and what he would do for the chance to find out. And since that kind of thinking was a danger any sane man could see coming for miles, he stopped.

Or at least he tried to stop, settling for reining Fargo around and riding hard all the way back to the barn, realizing along the way that no matter what he owed his men, this had been a very bad way to go about getting it.

3

BY THE TIME Wyatt reached the barn, Dr. Autrey had made it to the house along with most of his men, who'd been drawn to her car like calves to feed. The only one missing was Buck, who was waiting to take Fargo's reins and let Wyatt know what he was thinking with a shake of his head.

"What?" Wyatt asked, as if expecting a surprise. Buck was the only one he'd told about the true intent behind allowing the doctor to visit.

"Four days, huh?" The lanky foreman hefted the saddle and Wyatt's brightly woven blanket from the back of the horse and stored them away. "A Saturday I can see. Give her Friday to settle in and see the place. Saturday to talk to the boys. But four days?"

Having just had the same argument with himself, Wyatt didn't see how having it now with Buck would be any sort of help. He tugged off his hat, ran a hand back over his hair, then settled the hat once more into place, pulling the brim extra low on his forehead.

"We talked about what she's wanting to do, and I agreed that just a Saturday wasn't long enough to spend time with all you bowlegged has-beens."

"You being the king has-been and all, you need Sunday and Monday for yourself then, is that it?" Buck found the curry comb he wanted on a shelf beneath the hanging tack. "Do you not remember the poker game last Fourth of July?"

Wyatt remembered. The hands who hadn't headed to town for the big barbecue in the square had sat around the table in the bunkhouse kitchen, smoking big fat cigars while winning and losing the same money all afternoon.

They'd downed enough beers to float their own fleet, and revisited the good and bad of their years on the circuit, agreeing that four days was too long to stick with any one woman in any one town.

The trip down memory lane was a little too late to be any help. "I first suggested she get done what she could on Saturday and leave after breakfast Sunday morning. She said she'd like to stick around long enough to get the full flavor of the place."

"And you bowed down and told her yes."

Wyatt gave him the eye. Buck was thirty-eight to Wyatt's thirty-five and thought for some reason that gave him the right to say anything he wanted even though Wyatt was the boss. Or maybe he said what he did because they were things needing to be said.

Since the other man was also his best friend, he let him. "I didn't bow down *or* bend over." He added the latter to keep Buck from saying it since the look in his eyes made it clear it was on his mind. "She explained her thinking and her reasons for needing the time made sense."

"You Google-searched her, didn't you? You looked her up and decided you'd give your left nut to get your hands on her, and allowed yourself enough time to make sure it happened. And happened often."

"Leave my nuts out of this." Hands at his hips, Wyatt pulled in a deep breath along with the smells of damp leather, damp horse, fresh hay and not-so-fresh man. Him. Not the first impression he'd wanted to make, but so be it.

"This is as much for you guys as anything, remember?" Wyatt threw out a lot of the stuff he'd been thinking. "No one comes out here who's not buying stock, leasing stock, selling stock or training stock unless they're offering up supplies to help get all the rest of it done."

There was silence from Buck, so Wyatt went on. "I've kept the bunch of you so busy it's a wonder you haven't all up and put in your notice. You need more of a life than what you've got here. You deserve wives and families, if that's what you want, and this may not pan out, but I thought it worth a shot."

When he looked again at Buck, the foreman was waiting, his elbow parked on Fargo's rump, his hat low on his forehead, but not low enough to hide what was going on inside his skull. Wyatt didn't think he'd ever known anyone else who could call him on his bullshit without saying a word.

"There's a contest, you know." As if that was going to make a difference. "A reader from the paper wins a long weekend out here, relaxing, seeing what we do."

"Nothing about what we do here is relaxing," Buck grumbled.

"It's being billed as a rustic getaway. Maybe they'll be women and one of them can help you with that relaxing thing," Wyatt said, hearing a whole lot of laughter coming from the direction of the house, and his gut tightening up when he realized how much of it was female.

Buck glanced over Wyatt's shoulder in that direction. "And you? I'm guessing you've got four days' worth of relaxing planned?"

This time Wyatt didn't respond. Denying that the thought had crossed his mind would make him a liar. Admitting it would cause him no end of grief.

So all he said before he turned to make his way to the house was, "If you don't get that horse seen to, you won't be here for the next four days to know whether I've got anything planned or not."

WYATT was only halfway across the yard when the laughter began to die down. One at a time his men noticed his approach. Feet began to shuffle, heads to hang. Throats suddenly needed clearing.

If he hadn't been so irritated with himself over giving in to her request for four days, he would've chuckled and knocked them down a few pegs because goofin' like that was the kind of relationship he had with them. His fist was more putty than iron, and Silly Putty at that. It was part of what made them family, and was as important to the running of the ranch as was their shared background in rodeo. Every one of them had come from the same place, knew the same hardships of that life, and had chosen this one because it kept them close to a world that ran in their blood.

Bottom line, however, was that he'd seen her first. His men would get their chances to sit down and pour out their hearts. But after whatever it was that had happened between the two of them out there on the road, after that phone call where he'd heard so much longing in her voice, he'd be damned if he wasn't going to stake his claim in broad daylight.

And, as the thought crossed his mind, he realized Buck had hit the nail. All along in the back of his mind, he'd been making plans.

"Mornin'," he said, stopping in front of the porch, setting one boot on the bottom step, a hand on his thigh. "I'm thinking there's a lotta work around here that won't do itself while you all have your little tea party."

He didn't look at Dr. Autrey. At Tess. She didn't look at him. He stood where he was. She did the same, waiting until Duke, Rusty and Max—the long-winded one of the six—finished up their goodbyes. Only then did she turn and give him one-hundred percent of her attention.

Wyatt thought he'd braced himself, thought he was ready. He hadn't. He wasn't. And he didn't even have a porch rail to grab on to. It was all he could do to swallow the groan that rolled up from his chest when she looked at him. He'd never before had a woman stroke him without touching him at all.

She smiled with both her mouth and her eyes, her lashes long, the corners crinkling with all sorts of fun. Her lips were lightly colored, a soft pink that was not much more than nude, and her eyes…the soft green made him think of fields coming alive after the cold bare winter.

She held out her hand. "I'm Tess Autrey. From the way everyone vanished and the fact that I'd know that voice anywhere, I'd say you're Mr. Crowe."

"Wyatt," he said as his fingers closed around ones that were slender and cool. He held on longer than he should have. "Call me Wyatt."

"Wyatt." She made no move to pull away, frowning slightly and cocking her head. Her hair hung below her shoulders in a thick cloud that was either light-brown or dark-blond—he couldn't decide except to realize it really didn't matter. He still wanted to touch it, to see if it was as cottony as he thought it would be.

While he was lost in thinking about the texture of her hair, she seemed to come to some conclusion. "That was you, wasn't it? You were the one on the horse. The one I was watching."

He let her go instead of tugging her closer. If she wanted to be coy, to flirt, to act like she didn't know exactly who he was, then he was more than willing—and curious—to see how far she would go.

He nodded. "I was. I don't often get a break to take Fargo out and let him show me that he's still got game."

"He was amazing to watch."

Wyatt glanced toward the barn. "He does good work. Always has."

"One more member of the family?" she asked, her voice soft as if she were gentling him the way he gentled Fargo.

He found himself nodding as he thought over her question. "It's a big one here. Man or beast, doesn't matter. We all take care of each other."

She considered him as if she saw through the gaps in his story and knew his ordering his men back to work was all about taking care of himself.

But since she didn't call him on it, he didn't say anything to her about how long she'd stared at him out on the road before he'd turned to watch her watching him.

"I would think taking care of your own would be crucial, being as far out here as you are." She smiled again, but she also crossed her arms over her chest.

He wasn't sure which was more revealing, or which to believe. "Did you have any trouble finding us?"

"Oh, no. Not at all," she hurried to assure him. "I was just thinking how spoiled I am. Having everything I need or want just around the corner."

He liked that she knew the difference between needs and wants. Knowing what he did about her affluent background, he hadn't been sure if she would arrive complete with a sense of entitlement.

All he'd had to go on was the picture he'd found on the Internet, and the sound of her voice on the phone. He thought back to that night, how listening to her had him leaning back in his chair, closing his eyes and willing her into his lap as she talked.

"You learn to manage. Keep a large stock of non-perishables on hand, meat and bread in the freezer, fruits and vegetables canned or frozen. We make a trip into town for perishables every couple of weeks or so depending on how fast Teddy goes through the milk." He grinned, shook his head. "Lots of stuff we get delivered, but the milk? We're a bit far out for that kind of service."

She took several seconds to glance around the expanse of

the place, at least what she could see from the porch before looking at him again. "True bachelor digs, huh?"

"Guess you could say that."

This time she lifted a brow. "And no local bachelorettes to help out? Do some home-cooking? Add some sparkle to the windows and floors?"

"Woodson cooks. Skeeter cleans. They argue and fight like an old married couple, but they keep everyone fed and turned out in clothes their mommas would be proud to see them wearing to church."

She looked him up and down. "I'm curious."

Uh-oh. "About?"

"Whether after your experiences with the buckle bunnies on the circuit, you've chosen on purpose to keep women at a distance."

"You think we do that?" he asked, moving from the first step to the second until he stood only one beneath her on the porch.

"Nice try," she said with a laugh. "But I'm not buying it. You've made this place a refuge. Or a sanctuary. I'm wondering what you saw out there that sent you all retreating."

He weighed climbing the last step against staying where he was. She was assuming a lot, thinking there were any motives for them being here besides a shared love of the work they did and their history that made them brothers instead of the competitors they'd once been.

Their personal lives, sex lives, love lives…they'd never talked about keeping those things off the ranch but somehow had all come to the same conclusion that doing so was for the best. It had been a few years before Wyatt had noticed the toll that decision had taken.

A man could only chase away his loneliness for so long before he started looking for other ways to dull that potent ache.

But retreat?

He took the last step, moved onto the porch. Towering

over her, he met her gaze from beneath the brim of his hat. "Are you sure you're not just wondering how well you'll sleep on sheets washed by a man named Skeeter?"

Her mouth quirked, and this close he swore he did indeed smell springtime. "If you show me where I'll be sleeping, I can put that worry to rest."

4

HAVING TALKED to Wyatt Crowe on the phone when making plans for her visit had not prepared Tess for Wyatt Crowe in the flesh. He was big and muscled, tall—though she couldn't be sure how much of his height was his hat.

His hair was dark-brown, shaggy against his neck as if he hadn't taken time for a cut, and his eyes were sharp, aware, alert. The way he watched her, studied her, left her feeling as if she'd been pinned like a butterfly to a board.

The way his men had shown him deference made her wonder about the type of man he was, the type of boss, made her question his willingness to let her into a world of which he seemed highly protective.

Was there something he was hoping to get from her visit that could impact her plans?

Her suitcase in hand, he walked her into the house, pointed the way through the front room and followed her up the stairs. He didn't follow too closely. It was, however, just the right distance to put him at eye level with her ass.

She didn't know whether to hurry so that he didn't have a lot of time to stare, or to linger so that he did. To take her time, swing her hips, let him wonder and want.

He was gorgeous, he intrigued her, he was nothing like the men her mother kept sending her way. But she didn't know him; was she being stupid to tempt him without knowing more than she did? For all she did know, he'd sworn off women completely, or had left a long line of ex-Mrs. Crowes.

Before she could make up her mind—to flirt or not to flirt, what a silly thing to ponder—the decision was out of her hands. They had reached the second floor.

"This way," he said, leading her down the short hallway, his boots thudding on the hardwood floor as he walked, his face expressionless as he stepped around her, giving her no clue as to whether he'd noticed her ass at all.

Tess put a hand to her forehead, pushed her hair away from her face as she followed him, her own steps softer and lighter. She had to get a grip and do it now. The thoughts flitting through her mind were hardly professional, and she was here for reasons that were.

Okay, so he made her heart pitter-patter. If not her heart, then certainly her loins. She could either ignore the impact of seeing him in person, or use it as research for her column, putting herself into the boots of a buckle bunny and walking the proverbial mile.

Except she wasn't so sure that would work.

Earlier on the porch, she'd met Skeeter and Woodson, Rusty, Teddy and Max. She had yet to meet Buck, the foreman and ranch manager, but she couldn't imagine her reaction to him would be any different than her response to the hands who'd come to meet her.

They would be able to tell her what it was like living on the road, moving from one dusty small town to the next, finding women waiting, women willing to soothe their aching muscles, their tired minds, their bodies that were still able to perform.

She wanted to hear their stories, to understand what they saw in their sport's groupies, if anything, beyond the guaranteed sex, the warm, responsive partners who could so easily be won even if just for the night. She wanted to hear their

stories because of what the women had told her, but also
because of who these men were.

They were all rodeo cowboys who'd been successful in
their events, who hadn't tired of the sport but had been left
physically broken and with no option but to retire, who had
chosen to work the Triple RC because it kept them involved
in a world that had defined them for most of their lives.

But they weren't Wyatt.

Only Wyatt had caused her mouth to go dry, the small of
her back to perspire. Watching him on the back of his horse,
she'd known he'd be something. His command of the animal,
of his own movements, his body in the saddle, fluid, sway-
ing…she'd been duly impressed, her breath stolen.

Hearing about him from his men, she'd better grasped
the mutual respect she'd sensed in their first conversation.
Considering his employees' welfare made them the loyal
hands they were.

Only minutes earlier, she'd felt the power of his approach
without seeing him, and by the time she did, her chest had
been so tight, the ache to draw a breath so fierce, she wouldn't
have been surprised if she'd passed out at his feet.

It was fortunate that she hadn't. She would've hated to miss
out on that time on the porch, that tension, that wondering if
he would come up, if she should move down, that sense of
pregnant expectation, the waiting for her stomach to settle, her
heart to find a less spectacular rhythm…

"Here we are."

He set her suitcase just inside the door. She brushed against
his hip—oh, my, the hardness—as she walked by to place her
laptop case and oversized purse on the bed. She looked
around the room, rubbing her hands up and down her arms,
shivering from the contact and feeling uncomfortably weak
in the knees.

"It's perfect," she said, caught by the simplicity of the

space as much by the color. The paint was an off white, the wood trim a light oak, the only thing on any of the walls a fringed blanket woven in variegated blues, reds and greens that matched the spread on the bed and the throw rugs on the floor. "Very south of the border."

"The bathroom's across the hall, the linen closet beside it." He pointed to the desk that sat next to the door. "The house has WiFi thanks to Max, so you'll be able to check e-mail or whatever. The kitchen's at the back of the house on down the hall from the staircase, and Woodson should bring supper over for us around six."

She stopped herself from asking where his room was, and turned at that. "Bring it over from where?"

He lifted his chin, using it to gesture toward the other side of the house. "There's a big kitchen in the men's quarters."

"And that's where you all eat?"

He nodded, his jaw set, his lips pressed together, his eyes frowning darkly beneath the brim of his hat, the shadow keeping her from seeing their true color.

"Could we eat there instead of here?" she asked, wondering if he was already having regrets about her invading his space, disrupting his routine. "It would give me a chance to get to know everyone, and maybe see what time would be convenient to talk to your men individually."

He didn't answer right away. He stared at the floor or at his boots; she wasn't sure. Neither was she sure if he was second-guessing the involvement of his crew in her project. Or maybe, just maybe, he'd been looking forward to the two of them eating together alone.

The first she wasn't going to let happen. She'd charm, cajole, even coerce if she had to. This project might have started as a ploy to fend off her mother, but having interviewed the women, her interest in the men's side of the story was piqued.

And the second? If he wanted to get her alone, she was always open for dessert. "Whaddaya say, cowboy?"

He grimaced, grunted, but nodded and said, "I'll meet you on the back porch at six."

SUPPER, dinner, whatever the cowboys called it out here on the ranch had been amazing. Homegrown and fresh-canned green beans with onions, potatoes mashed with sour cream and the skins, chicken baked with a crust of cornmeal and sage.

And then dessert. Banana pudding with whipped cream and dozens of soft vanilla wafers.

She was stuffed.

The time she'd spent with the men as a group had been invaluable. It had also been noisy as hell. She couldn't remember when she'd laughed so hard she'd nearly snorted food up her nose. She'd also gotten a good feel for who would be open to talking to her one-on-one, and who might need coaxing to open up.

Talking to a woman—her—about how they'd slept with others whose names they'd never known wasn't something all of them were going to be comfortable with, even though she'd assured them she wasn't here to judge.

A couple of them seemed as if they'd be more willing to share their tales if she interviewed them together. Counseling was often done similarly and for the same reason: knowing they were not alone in their experiences gave the participants a level of comfort they otherwise lacked. Putting the same tactic to use here might work.

But the one she was most curious about was Wyatt.

He'd sat down the table from her on the opposite side, and hadn't joined in the dinner conversation at all. He'd grinned to himself—oh, but she loved his smile and his laugh—or chuckled under his breath at the ribbing that had gone on, but he'd waved off personal queries and deftly reflected the digging barbs thrown his way. There was something he didn't want her to know. She was determined to find out what it was.

The entire group had stayed at the table long past the end of the meal, and when she and Wyatt had finally set off for the main house, the sun was completely down, the moon in its place and shining brightly in the velvet canvas of sky.

Walking beside him now, she made no attempt to hurry, enjoying the brisk air that frosted when she breathed, the scent of that very same cold, of the earth chilling as the temperature fell, of the animals snorting and huddling close in the pasture.

"You cold?" Wyatt asked, looking over at her.

She nodded, shivered, tightened the belt of her sage-green cardigan. "Yes, but it feels wonderful. At home I'd be huddled beneath a lap blanket, drinking hot tea, basking in the warmth of central heating. This is a different kind of cold. Invigorating. Lovely."

She thought she saw him nod, the brim of his hat seeming to dip…unless what she was seeing was shadows, tricks played by the moonlight as she tried to sneak peeks at his face.

"If it gets to be too much," he told her, "I can rummage up the tea and the blanket. But for heat, it's propane or the fireplace."

She stopped. He stopped. Their eyes met, and after several heartbeats of seconds, she smiled. "If you've got tea and a fire, I wouldn't even care about the blanket. Of course, I wouldn't say no to toasted marshmallows.

"But most of all," she said, taking a monstrously frightening leap of faith and hoping for a net at the bottom just in case she fell. "Most of all I'd like you to stay and enjoy it with me."

It took him no time at all to grin. "I'd planned to all along."

5

"I TAKE back what I said about you all retreating."

Wyatt suppressed a smile. They might have been doing just that, but it had never been a conscious surrender. This was just the life they all loved. One lived in the present, the baggage of the past left unclaimed. "Yeah?"

"Well, at least hiding out from women," Tess said, animated. "Your crew are incredible flirts."

She wasn't telling him anything he didn't know. "Think so?"

She nodded. "But I'm quite certain you're hiding out from something. And that's you specifically, not you in the plural meaning all of your men."

While he stared at the flames licking their way through the kindling to the wedges of split oak, his smile twisted in irony. If he hadn't wondered before, now he knew. He was in for a hell of a weekend.

Tess had brewed the tea while he'd laid the fire. He hadn't run across any marshmallows, but had found a bottle of rum. Even if she didn't want any, he didn't see himself making it through the rest of the evening without it.

Watching her at the supper table had been as telling as it was excruciating. Telling because it was obvious how well she had chosen her field. She was a people person, empathetic, a good listener, giving her full attention to whoever had the floor. He'd never seen his men so engaged.

Sure, sitting down to eat with a gorgeous woman had a lot

to do with the bunch of them, even Buck, having such a good time. But Wyatt had seen them all in the company of other women—many of them the women Tess was here to ask about—when none of them could find much to say.

Tess made the men feel safe, as though what they had to say mattered, as though *they* mattered—not as a team, the hands who managed the Triple RC, but as individuals. She had earned their trust and their respect over that one very long meal. And that was where the excruciating part came in.

She wasn't the type of woman he could love and leave. Tonight's dinner had proved that. He hadn't learned much about her personally; she'd kept the conversation focused on the men. But what he had learned meant he'd just signed on for four very long days.

Oh, yeah. Rum was definitely called for, he mused, grateful he'd carried the bottle to the big empty house's main room. He hadn't built a fire since Christmas when his folks were out to the ranch. It hardly seemed worth the effort to do it for himself, but now he was glad he'd made the suggestion.

Tess sat on the floor in front of his big recliner as if she were better able to feel the heat from there than curled into the corner of the chair. He was quite sure if she had, the light wouldn't have reached her halo of hair, threading like ribbons through the strands.

And why she had him stupid-dizzy and wanting to touch her hair was something he couldn't afford to examine too closely. What he had to keep in mind was that this wasn't a rodeo, he wasn't a champion and she was not a bunny looking for a good time.

He sat on the steamer trunk that served as a coffee table. It was closer to her than the sofa, but not as close as he'd be were he to sit on the floor and lean back against the trunk, his legs stretched out toward the hearth. When he twisted the top from the bottle and offered to pour, she nodded, and he added a splash of rum to her tea.

"So are you going to tell me what it is?" she asked after she'd sipped and sighed. "Why you're out here keeping a low profile when I picked up more than a few hints over dinner that you're a high-profile guy?"

He figured this was as good a time as any to remind her that she'd agreed not to name names, and in exchange for that consideration, he might even give her the answer to what she was asking.

"I *was* a high-profile guy." The room his folks used to sleep in was where all Wyatt's trophies and buckles were on display in glass cases. Right now he was really glad he'd moved them out of here. "I guess I still am. It's just that out here it's not such a big deal. For the most part, I work behind the scenes and let Buck do all the talking."

Tess tucked her legs to the side, wrapping the blanket she'd found folded on top of the trunk more tightly around her shoulders. She brought her mug to her mouth, but before drinking, asked, "Who are you then?"

Elbows braced on his knees, he stared down into his mug, watching the reflection of the flames dance on the surface of the golden-brown liquid. He lifted and drank, gathering his thoughts as the pungent tang of the rum warmed his throat on the way down.

"I've won more professional bull-riding championships than any other rider ever has." Though after the beating he'd taken from the seventeen-hundred-pound monster Brangus named Baby Shakes, his records were up for grabs. "They called me Lawman, something about letting the bulls know who was in charge."

Tess held her mug in both hands, her eyes wide as she listened. "Or maybe something about the name Wyatt belonging to Wyatt Earp? One of the legendary lawmen of the West?"

"Yeah," he admitted. "That, too."

She tilted her head toward the fire as she considered him. "Does that make you uncomfortable? Having a legendary status of your own?"

"Nah. There was a lot of pressure, sure. Could I do it one more time? When was I going to wash out or meet my match? But in the arena?" He shook his head. "All that goes away. It's only you and close to a ton of pissed-off bull aiming to use you as a punching bag. You think of anything but the ride, and you won't make it two seconds, much less eight."

"Eight seconds." She sighed, sipped her tea. The light from the fire washed her skin in gold, picked up bright sparks of color in her cheeks. "It sounds like little more than the blink of an eye."

"Trust me. It can be a lifetime." He added another splash of rum to both of their mugs, then another to his for good measure. He didn't mind talking about rodeo at all. But talking about it to a woman with this one's intuition wasn't the easiest thing to do.

He didn't dwell on those days or want them back. They were a part of who he was, sure, but he'd moved on. This was his life now, his home. The ranch was as important to him these days as the rides had been in the past. And he didn't want what had gone before to be what he was judged on now.

That was why Buck acted as the mouthpiece for the Triple RC, and why Wyatt himself had grown to accept being a bit of a recluse. It was unintentional, not a lifestyle he'd ever planned for, but leaving his celebrity behind made it easier to trust that he wasn't being used for his name.

"I'll bet you were a hit with the bunnies," she finally said as if reading his thoughts.

"For a few years there? You bet." Why deny a truth that was so obvious? "The only nights I spent alone were those on the road when we drove straight through from one town to another. The rest of the time there wasn't enough of me to go around. I don't know if it was the bulls or the bunnies who wore me out in the end."

She seemed to take that in, mulling it over and considering what she wanted to do with his admission. Whether to kiss his ass good-bye right here and now, or forgive him a past life that had branded him as less than a saint.

After a long minute spent studying his face, she said, "It won't work, you know."

He tried not to squirm under her scrutiny, or her insight. She knew what he wanted. And his insight told him she wanted the same thing—and had since that second phone call. They were headed to bed. How soon it would happen and how long it would last were the only things to settle.

"What won't work?" he finally gave in and asked.

"You're too smart a man to ever have jeopardized your career for sex. I understand groupies. All sports have them. But athletes who want to stay in the game know where to draw the line."

She let the blanket fall to the floor and got to her feet, coming to sit beside him. "If you're wanting to scare me off, you'll have to do better than that."

Wyatt could've shifted so that their thighs pressed together—there wasn't more than an inch between—but he didn't. He stayed where he was, enjoying the heat of having her near, the anticipation of having her nearer still.

Sooner. He was pretty damn certain it was going to happen sooner, though he wasn't going anywhere if she had later in mind. "I hadn't thought so much about scaring you off. It was more about letting you know who I was."

"Isn't *was* the operative word here? Because if that's still who you are, you wouldn't let Buck do all the talking. You'd keep your profile as high as it ever was and have the bunnies lining up at the gate."

He set his cup aside, got up to tend the fire, knowing that

no matter his good intentions, it was way too late to put any distance between them. Yeah, she'd agreed that he wouldn't be profiled for her article or interviewed for his take on the rodeo life. Even so, she'd been here less than twelve hours, and she'd already figured out more about him than he'd told anyone in a very long time. It was going to make her four days on the ranch seem like four years.

That should have bothered him more than it did, but instead of figuring out why it didn't, he decided to tell her as much of the truth as he could manage without choking on the words.

6

"I'M DONE with both the bulls and the bunnies," Wyatt said as he came back to sit beside her, closer this time, his hip brushing hers, his arm pressed to hers. "My body can't take the abuse of the first, and I'm not interested in the second since most of them are only interested in the Lawman, not in the Triple RC or in me."

Tess didn't say anything, but she understood. She'd lost count of the men she'd met who were more interested in her society connections than in the work she did, or her love of gritty action flicks, or the fact that a long walk on the beach was honestly her idea of a perfect date. Oh, yes. She definitely understood.

She lifted her drink, realized it was nearly gone, decided this conversation—or was it a confessional?—called for more rum and held out the mug, ignoring the arch of his brow as he poured her a refill.

She thought his eyes were dark blue. She'd been sitting too far away at dinner to tell, and now the only light was that of the fire which burnished everything in shades of copper and bronze. Then again, she could very well be looking at him through eyes hazy with the heat of lust.

Since seeing him on horseback and watching his body move—already knowing his voice and what the words he said did to her, how he so easily coaxed her to open up—she'd been counting the minutes until they could get through the pleasantries her arrival required so that she could feel his hands on her skin.

The wait shouldn't have been this hard. She shouldn't have been this anxious, this antsy. This ready to sleep with a man she'd only just met and didn't really know…and how did that make her any different than the women who had followed him from rodeo to rodeo?

She silenced a rising groan and hoped he'd given her enough to drink. "I thought you said I wasn't doing a very good job of scaring you off."

"If you're talking about me having a little tea with my rum, that's not about you at all," she replied, and it was only a tiny white lie.

He added more to his drink as well, before setting the bottle off to the side and moving from the trunk to the floor. When he held out a hand, she took it, and slid down to sit at his side, not minding at all when he rested their joined hands on his thigh.

"So tell me, Doctor. What's driving you to drink?"

His leg was solid muscle beneath her hand, his fingers strong laced through hers. She was relaxed, liquid, just this side of intoxicated as she weighed how much of the truth was smart to reveal.

"Believe it or not, my mother. Or at least her quest to see me married into the right family. Not to the right man, mind you, or even to a man I might like, but to the right pedigree."

"I did some checking on who you are," he confessed, though he didn't sound the least bit apologetic. "After you called. I didn't want to be taken for a ride."

She didn't blame him. "You contacted the references I gave you?"

He nodded and ran his thumb over her knuckles. "I can see why your mother might worry about strays roaming the yard. You've got quite a pedigree of your own."

Damn lot of good it did her.

"Does your mother know where you are?"

She gave him a sideways glance. "Isn't that something you'd ask a teenager?"

He laughed, the sound throaty and earthy, and just a little bit drunk. It slipped beneath her skin, into her veins and melted her. Just melted.

"I meant," he continued while she pulled herself together, "what would she think about you drinking rum in front of a fire with a mutt of a cowboy?"

Funny. She'd just thought of herself as a mutt earlier today. Her thoughts, however, had been about her likes and dislikes while he seemed to be comparing their "breeding"— the very thing her mother obsessed over, and that Tess wanted so badly to escape.

"Considering I ditched one of her fundraisers to work on this article, she's already unhappy with me." Big fat understatement. "If she knew I'd been lured into a compromising situation, I'm sure she'd call out the dogcatchers."

He chuckled and squeezed her hand. "So, now I'm the one doing the luring here? Is that it?"

She found herself smiling, warming, whether from the rum, the fire or his touch she wasn't sure. "Aren't you the one who supplied the booze?"

"I didn't have any marshmallows," he said with a shrug. "Besides, I wasn't the one who made a roomful of curmudgeons fall in love with me over supper."

Oh, no. She wasn't going to take all the blame for where they found themselves. "You want to talk about luring—what about you on the back of a horse all muscled and fluid, and staring like you wanted to chase me down?"

"I did," he said, leaving it at that, leaving her to wonder if she should press or let things simmer, leaving her to wonder, too, if waiting was what she wanted, or if she was ready to turn the temperature higher right here and right now.

They sat quietly for several minutes, enjoying the fire, the company, the warmth of the alcohol and the way it lowered inhibitions. At least she was enjoying that last part, thinking how much larger his hand was than hers, and how much she'd love to have him do more than stroke his thumb the length of her index finger again and again.

But she didn't want to break the spell, sure she'd say the wrong thing, make the wrong move. Scare him off and ruin the whole weekend. If she went home too soon, she'd be going without her story, and her mother would find some event for her to attend to replace the one she'd managed to dodge.

No, she needed to get her research done before she even thought about leaving. Her real research, interviewing the men. Not this sitting-beside-a-cowboy-in-front-of-a-fire research that wasn't about her story at all but was about how ready she was for…did she even know what for? Or why he was the one who had stirred this need?

She took a deep breath, released it on a long slow sigh, and dropped her head back against the trunk, closing her eyes, her lips parted. She'd needed this, this doing nothing, this getting away. She hadn't known how much until now.

Work kept her more than busy, and her career was not one to take it easy on the stress. She carried her clients' problems home on a regular basis. And much as she wished her mother would stay out of her personal life, she admired the energy Georgina poured into her causes, and so she devoted as many hours as she could to the same.

And then there was all the keeping up with her best girl-friends and their busy, busy lives. True downtime was as much a part of her fantasies as was finding the right man, one enamored of her, who would have loved her just as much if he'd found her living in a box on the street with a dozen stray cats her only connection to any sort of society, instead of in her trendy condo.

Okay, that was going too far. Even she could see that. But there were times she wondered if her place in the world would actually doom her to a life alone, or to a marriage that was solely about convenience and companionship when she so wanted to be loved....

"Hey, sleepyhead. Let's get you to bed before your snoring wakes up every animal in the barn."

What was he saying? Snoring? Her eyes popped open. She felt heat rise to color her face, heat that had nothing to do with the dying fire or the haze of lust. How long had she been drifting? And did she really snore?

"What time is it?" Besides time for embarrassment.

"Time to go to bed."

"Together?" Nice...

He was still holding her hand, and he brought it to his mouth, pressing his lips to her fingers. "Is that what you want?"

Had any question ever been more loaded?

If she told the truth, it would make it hard to pull off this assignment with any sort of professionalism. And if she lied, well, he'd see the truth anyway. Changing the subject seemed the smartest thing to do.

"I'm sorry. I think I should have stuck with the tea. I'm usually not this unprofessional." Or this...easy. This...hungry.

He hadn't yet released her hand, and the fire she saw in his eyes wasn't dying as quickly as the one that had warmed her feet. "You're not on call. I figure even psychologists are human."

"Some of us, anyway," she said, getting up off the floor, appreciative of his teasing because she was in no condition to trust herself with this man. "The rest are around-the-clock therapy machines."

He took her mug from her hand, put it with his on the hearth and then stood. "If I need counseling at 3:00 a.m., I'll know not to give you a call."

At 3:00 a.m., she'd be much more inclined to provide him

another service, but she managed to keep that thought to herself and take the arm he offered, walking beside him as he escorted her to the stairs.

Once there, he let her go and followed for the second time as she made the climb. If he was watching the sway of her hips, it would only take his mind off the things she'd said that she would like to take back. She added a little extra wiggle just in case.

Tomorrow.

She'd wake up tomorrow, this night behind her, and get back to the business she was here to do. She wouldn't be starting off the day watching a cowboy on horseback move as if he and the animal were one.

They reached the door to her bedroom. She stopped there, but delayed walking through. Though it had to come to an end, she wasn't ready for the night to be over.

She backed a step into the room, her hand on the jamb, the open door behind her, and said, "Goodnight. I'll guess I'll see you at breakfast?"

"You will if you're up at four-thirty."

"Four-thirty?"

He nodded, his eyes dark, stormy, aroused, and his lashes so very long. "I usually come in for coffee around eight, but if I miss you, just make yourself at home in the kitchen. Eggs, bread, cereal, juice. Whatever you want. It's all there."

"Thanks," she said, wondering what he'd do if she told him exactly what she wanted. "Eight I can do. And after cleaning my plate more than once tonight, coffee and juice will be about all I'll want."

"Okay then," he said, but did so without making a move down the hallway toward his own room, or even back the way they had come. "Coffee at eight."

She nodded, waited, nodded once more, and then smiled.

He looked away, his pulse throbbing at his temple, then looked back and, muttering under his breath, stepped into her bedroom and backed her into the door.

7

HE'D TOLD himself hands off, so he planted them against the door above her head and held her in place with his body. He waited for her reaction because if she told him to skedaddle, he'd be on his way.

He was hoping she wouldn't. He wasn't going to take her to bed, not yet, not until this heat between them became exquisitely unbearable, but he wasn't ready to crawl between his own sheets alone.

And so he waited, watching her breathe, her chest rising and falling more rapidly as the seconds passed.

When she caught at her lip with her teeth, wetting the spot with her tongue, when she moved her hands from where she'd curled them at her hips to his waist, he knew it was time to do what he'd been waiting to do all day. He lowered his head as she lifted hers, and he kissed her.

He meant to be gentle, to keep it soft and sweet, to promise her that what they'd shared today was only the beginning and that there was so much more to come. But gentle wasn't going to happen. She dug her fingers into his sides and told him she wanted more right now.

He was enjoying flirting with her mouth, teasing one corner with tiny kisses, catching her bottom lip between both of his, breathing her in, that fresh green scent of springtime. But he didn't mind giving her what she wanted, so when she parted her lips, Wyatt opened his over them and slipped his tongue between.

The noise that rattled in her throat was half whimper and half groan. He couldn't help it, he pushed his hips into the cradle of hers. When she squirmed against him, he had no doubt that she'd felt the change in his body. He was hard, and growing harder. He wanted her and saw no reason not to let her know how much.

Her mouth was wet and giving, and she wasn't the least bit shy. She kissed him fiercely, using her hands to bring him close, her tongue to sample his, telling him with lips that pulled and sucked that he wasn't giving her enough, that she wanted to taste him in other ways…

Or so went his fantasy of her dropping to her knees, opening his fly and taking him into her mouth.

It had been so long, and he could have easily stripped the both of them bare and spent the rest of the night buried deep inside her body, his cock filling her, her sex hot and tight and sucking him deep. But he wasn't on the circuit anymore, and she wasn't there for one night to have a good time.

The kiss he could blame on the fire and the rum and still wake up tomorrow with his conscience intact. And as much pleasure as they were sharing here, both fully dressed, he wanted to be sober and sure when they got naked.

So he eased back slowly, first his body then his mouth, finally lifting his hands from the door where he'd kept them like the Boy Scout he was. He was breathing just as hard as she was, his frustration pounding in his ears and behind the fly of his jeans, but he was doing the right thing. He saw in her eyes that she knew it, that she appreciated him pulling this runaway beast to a stop.

"Get some sleep," he told her.

"I will," she whispered to him, her voice so soft, so torn, aroused and at the same time relieved. "I'll see you in the morning."

He nodded, backed his way out of the room, wanting to tell her this wasn't over, but her expression had already told him the very same thing.

FOUR-THIRTY came way too early. In fact, Wyatt didn't make it out of bed until after five. He ran late with everything for the rest of the morning, and he missed having coffee with Tess. When he did finally catch up with her, lunch had come and gone.

She was sitting on the rocking bench in front of the bunk-house talking to Buck. Or Buck was doing the talking and she the listening—so intently she didn't look up from Buck's story until he paused in the telling of it at Wyatt's approach.

"Afternoon, boss. Good to see you could make time in your busy schedule for your company here," Buck said, getting in the dig before Wyatt had a chance to explain to Tess what had held him up.

He pushed his hat off his forehead, crossed his arms and leaned a shoulder against one of the porch beams. "It's called ranching. You know, the work we do? Work being something I'm certain Dr. Autrey understands, though I'm thinking the rest of you aren't going to get much of anything done today with her being around."

Buck looked at Tess and spoke to her in an aside, pointing at Wyatt as he did. "The man brings a pretty thing like you out here and then blames us for not having a head for horses. Hurtful, I tell ya. Just plain ol' hurtful."

Wyatt finally glanced away from drama queen Buck Donald to Tess. She was smiling at the ranch manager, but the smile wasn't the one he'd seen last night. This one was nervous, as if she wasn't yet ready to face him, or wasn't sure what all had happened when they'd last been together.

He started to order Buck back to work—something he didn't think he'd ever done in their years together—but was saved from that folly by the sound of a diesel engine as a truck and trailer stopped at the gate.

Buck pushed up to his feet, still shaking his head in faux misery. "Dr. Autrey, it's been a pleasure, but since the boss is watching, I'd best go take care of business before Wyatt here has to show his face in public."

"If you have some time later, I'd love to talk more," Tess said, standing as Buck stepped off the porch. "You need to finish telling me about that night in Las Vegas."

"It's a date," he said, giving her a quick wave before turning away, buttoning up his denim jacket, then crossing the ranch's main yard.

Wyatt stayed where he was; waiting for Tess to acknowledge him instead of looking down at the porch boards and tugging on the hem of her pale-yellow sweatshirt the way she was doing, before finally stuffing her fists into her jeans pockets and hunching her shoulders against the cold.

"I—" was all she got out before he took the cue.

He vaulted onto the porch and hustled her into the big kitchen where they'd eaten dinner last night. Once out of the cool air and into the interior warmth, she seemed to find her footing. "About last night—"

He cut her off with a shake of his head. "Don't tell me you're sorry."

Her head came up, her chin high, her eyes bright with as much worry as pique. "I'm not sorry, but I didn't want you to think—"

Again, he didn't let her finish. "I didn't think anything that you need to worry about."

She screwed her mouth to one side and frowned. "Oh, thanks. Now I'm going to wonder for the rest of the day what you *were* thinking."

"Then we're in the same boat," he admitted, because he'd

wondered what she'd had on her mind when he'd left her at her door. "You getting what you need from the men?"

She nodded. "I've only talked to Max and Buck, but they've been very forthcoming."

"They're under orders to be," he told her, exaggerating the truth. The men, when presented with the proposition, had been more than willing to talk.

Her arms around her middle, she swayed from side to side, looking up at him coyly. "And what about you?"

"What about me?"

"Do you really not show your face in public? Like Buck said."

Damn the man. "I'm showing it to you."

"I'm one person. And we're on your ranch."

He shrugged off the topic, expecting her to press.

She didn't disappoint. "You're not the one who goes to town for milk and perishables, are you?"

"No need," he told her truthfully. "Woodson does the shopping."

"And Buck deals with the stock deliveries?"

He wasn't particularly enjoying this line of questioning. "He and Max."

"Tell me something, Wyatt."

Nope. He wasn't enjoying it at all. This time he was the one who crossed his arms.

She looked up at him with too much know-it-all in her expression. "When was the last time you left the ranch?"

"Do you know how big the Triple RC is?" he said instead of giving her an answer.

She wasn't so easily mollified. "It's still all the ranch. The same buildings. The same people. The same scenery. The same work to be done every day."

Ah, but that's where she was wrong. "The work may be the same, but it's always different depending on the time of year, how many animals we're raising, selling, taking delivery of. And the scenery can change from one day to the next with the weather. Things don't look the same under gray clouds as they do under bright sun.

"And if you're on horseback, you'll see things differently than you would from behind the wheel of a truck or on foot. Some days we work twelve hours, some days twenty-four. Yeah, it's still all the ranch, but the day-in and day-out is never the same."

He barely got the whole speech delivered before she dismissed it. "That's no reason not to show your face in public."

Psychologists. Lord love a cowboy and his horse, but they were a nosy species, digging into a man's head, looking for things he kept buried there for good reason.

He'd told her that he wanted to separate the success and the reputation of the ranch from that of the Lawman. Told her, too, that the Triple RC kept him busy enough that he never had reason to leave, though he hadn't filled her in on the fact that he did hit the livestock sales and auctions with Buck.

He figured that was plenty, that she didn't need to know how he'd brought a woman here once, one he'd thought he'd love till they died in each other's arms, sap that he was. Telling Tess that his injuries—the broken leg, pelvis, hip, ribs and nearly broken spirit—had also been the end of that relationship didn't sit so well.

Neither was he liking how easily she fitted in here with him, with his men, loving the house and the land without a complaint about the hours or the dirt or the smells that could turn a stomach as well as a nose. Yeah, she'd only been here a matter of hours, but he knew that when she left, he was going to feel it in a mighty big way.

He gave her the only answer he figured he owed her. "I can't think of any reason I should."

"I can think of several."

Of course she could. He glared down. "Would that have to do with you being a psychologist?"

And then she blew him right out of his socks. "Not as much as it has to do with me being female and wondering why no woman has snatched you up." ·

8
___

TESS watched him struggle to find a response he could live with. Then again, he could have been struggling to get out of answering at all, not wanting to share something that personal. But somehow she didn't think so.

Something made her think that he'd kept himself bottled up in solitude for so long that he wasn't comfortable letting anything of himself out. And that couldn't do anything but put off a woman's interest.

What she hadn't expected was for him to turn the question around on her. "What about you? You're degreed, successful, an amazing kisser and that car you drive speaks clearly about the money you come from—"

She held up a hand, cutting him off. "That car is all about the money I make, cowboy. Remember the degreed and successful part?"

Again with the tactical evasion. "Mostly I remember the kissing part."

Well, if he insisted on bringing it up…

She didn't think she'd dreamed or imagined how good he'd tasted, the wonderful movements of his mouth over hers, his tongue doing all the things a tongue should do. But knowing that what they'd shared stuck in his mind as well thrilled her beyond reason.

She looked down, stared at spots worn through the speckled flooring. "The kissing part was not the smartest thing in the world we could've done. If I want to present an unbiased look at the cowboy's side of the story, I need to maintain a certain detachment."

His boots scuffed against the vinyl as he shifted his stance. "You're not allowed to feel passionate about your subject?"

"Subject matter, sure. Not the subject himself." Though how easy had it been to do just that? And, oh, how much more passion did she have to give.

"Ah, but you're not interviewing me, remember?" he reminded her with no small hint of how he enjoyed his upper hand. "The deal was that you only talk to my men."

An agreement she regretted making, but how could she have known he'd be the one to rouse her curiosity the most?

Sidestepping the topic of the kiss, she queried him about more of last night's conversation. "Then since you're not a part of my column, there's no reason for you not to tell me what turned a high-profile guy into a loner."

She wanted to know. She really wanted to know. She didn't believe for a minute it was only about the women who wanted to mount him as a trophy...so to speak.

He walked across the room to the coffeemaker and sniffed at the liquid in the stainless-steel carafe. She knew Buck had put the pot on to brew before they'd talked, so when Wyatt offered to pour her a cup, she accepted.

Tess didn't need the caffeine; her stomach was already in knots, her energy wired high. But fixing the cup the way she liked it kept her from pressing him for a response. She had to give him time. Time and patience would get her what she wanted.

Once they'd both added cream and sugar and were sitting across from one another at the end of the table, he began. "I haven't made a conscious choice to be a loner. I don't even think of myself as one, though I can see why you might."

She didn't say anything to that, just wrapped both hands

around her mug and lifted it, blowing across the surface as she waited for him to go on.

"We deal with stock contractors, event coordinators, others with a vested interest in rodeo. For the most part, they're good people, but like with anything, a few bad apples spoil the barrel for the rest." He spun his cup back and forth on the table, from one hand to the other. "They want favors and perks, and they'll use any connections they have to get things to go their way."

"And you don't want them coming to do business with the Lawman. Or looking to be given any advantage for old times' sake," she said, beginning to understand more of what he probably faced on a regular basis—or would have faced had he not taken steps to remove himself from the picture.

He nodded, still toying with his mug. "I want them to come here to do business with the ranch, not with me. Our reputation needs to be based on the quality of the work we do here, and that of the stock we provide."

"Just to play devil's advocate—" because it was what she did often in her line of work "—wouldn't your old reputation bring you legitimate customers and inquiries as well? From people who would trust your judgment and prefer to do business with someone who has an inside track?"

He drank, then returned his mug to the table, shaking his head. "It would, but this way has worked well for us. I don't need the ego stroke of having my name attached to the ranch. Running things the way we've been doing seems to be the best solution all the way around."

"Plus, it does keep the hard-core bunnies from stalking you," she said, digging a bit deeper, a bit more pointedly, hoping he didn't shut down since she'd agreed not to include him in her interview.

He clamped his mouth shut as if there were a story in there wanting to get out. So, of course, she pried further. "Did it make you feel like a rock star? Knowing they'd be waiting for you after every performance?"

Even though he had to know exactly what she was doing, he answered her seriously, surprising her by not dodging her questions. "For a while, sure. But there's a point where it gets… eerie, I guess."

Eerie? "How so?"

"It feels like you've picked up a stalker instead of an admirer. Most of the women know the score. They don't want anything but to have a good time. Others don't understand the way the game is played."

He was talking about the ones who wanted more than a night or two in a champion's bed. Tess had met them. They thought sleeping with a cowboy was more than an exchange of sexual favors. They thought they were giving the men something they couldn't live without, couldn't get from anyone else, were on the road hoping to find.

They formed wrongly motivated emotional attachments. They role-played, forgetting the line between real life and make-believe. Some grew obsessive, and obviously Wyatt had run into the type who didn't want to let him go.

From where she was sitting, Tess had to admit she wouldn't have a lot of trouble walking a mile—or ten—in those women's shoes, and she hadn't yet spent time in his bed—a thought she cut short before it got her into trouble.

Then he surprised her by adding, "And there are some who'll drop a cowboy the minute he loses a title or an event. That's all they want. His limelight."

Well, now. That was unexpected. She'd hadn't thought about the possibility that his retreat, his reclusiveness was about being hurt emotionally as much as physically. "What do you do now for companionship?"

He snorted. "By companionship I'm assuming you're talking about sex? Not the camaraderie I share with the guys?"

She forced a careless shrug and stared at her coffee, trying to make less of the subject than it seemed to be. But now she had to admit to wondering whether his heart was as free and clear as his body. "Not that it's any of my business…"

"It's not."

Arrogant man. "And not that I'm going to use the information in my article…"

"You're not."

Bossy man. "It's just that I was wondering…"

"You were wondering if you'd be stepping on anyone's toes if we slept together."

Intuitive man. "Not that it's going to happen…"

"Sure it is. We both know it is."

"Oh?" The way he said it, as if there was no question that they'd end up in bed, was as intoxicating as last night's rum, as warming as the fire she'd watched flicker and spark while she'd sat beside him.

He went on, "It's been coming on since the road. That's where it started. You watching me. Me watching you. Or before that, with the phone call, and you telling me that celibacy was for the birds."

He paused as if giving her a chance to deny the obvious, continuing when she remained mum. "C'mon, Tess. Isn't that how most of these things work?"

She loved hearing him speak her name. Loved the gritty edge to his voice, how he used the one word, rawly spoken, to take this conversation from impersonal to intimate. Then again, she'd gone there when she'd asked about his sex life, and told him about hers.

Her stomach tumbled. "You've had a lot more experience with being watched than I have. You tell me."

"That's not the sort of watching I'm talking about," he said, his tone low, potent, intense. "Not performing. Not in an arena. Not with an audience."

"Then what?" she asked, because as much as she loved listening to him, she loved even more the way he was looking at her, watching her now.

"In a bar. You're sitting on a stool, or at a table with your girlfriends. Especially with your girlfriends, talking, laughing. You attract a man's attention. You make eye contact. Now *your* attention is divided.

"You can't keep up with the conversation at the table because you're wondering what he's thinking, if he wants to meet you, maybe have a drink. But neither one of you make a move. You're both caught up in the watching."

When he stopped, she was finally able to draw a breath. Her skin beneath her sweatshirt was hot and damp. Her heart was spinning in her chest. Oh, what was he doing to her? "How would you know I'd be thinking any of that?"

His eyes flashed, the color that of stormy skies. "A woman I once knew. She told me that's how it was."

That woman he'd known—she'd been pretty damn on the mark. Tess hadn't experienced it often, but there were a couple of incidents she'd often looked back on, wondering what might have happened had she made a move, left Claire, Alexandra and Windy behind and met the man watching her from his table.

But all of those memories paled in the face of having Wyatt watching her now. And she couldn't deny her curiosity, her arousal, or keep from asking him, "What about from the man's point of view? What's going on in his head all this time?"

Wyatt set his mug on the table, placed his hands on either side as if the contact with the wooden surface was the only thing keeping him in his chair, the only thing keeping her safe.

"Are you sure you want to know?" he finally asked, and Tess didn't hesitate.

"Yes."

9

WYATT LOOKED into her eyes. He had to know, had to be sure she knew what her answer meant. He wasn't going to hurt her or frighten her or force her to do anything except to face the truth of his wanting her. Anything that might happen between them because of it would be her call.

He started slowly. "I would be thinking about walking over to you and offering you my hand."

"And if I took it?"

"I'd pull you to your feet. What happened next would depend on whether or not we're really in public or whether we've moved into my fantasies."

"What if it's the here and now?" she asked, her voice breathless and husky, as if her anticipation of his response had taken her into a fantasy world of her own.

Ah, hell, he thought, realizing she'd just given him the go-ahead he'd wanted. She was smart and sexy and easy to talk to, and the minute they took things any further, he'd be in over his head.

And after all he'd done to protect himself and his privacy, to keep from getting involved and ending up plastered face-first in the dirt…after all of it, he was falling for a woman who wasn't going to be around but four days.

Four days.

And he'd been worried about *her* wanting more time.

Wyatt reached across the table for Tess's hand, and once

her palm was flat to his, he closed his fingers and got to his feet, holding her while he circled around to her side and drew her up against him.

She didn't resist when he moved his hands to her waist and lifted her to sit on the table's edge, but instead parted her legs, inviting him between, and hooked her heels behind his thighs to make sure he stayed.

He had no intention of going anywhere unless he dragged her out of the kitchen to bed. But he didn't mind at all that she wanted him close. Or that she slipped her fingers through his belt loops, refusing to let him go.

"For being all about the here and now, I gotta say this is a hell of a fantasy," he said, his voice tight and raspy, an ache in his throat. He rested his hands on her thighs just shy of the crease at her hip.

"I'd say it's a hell of a reality," she told him, doing that thing with her lip and her teeth and her tongue, that thing that made him ache. "You're certainly not what I was expecting to find during my visit."

He let her words settle, surprised that his first reaction wasn't to close down, that his second wasn't to bolt. Still, he had to know— "What do you think you've found?"

"I don't know. A kindred spirit, maybe? You get what it's like not to trust easily, to wonder what's behind someone's interest, whether their motives for being with you have anything to do with who you really are, or if it's only about what you can give them."

It was the truth, all of it. He appreciated that she understood. "You know you haven't once questioned mine. I told you I'd looked into you. Aren't you worried that I might be after more than getting you into bed?"

"No," she said, tugging his belt loops. "You agreed to let me come before you knew any of that. And you have no reason to need my family's name and social connections."

"What about your money?"

She knew he was teasing her. He saw it in her quirky smile. "I'm only guessing here, but I doubt you have need of that either."

"So where does that leave us?"

"With the rest of today, tomorrow and Monday to enjoy this fantasy," she said, suddenly pragmatic.

He frowned. "I thought you said it was reality."

"I changed my mind."

"Why?"

"Because if it was real, we wouldn't be dealing with a time limit."

"We don't have to."

"Even though you set it?"

"I changed my mind." Four days wasn't going to be enough time.

"Maybe you should wait and see if I'm any good in bed before you do that."

"No need," he said, shaking his head and sliding his hands beneath her sweatshirt, settling his palms on her rib cage just beneath her breasts. "A man doesn't have to get a woman into bed to know if she'll be a good time. At least the kind of good time worth having. One that's about more than a handy warm-and-willing body."

She sighed, shivered. "The best sex really is between the ears?"

"Like I said. The kind that's worth having."

"And you like what goes on in my head?"

More so that she could possibly imagine. Talking to her had given him more pleasure than any exchange—physical or otherwise—he'd had with a woman in a while. He nodded, then dropped his head close to her shoulder, his mouth to her neck at the band of her shirt.

She moaned, tilted her head to the side as he nuzzled, giving him more access and more reason to go on. "I'm not sure we have much in common. I don't know a thing about rodeo."

"I can teach you." He nibbled her skin, bathed the spot with his tongue. She tasted like early-morning mist and water, clear and pure.

She moved her hands from his belt loops to his waist, gathering the fabric of his shirt in her fists. "What if I don't really care about rodeo?"

"I know enough for both of us."

"It won't work. My practice is in Houston."

"You can commute."

"It's too far. And I love my condo."

"I can commute."

"No you can't. You live and breathe this place."

"Right now, I want to live and breathe you." He wanted it more than anything he'd wanted in years, more than he'd imagined wanting it when he'd seen her on the road that morning.

"That's fine. It's just a fantasy, remember?" she said, her hands creeping up his sides, her fingers walking along his ribs, his chest, reaching for the snaps on his shirt, popping one, then another—

Steps sounded on the porch outside.

Wyatt jumped back as if dodging the horns of a bull. Tess leaped off the table, straightened her sweatshirt, patted down then fluffed her hair. Wyatt picked up their mugs and carried them to the sink.

He was rinsing them and willing down his erection when Teddy Jacobs opened the door. The young cowboy had been a champion steer wrestler until one of the animals had taken a liking to his boots and tried to make room for his own hoof by slamming Teddy's ankle out of the way.

"Want a cup of coffee, Teddy?" Wyatt asked. "I was just going to get another for Dr. Autrey here."

"It's Tess, please. Just Tess."

"Sure," Teddy said, pulling his hat from his head and worrying the brim in his hands. "Sorry if I'm early. I finished up with the stirrups needing mending and decided to head on over."

"Your timing is perfect," Tess told him. "Besides, this needs to be convenient for you more than for me. I don't want to get in the way of your work schedule. Your boss was just checking to make sure I kept that in mind."

Wyatt set the freshly poured cups on the table, slapped Teddy on the shoulder and headed for the door. He turned to Tess before leaving and said, "I may not make it to supper tonight, but I'll check in with you when I get back, see if there's anything you need before calling it a night."

He didn't wait for her to answer. He saw all he needed to see in her eyes.

IT WAS almost ten by the time Wyatt finished for the day, got Fargo brushed down and bedded, and began making his way from the barn to the house.

He'd spent a lot of hours this afternoon thinking about what had happened in the kitchen with Tess, how they hadn't crossed a single line of impropriety, yet how he couldn't get the heat of the moment off his mind.

Yeah, he'd nuzzled her neck, breathing in that fresh springtime smell that he thought was just her scent rather than any soap or shampoo or perfume. And, yeah, her fingers had teased him, had reached to undress him, but she hadn't done anything more than play with his snaps.

He'd had his hands beneath her sweatshirt, and the skin of her stomach had been so warm and beautifully soft, but he hadn't gone up or down into forbidden territory. And still he couldn't remember another woman ever bringing him to a boiling point with such innocent contact.

What that said about his feelings for her, he couldn't be sure. It was too soon, or so he told himself, thinking love at first sight too crazy a concept to possibly be true. Lust, sure. That he had no trouble believing in. So it didn't make sense that from the bottom of his heart he felt more. He really, truly felt more. And that scared him in ways he couldn't put into words.

He was halfway across the yard when he caught sight of Tess at the back fence, her feet on the bottom rung, her crossed arms hooked over the top one as she stared off into the darkness. He changed direction midstride, slowing as he closed the distance between them, clearing his throat softly so he wouldn't frighten her with his approach.

She didn't turn, but she did step down to the ground, curling her fingers over the fence board and resting her cheek on her hand. She smiled when he finally reached her. "I didn't realize talking about fantasies was going to scare you off for the rest of the day."

Wyatt braced a boot on the bottom rung, pushed his hat off his forehead, and held the top of the post with one hand, as close to her as he could get without more than the fabric of their clothes touching. "Believe it or not, I was working. And I didn't have an easy time of it out there all day knowing you were waiting here."

He stopped himself from adding, "for me." He wanted to be sure she was in this as completely as he was, and that she understood he'd been serious when he'd told her he'd changed his mind, but he knew that if he went too fast, pressed too hard, it wouldn't take much to send her running.

"Me waiting for you. Is that still part of the fantasy from earlier?" she asked, her voice soft, her eyes warm, both inviting him to take her inside.

He would. He wanted to get her out of the cold, into the shower and then into his bed. But he wasn't going to lie. Not when this was the most important step he'd taken toward starting a relationship in years.

And so he shook his head. "No. No fantasy. It's one-hundred percent reality. You just have to let me know if you're ready for that."

10

SHE WAS ready to make love to him. That much she knew. He was physically gorgeous, yes, but she was drawn to him by much more than the fit of his jeans and the width of his shoulders.

She'd been as honest as possible when she'd told him she felt she'd found a kindred spirit who understood why she found relationships so hard. She just hadn't told him that she saw everything she wanted in him.

Knowing she could trust him in that one regard made opening up to him so easy. It was no guarantee that she wouldn't get hurt, yet getting hurt was a risk that came with all emotional involvement.

But was she ready for what he was asking? For what he wanted? The only answer she had was that she was ready to try, and so she moved away from the fence, took a step toward him and held out her hand.

Instead of taking it, he wrapped an arm around her shoulders and pulled her close to his body. She leaned into him, one arm around his back, one hand reaching up to hold his as they walked toward the house.

She hadn't noticed the cold when she'd been outside enjoying the twinkle of the stars splattered across the sky for unending miles, but once the warmth of the house began to thaw her fingers, her ears, the tip of her nose, the shivers set in and rattled her.

Wyatt reached his free hand across her body and rubbed up and down her arm as they made their way through the dark kitchen. "What were you doing outside with only a sweatshirt anyway? It's going to drop close to freezing tonight."

Shaking all over now, she hated to let him go, but had to in order to climb the stairs. "It didn't seem that cold when I went out."

"Lost in thought?"

She nodded. She'd been thinking about him, this place, if there might honestly be a way they could continue to see each other after this weekend, or if all their teasing about commuting was just that—nothing but a joke. What would she be willing to give up to have him in her life?

"You're not going to share the details?"

"A girl's got to have some secrets," she said as they reached the second-floor landing.

"Hmm. Not so sure I like the sound of that."

"Think of it this way. If I tell you everything now, what will you have to look forward to?"

Huffing at that, he took hold of her elbow and led her to the bathroom, grabbing towels from the linen closet. "What I'm looking forward to right now is smelling a little less like someone who spent the past few hours riding through a herd of cows getting ready to drop their calves."

She pushed open the bathroom door. "Would you like some help with that?"

He growled his answer, propelling her into the white-and-yellow tiled room and kicking the door shut behind them. He tossed the towels to hang over the rack, and stood on one foot then the other to tug off his boots.

When he reached for the snaps of his shirt, Tess stopped him. She wanted to see his body, to touch him, to taste him, to breathe him in. She wanted to learn the texture of the hair on his chest, his head, between his legs. She wanted to see how the skin at his throat tasted differently from that of his chest and belly. But she didn't want any of it to happen so fast that she missed enjoying a single moment.

And so she started on his shirt, pulling the tails from his waistband and popping the snaps one by one. He let her do that much, but then he grew impatient, shrugging off the heavy denim and reaching for the hem of the plain white T-shirt he wore beneath.

She could have stopped him, could have inched the fabric up his torso and chest, revealing the skin beneath slowly, but she let him strip the shirt away, thrilled to see how anxious he was to have her.

And, oh, but his chest was beautiful—broad and finely muscled, covered with a mat of dark hair that grew less thickly over sharply defined abs before trailing down to disappear beneath the jeans he still wore.

She reached out because she couldn't resist, dragging her fingers up his stomach to his chest, threading them through his hair and tugging, finding his nipples and pinching them lightly, massaging the flesh covering his pectorals until he groaned.

He wasn't a patient man and only gave her a minute to play before reaching for the lower band of her sweatshirt, skimming the garment over her head and saying, "My turn."

She stood there in her jeans and a bra of lemon-colored silk. It wasn't particularly sheer, but she could see her reflection in the mirror over the sink, and knew exactly how dark and tight her nipples appeared. If he couldn't tell by her body's reaction how much she wanted him…

Wyatt's eyes seemed to sizzle as he stared, as he watched her reach back to unhook the clasp, as he took in the bounce of her breasts when she shimmied free of the straps and the bra dropped to the floor.

His chest began to rise and fall rapidly. His eyes dilated. His nostrils flared as he searched for her scent. She didn't have to lower her eyes to know he was fully aroused. She'd felt the strength of his erection last night when he'd pinned her to the bedroom door, and his expression burned now as it had then.

She couldn't wait anymore. They had to get this first coming-together behind them, relieve the tension so they could spend hours taking things slowly. Reaching into the tub, she turned on the water, jerked the curtain almost all the way shut, and hit the lever that sent the water from the faucet to the shower head above.

That done, she fumbled for the buttons of her jeans. While opening her fly, she kicked out of her shoes and socks, then peeled off both her pants and panties. She didn't look at him, though she heard all sorts of grunts and groans as he got rid of his clothes, but stepped into the tub and lifted her face to the spray.

She listened to the slide of the curtain on the rod as he pulled it open then shut it behind him, and suddenly the tub that had seemed so roomy closed in on her, leaving her feeling as if this moment in this place was her whole world. As if nothing had existed before Wyatt Crowe walked into her life. As if what happened here would change her forever.

Oh, but she was ready for it to happen. What Wyatt had given her in the last two days was what she'd never found in the men she'd dated to make her mother happy. He wasn't interested in her pedigree, her social status, her family's wealth.

He didn't care that she knew nothing about rodeo, that she had no intention of ever getting up at four-thirty in the morning, that she could chow down with the hungriest of his men. He wanted her for being Tess.

And for him, that's exactly who she wanted to be. Herself—giving him all the things she'd never wanted to give to anyone before. Especially her love. She turned, slicked back her hair from her face, and finally opened her eyes.

He had one hand on the curtain rod, one braced flat on

the tiled wall. He was staring down at her, watching her, his eyes fiery, the tic in his jaw proving how close he was to losing control.

She wanted to see what it would take, how far he could stand for her to go, so she reached for the soap, lathered a head of suds in her hands and slipped her palms beneath her breasts, cupping their weight, toying with her nipples, her bottom lip caught between her teeth.

Wyatt closed his eyes, dropped his head back on his neck, his throat and shoulders tense. Tess glanced down at his erection, took a deep breath and wondered why she was playing games and drawing this out when he was what she wanted—and when she wanted him so much she thought she'd die with the need to have him inside her.

She didn't wait for him to regain his composure. She took him in her soapy hands, wrapped one leg around his hip and stood on her tiptoes to guide him into place. Once he realized what she was doing, he took over, reaching for a condom he'd left on the counter and having a much better idea of how this balancing act should work.

He hooked his hands behind her thighs and hoisted her up as he drove forward, nearly slamming her into the wall in his need to have her. He entered her in one long stroke, and she gasped as he filled her, looping her arms around his neck and holding on for the ride she knew wouldn't take either of them long.

He felt as if she'd been waiting for him forever, the fit of him perfect as he stretched her, as she tightened around him, her contractions causing him to make a lot of sounds that were nothing if not base and raw, sounds that she would've echoed had she been able to find her voice.

She couldn't find anything but sensation. The water steamy around her like a cloud, beating against her legs, her side, stinging her skin. His muscles beneath her hands flexing. The scent of damp skin and soap. And the picture in her mind of his erection, the girth, the length…the realization that she had all of that inside her now.

He shifted his weight more evenly, leaning heavily into her, nearly crushing her, and she didn't even care. She loved bearing up his body with her own, giving him that cushion, that support, that comfort. The friction of his skin against hers, the slick slide of their bellies together, the damp hair of his chest rubbing over her breasts was almost too much stimulation to process. And she wouldn't have changed a thing.

His thrusts were powerful, spreading her open, the base of his cock grinding against her clit, his hair there scratching against her, stimulating, tickling, bringing her to the edge so quickly that she went over in a spectacular fall that she thought would never end.

He came then, his orgasm following hers, a storm, a surge, exploding into her and taking her with him again into a swirling, spiraling completion that left them both too short of breath to stand.

"THAT SHOULDN'T have happened so fast," he said, shifting his right elbow closer to her head where her hair lay in damp ringlets on his pillow.

She sucked a sharp breath as the motion had his erection hitting just the right spot inside of her. "Who says?"

"Me, for one." He brushed back strands of hair that had fallen into her eyes. "I like to take things slow. Get a lot more out of the experience than one quick blast."

"Isn't that what you're doing now?" she asked, reaching up and tugging on his locks, long against his neck. She liked the length, the way he looked more outlaw than lawman. "Making up for being so quick on the draw before? Stop apologizing."

He narrowed his eyes. "How 'bout if I place blame instead?"

"On who? Me?"

"It sure as hell wasn't all my fault, the way you were getting yourself off."

She liked that he'd enjoyed watching her, liked that her plan had worked. "I was taking a shower. You know, washing, soaping up my breasts."

"A shower my ass." He thrust again, nearly taking her off the bed.

It took several seconds to find the will to speak. "I showered your ass, too. Along with every other part of your amazing body."

"You did, didn't you?" He settled more of his weight in the cradle of her hips, rubbing the base of his shaft against her swollen clit. She tingled, she ached, her heart swelled. "You did a damn fine job."

"Thank you, kind sir." She dug her fingers into his buttocks and urged him further along the length of her body.

He complied, sinking as deep inside of her as was possible for him to get. "Is that better?"

"It's perfect." Too perfect. Perfect bliss. Heaven. She groaned. "I could get so used to this."

"You can have it any time."

Had he come up with a magical solution to merging their separate lives? Could she even think about that at a time like this when she was so close to coming for what, the fourth, fifth time? "How so?"

"Commute."

"That's not fair." He rolled his hips; she shuddered beneath him. "And that's really not fair."

"Just don't want you to forget me," he said, looking down at her with eyes so soft, so filled with emotion that her throat threatened to lock around the words she wanted to say.

"That will never happen."

He dropped a kiss to the tip of her nose, a tender touch,

so gentle. "That's good to hear, because I plan to see that you don't."

She arched upward, dropped back to the mattress, hurting with the way she wanted him now, the way she wanted him forever. "This plan of yours. I'm going to assume that includes you not forgetting me?"

He leaned to one side and brought his free hand up to cup her breast, to run his thumb teasingly across her nipple before sliding his fingers down between their bellies to where their bodies were joined.

Tess cried out, her arms reaching to both sides of the bed, her hands gripping the sheet as she came. She lost herself in the sensation, knowing that he came with her, but so drunk with what she was feeling that she couldn't spare any of herself to help him along.

When they had both finished and collapsed together, exhausted, he whispered into her ear, "In a million years, a million lifetimes, I will never forget about you."

11

TESS SPENT all of Sunday talking to his men, and Wyatt spent the same time watching her. She amazed him, how natural she was with everyone, how easily she got them to open up about the women they'd been with in the past.

Women who'd given them a good time but nothing else.

Women who in the end, hadn't meant a thing.

Women who'd taken what they needed and no more.

Having shared the same experiences as his crew, Wyatt couldn't believe the difference Tess made in the morale around the ranch. He would've thought he'd hired on a whole new staff, what with the way everyone's steps seemed to be lighter, the lift of their lips smiles not snarls.

Agreeing to this whole contest with the article and the getaway weekend had been a freakin' brilliant plan. Whether or not they wanted to admit it, his men had realized it would be good to have their own women around. Especially since Tess was all his.

It was Monday, now, and she was packing to go. The men had gathered around her in front of the house, helping her with her bags, with packing her car, making sure she had coffee for the road and a map to get her where she was going. If Wyatt had his way, she wasn't going to go anywhere for long.

He'd left her in his bed this morning and ridden out on Fargo, knowing he couldn't tell her goodbye in front of a curious audience when he didn't plan to tell her goodbye at all. He'd meant what he'd said. A million lifetimes wouldn't be enough for them to share.

In four short days she'd won his heart.

The things she'd done to his body he wanted to do with her over and over again. But her interest in him, her teasing and flirting, the talking they'd done after making love the last two nights, staying awake until the wee hours and having the days drag until they could be together again...

He didn't want that to end. In fact, he was thinking it was something he'd like to do for the rest of his life. The fact that they barely knew one another, well, they had a lifetime to remedy that.

From the pasture that ran alongside the road—the same one he'd been working in the day she arrived—he saw her coming and urged the horse into a gallop, staying far ahead of her car. Once he reached the gate, he leaned down to open it, maneuvering it closed from Fargo's back.

And then he waited for her in the middle of the road.

She slowed when she saw him, coming to a complete stop in a repeat of Friday's encounter. Even through the windshield he could see her fighting a smile. It made it hard for him to keep a straight face as she climbed out of the car.

"I thought this morning was the only goodbye I was going to get from you," she said, having a hard time keeping her voice from cracking.

He'd made love to her, both of them still half asleep, before getting out of bed. He planned to make that a regular occurrence. "That wasn't a goodbye. It was to hold you until I could come up with a solution."

"A solution to?"

"This commuting thing."

"I see," she said, reaching in to turn off the ignition then walking around the front of the car and leaning against the hood. "And did you? Come up with one?"

"I think so." They hadn't talked much about what they were going to do after today. Or at least they hadn't talked seriously. But even the teasing they'd done hadn't seemed so much a joke as it had desperation.

He only hoped she bought into his plan. "I know you see patients during the week. And I work, well, every day. So I was thinking, that if you'll come out here on Fridays and stay till Monday, I'll come in on Tuesdays late and leave early Thursday morning."

She crossed her arms, considered him more than his suggestion. It didn't keep him from holding his breath as he waited for an answer that would change both their lives. "That would mean you wouldn't be at the ranch at all on Wednesdays. Could you deal with that?"

"It would also mean I'd get to see you seven days a week, even if we'd only have a few hours during a couple of them. So, yeah. I can live with anything to make that happen." And that was the God's honest truth.

She pushed off the car, came a few steps closer, scuffing the toe of her shoe in the road's dirt like she was wearing old boots instead of designer footwear. "Do I have to learn to ride a horse?"

The smile that split his face fairly ached from the way it stretched his skin. His heart pretty much ached the same. He slid from the back of the horse, dropping Fargo's reins to ground-tie him, and met her halfway between their two rides. "Only if you want to."

"And you." She stopped in front of him, toyed with the snaps on his denim shirt, popped one, another, only stopping when he wrapped his hand around her busy little fingers. "When you're with me in Houston, are you going to show your face in public?"

He couldn't wait to take her out on the town. "I figure you'll be wanting to show me off to your friends."

"That so, cowboy?"

"That's so, city girl," he said, sliding his hands into her hair and bringing her mouth to his for a kiss that rocked his world until he couldn't see straight.

When she finally pulled away breathless, laughing, she asked, "Tell me something. Is it really possible to have sex on the back of a moving horse?"

What the hell? "You been reading some bad porn or something? Because I value my privates too much to give that a try."

She laughed. She doubled over until tears streamed from her eyes, tears he was damn certain were about more than what he'd just said. "Oh, Wyatt Crowe. I think I love you."

"I think I love you, Tess Autrey," he said. "And for you, I might even give that horse thing a try…"

I CAN STILL FEEL YOU...

Cara Summers

To Dawnelle Jager—my colleague and very good friend. You gave unconditional love and support when I needed it most. You're the best!

1

"TURN and face the camera, Macy."

Recognizing the director's voice, Macy Chandler did exactly that. She knew him only by his first name—Danny. She'd met so many people from the TV station in the past week that first names were about all she could manage, and right now, thanks to the lights aimed at her from several directions, she couldn't see any of them. Danny and the rest of the crew were dim shapes crammed into the space beyond her food-prep island.

"You aced the first segment," Alan murmured. "One down and two to go."

Her assistant and very best friend, Alan Garner, stood in the shadows to her immediate right, looking cool and elegant in spite of the heat from the lights.

"FYI—I heard one of the crew say that you're a natural." Alan had been her own private cheerleader since their junior-high days. As Macy checked the ingredients he had laid out for the next dish, he began to hum "Everything's Coming Up Roses."

Immediately, her nerves began to settle. Everything *was* coming up roses. Her personal chef business, Some Like It Hot, had been steadily gaining a reputation in the Austin area, and three weeks ago, Kate Sinclair, editor of the "Sex in the Saddle" column in the *Austin Herald,* had called and asked her to provide the prize for a Valentine's Day contest. The newspaper's corporate owner, Deep in the Heart Communications, was sponsoring Valentine's Day promotions in its papers in three Texas cities—Houston, San Antonio and Austin. The goal was to increase circulation. Each city had to create its own contest and the staff at the paper that received the most entries was going to receive a bonus.

When Kate Sinclair had proposed her idea of offering three separate prizes—"Brunch in Bed," a "Pleasurable Picnic," and a "Sexy Supper," Macy had jumped at the idea. Kate had also contacted a local TV station and convinced them to join forces in the promotion. The TV station had agreed to film Macy preparing each recipe, and the paper was publishing them to increase circulation even more.

That, in a nutshell, was how a TV crew had ended up in her kitchen on a hot Sunday morning. The televised segments of the "Pleasurable Picnic" airing during the past week on *News at Noon* had been so popular that the contest entries for the remaining two prizes had flooded the *Herald* office. Everything had happened so fast that Macy had an urge to pinch herself to see if she was dreaming. But the TV lights were real enough. So was the trickle of sweat running down her back.

"Give us that five-hundred-watt smile, Macy," the director said.

Once again, Macy did what she was told.

"Quiet. Ready on a count of five."

"Wait!" A pretty young makeup woman stepped into the lighted area, dabbed powder on Macy's nose, then disappeared into the shadows.

"On five," the director reminded every one. "One, two…"

There was nothing to worry about, Macy told herself. Hadn't she practiced the preparation of each dish over and over again with Alan as her test audience? And the asparagus was the simplest course for her "Brunch in Bed."

"Don't forget to tell them about the French bridegrooms," Alan whispered.

"Three, four, five."

"Why asparagus?" Macy winked into the camera. "And well you might ask. Isn't that the veggie you used to try to get the dog to eat when you were a kid? But there are several reasons to include asparagus on our 'Brunch in Bed' menu. For starters, because it's finger food, and there's nothing quite as sexy or seductive as feeding your lover."

She picked up a piece of asparagus. "But first you want to eliminate the tough ends. Just bend the vegetable." She snapped the stalk in two. "Now you break all the others where they snap naturally." While she talked, she spread the asparagus on a foil-lined cookie sheet, then drizzled them with olive oil and sprinkled them with chopped chili peppers.

"Now we come to the second reason for asparagus. It will give you and your lover a chance to play with your food and to learn how that can stimulate all of your senses."

As she demonstrated how to "play" with the asparagus by using her hands to toss it in the oil and spices, Macy continued, "Of course the best reason to include these little green stalks in any seductive brunch is their reputation as the most erotic vegetable. Nineteenth-century French bridegrooms were required to eat several courses of them on their wedding nights because of the power of asparagus to arouse." After popping the cookie sheet into the oven, she turned and once more winked at the camera. "And you thought you had to depend solely on oysters."

There was laughter and a round of applause from the crew as the director called, "Cut."

RANGER Cade Dillon stopped short in the doorway of Macy Chandler's kitchen. It took him a moment to absorb the TV crew and the lights, another to figure out that a cooking show was being filmed. The sharp stab of fear that had caused him to sprint up the front walk gradually eased.

His partner, Nate Blackhorn, had told him that Macy had been appearing on the *News at Noon,* but he hadn't expected to find a TV crew filming in her kitchen. Her front door had been wide open—anyone could have walked in. He had. So could Elton Leonard, the eccentric and slick bank robber Cade had been chasing for the past two years. He could have been too late.

Cade quickly scanned the crew standing elbow to elbow in Macy's small kitchen. Behind the island, two people were deep in conversation with Macy, blocking her from his view— a short balding man with a long ponytail who Cade didn't know, and a taller man he recognized as Macy's assistant, Alan Garner. Alan was tall, blond and handsome, and Cade knew that he was in a long-term relationship with his partner, Martin. Cade purposely didn't look at Macy; instead, he shifted his attention back to the crew. Only when he'd satisfied himself that Leonard was not present did he lean back against the doorjamb.

Elton Leonard was back in Austin. An informant had spotted him in the area three days ago, the same day Cade had received another anonymous e-mail—PS, This is Austin.

Cade had been receiving the cryptic e-mails—sometimes a country-and-western song title, such as "PS, This is Austin," and sometimes an old saying—ever since Leonard had jumped bail and disappeared from Austin two months ago. The gut instinct Cade had honed in his fifteen years as a Texas Ranger told him that Leonard's return spelled big trouble for Macy Chandler.

Before Leonard's arrest, the media had dubbed the unknown perpetrator of a string of Texas bank robberies "Clyde without Bonnie," thus romanticizing the exploits of one of the most elusive criminals Cade had ever run into. In the beginning, Cade had been the only one who'd suspected that Elton Leonard, a reclusive and purportedly brilliant heir to a fortune in Texas oil, was "Clyde."

Leonard wasn't a large man, and in his rare public appearances, he wore glasses and projected the image of a rather harmless nerd. But Cade had learned that one of Leonard's talents was his almost chameleon-like ability to shift himself into different personas. When he donned a disguise, he practically *became* another person.

Leonard's other characteristic—the one that was going to lead to his downfall—was his arrogance. He had a vast collection of cars and he'd used them to make his getaways. Twice a witness had gotten a partial plate number, and both times Cade was able to link the numbers to one of Leonard's cars. It hadn't been enough to make an arrest, but it had certainly pointed a finger.

In Cade's opinion, robbing banks was a game to Leonard—a way of proving that he was smarter than the police and the Texas Rangers, a way to demonstrate that he was above the law. But his last bank robbery in Austin hadn't gone so well. First off, he'd shot and killed a bank guard, and then Macy Chandler had spoiled his fun by pulling her catering van into an alley behind the bank just in time to see Leonard exit the building, change out of a disguise and drive away. Because she'd thought the behavior odd and more than a little suspicious, she'd noted the license number. Leonard had once again been driving one of his own cars. Later Macy had picked him out of a lineup, and Leonard had been charged with armed robbery and murder. Cade had made the arrest.

"Ready everyone?" The short, ponytailed man Cade figured for the director backed around the island.

"Give me a moment." A cameraman moved closer to Macy, and Alan Garner rearranged some dishes on the island counter. One of the crew members adjusted a light.

Thanks to Macy, Elton Leonard had run out of luck. His team of top-flight attorneys hadn't been able to prevent the indictment. If the billionaire hadn't jumped bail and disappeared, he'd be behind bars right now. And if Cade hadn't been distracted by sleeping with his star witness, Macy Chandler, Leonard might never have succeeded in skipping out of Austin.

"Ready on five," the director said. A hush fell over the room.

That was why Cade had kept his distance from Macy Chandler for two months—so that he could do his job. The attraction they'd felt and acted upon had been too intense, too consuming. She'd interfered with his work which was getting Leonard behind bars.

That's what he'd told himself night after night when Macy had filled his dreams until he ached.

"One, two."

He'd given the same explanation to his partner, but Nate wasn't buying it. He had told Cade flat-out that he was running scared from the only woman who'd ever gotten past his guard.

"Three, four, five."

Macy winked and aimed her smile at the camera. For the first time, Cade fastened his gaze on her, and once he did, he simply couldn't look away. Time seemed to slow. The people around him seemed to fade and the air grew thick. He had to remind himself to breathe. It was the same reaction he'd had on the day she first walked into his office.

She looked just the same as the picture he'd carried in his mind for the past two months—tiny, blond and radiating as much energy as Disney's Tinkerbell.

Experimentally, he shifted his gaze to her hands and studied her precise movements as she used her fingers to crumble butter into a bowl of flour. That's all it took for him to recall just how those strong hands had felt moving over his skin. His own hands itched to touch her again. His gaze shifted unwillingly to her mouth, and desire clawed its way into his center.

He drew in another breath and released it. Okay. Nothing

had changed. Staying away from her hadn't gotten her out of his system, so what was he going to do?

Certainly not what he'd done two months ago when he'd let his adolescent hormones rule. He hadn't even managed to keep his professional distance for twelve hours. And once he'd given in to the temptation to kiss her, he simply hadn't been able to stop. The first time they'd made love had been in the backseat of his SUV. It had been crazy and fabulous. And— once he'd been able to think more clearly—terrifying.

She wasn't even his type. She was barely five-one and slight. He knew for a fact that the counter she was working at had been built to accommodate her diminutive size. In the glare of the lights, her hair was caught between red and gold, and she wore it nearly as short as a boy's with spiky bangs across her forehead. For practical reasons, she'd explained to him. She had no time to fuss.

In Cade's opinion, there wasn't any need to fuss. She had a natural prettiness—if you liked petite blond cheerleader types. Problem was he never had. He preferred long hair on a woman and he'd always leaned toward taller, leggier and more amply proportioned brunettes. In his experience, blondes were very high-maintenance, and in his line of work, he didn't have time for high-maintenance. Women had always occupied a peripheral place in his life, the only exceptions being his mother and two sisters.

Once again, Macy looked into the camera and, Cade could have sworn, directly at him. The punch he felt low in his gut was powerful and in that instant he wanted her mindlessly. It wasn't until she broke the connection that he remembered to breathe.

Okay. To borrow a phrase from Yogi Berra, it was going to be déjà vu all over again. And he simply couldn't let that happen. Macy's life could be at stake.

2

MACY WAS halfway through the chocolate chip scones when she experienced a prickle of awareness that began at the base of her neck and radiated everywhere. There was only one person who had ever made her feel that way: Cade Dillon, the man who'd... No. She was not going to go there. She had a show to finish.

Gathering all of her powers of concentration, Macy focused on her mental script, the one she'd performed several times for Alan, but the feeling of sensual awareness only increased while she filled mini paper muffin cups and highlighted the history of chocolate for her audience. After all, no Valentine's Day meal would be complete without chocolate.

When the segment was completed, and the crew finally turned off the lights, Macy wasn't surprised to see the tall, lanky Ranger Dillon leaning against the kitchen door frame. Of course, she'd known that their paths would cross again. Billionaire bank robber Elton Leonard was still on the loose. Even though he'd killed a bank guard, the media was still romanticizing his story, referring to him as "Clyde" and hyping the way he was leading the Texas Rangers on a merry chase across Texas.

She'd told herself that she was prepared for her inevitable meeting with Cade Dillon. She'd also convinced herself that when they did meet, the irresistible sexual attraction that had flared between them would have faded. But the intense awareness that she'd always felt in his presence certainly hadn't. And why should it when she hadn't been able to stop thinking about him? Or wanting him. There hadn't been a night since he'd left when she hadn't dreamed of what he'd done to her, what they'd done to each other in the three days that they'd spent together.

Try as she might, she couldn't prevent herself from studying him for a moment. He looked the same—broad shoulders, narrow hips, long legs. She managed not to look at his face. But there was no need since his features seemed to be etched permanently into her mind. His eyes were smoky gray and very intent. He had the face of a warrior—tough, with sharp-edged cheekbones, a strong chin, and a mouth—

"Great job!" Director Danny brought her back to the present by gripping her shoulders and air-kissing both her cheeks. Then he glanced at his watch. "It will take us about half an hour to set up the cameras at winner number two's house. So you'll have a little time to pack up the food. Need some help?"

"No, we've got it covered," Alan answered for her.

"See you," Danny said, giving them a little finger wave as he left the kitchen.

Then in a low voice only she could hear, Alan said, "FYI— Ranger Hunk is here."

"I know." Macy barely breathed the words. Out of the corner of her eye she saw Cade walking toward her. Not that she needed to see him—she could feel him. She drew in a deep breath. She could deal with this. After all, she'd just shot her second TV cooking show. She'd picked up five new clients since the first TV segment had aired. "I can handle him."

"I'll just bet you'd like to handle him," Alan murmured. Then he started humming "Everything's Coming Up Roses" again.

"No way," Macy muttered under her breath, pushing down the urge she had to bolt from the kitchen. No way, no how. Macy Chandler didn't run.

"Ranger Dillon." Alan stopped humming to nod at Cade. Then he turned to Macy. "I'll just start loading the car."

As Alan left, Macy stiffened her spine and summoned up her brightest smile. "What can I do for you, Ranger Dillon?"

"I want to talk to you about Elton Leonard."

"Okay." He was here on business. That was crystal-clear in the coolness of his tone, the flatness in his eyes. *Good. Keep it professional. Pretend that you've never touched that body or learned its pleasure points. And ignore the little band of pain tightening around your heart.* "If you've come to tell me you've arrested him, I'll definitely do the good-citizen thing and testify at his trial."

"I haven't arrested him yet."

Her brows shot up. "Then why are you here?"

Cade regarded her steadily. The coolness of her tone annoyed the hell out of him. She might have been talking to a stranger. Surely she must be feeling just a little of what he was. Unable to resist, he reached out to brush a strand of hair off her forehead. Her sudden step back and the flush that rose in her cheeks pleased him. The fact that his throat went dry as dust didn't.

"You haven't answered my question. Why are you here?"

If her tone had been cool before, it was icy now.

"Leonard is back in Austin. You're the only person who can testify that he robbed the First Trust Bank. If he eliminates you, the D.A. will probably drop the charges. Then he's a free man, and he can resume his old life."

"You think he intends to kill me?"

"He killed that bank guard to keep from getting caught."

She lifted her chin and clasped her hands together on the counter. "And you're telling me this because?"

Her eyes were steady on his, but Cade noted the rapid beat of the pulse at her throat and the whitening of her knuckles. The tough outer shell she projected was something he admired about her.

The day she'd come in for the lineup, she'd been so cool and composed watching the men file in, and she'd picked Leonard out right away. No one who hadn't been studying her closely would have noticed that her hands had trembled when she'd clasped them together. Her knuckles had been white that day too. Her air of bravado was all the more attractive once you caught glimpses of the vulnerability that lay beneath.

Something inside Cade softened and he nearly reached to take her clasped hands in his. "It'll be all right, Macy. I'll put you into protective custody until I can catch him. I have a safe house all set—"

"Whoa." She raised a hand. "Stop right there."

The sudden heat in her eyes nearly had *him* backing up a step.

"No way, no how are you putting me into a safe house."

"Macy, listen to reason."

"No, you listen to reason, Cade Dillon. I have a business to run, clients to please—and I have another TV show to shoot on Tuesday."

"Take a break. Give me a week, two at the most and you can film your show then."

"Are you kidding? The corporation that owns the *Austin Herald*—you've probably heard of them—DITH. They're running these big Valentine's Day contests connected to their 'Sex in the Saddle' columns in Houston, San Antonio and Austin. And the papers are all competing with one another. The *Austin Herald* has a very good chance of winning."

Cade hadn't heard of the corporation, but he'd heard his sisters and his mother discussing the hugely successful column.

"Three sexy meals from Some Like It Hot are the grand prizes here in Austin. Even a busy Texas Ranger with bank robbers to chase must be aware of the importance of Valentine Day—you know, the big February holiday—candy, flowers, romance…"

Pausing, she cocked her head to one side. "Well, maybe

not. But the shows can't be postponed. Besides, thanks to this contest my business is on a roll. I've booked five new clients since the first TV segment aired this past week. And every day Alan is taking calls asking if we'll do takeout. He says we ought to change our name from Some Like It Hot to Aphrodisiacs to Go."

Cade felt his own temper begin to rise. "Your TV appearances also make it very easy for Leonard to stalk you. He's not the romantic figure the media has painted him. In the two years I've been tracking him, I've been able to create quite a profile. Among his other sterling qualities, he has an ego the size of Texas, and you're the one who brought him down. For the sake of his pride alone, he'll come after you. And he's already killed once."

For a few seconds, silence hummed between them.

Macy spoke first. "Excuse me. I could use a cold drink." Whirling away, she strode to the refrigerator and pulled out a can of cola. "Want one?"

"Sure." Cade had to move fast to prevent the can she tossed at him from slamming into his chest. "Look. This is serious. With your face on TV screens, you might as well have painted a target on your back. I half expected to see Leonard in the crowd in your kitchen."

"So?" She took a long drink of her cola. "What's the problem? If Leonard *had* been here, you could have arrested him. Your precious case would have been closed."

Cade tightened the reins on his temper. "Macy—"

Alan stepped through the doorway and cleared his throat. "The car's loaded."

Neither Cade nor Macy spared him a glance.

It was Macy who broke the silence. "Good day, Ranger Dillon."

She set her empty can on the counter, then sailed past Alan and out of the kitchen.

"She's pissed," Alan said.

Cade set his cola can down next to hers. "I'm a trained investigator. I got that much."

"I couldn't help overhearing part of your conversation. You're pretty sure that Leonard wants to get rid of her."

"Yeah." Cade met Alan's eyes and narrowed his. "What is it?"

"Maybe it's nothing, but the day before yesterday— Friday—we'd just finished shopping at a fresh-air market. It was crowded, lots of jostling. I didn't think anything of it at the time, but Macy got shoved into the street. A car missed her by inches."

Cade's stomach clenched. He hadn't gotten back into Austin until yesterday. Macy could have been already injured or—

"You think it could have been Leonard?" Alan asked.

Cade met the man's eyes steadily. "Yeah." Once again Elton Leonard was a few steps ahead of him.

"You're not going to get her to go into a safe house."

"No."

"Is protecting Macy and catching Leonard the only reason you came back?"

Cade didn't speak. It wasn't a question he'd fully answered for himself yet.

"I thought so." Alan gestured for Cade to follow as he started toward the door. "One thing you ought to know. You hurt her. She's recovering. She's had some practice snapping back from the jerks who've dumped her, but I was worried about her this time."

Turning his head, Cade studied Alan. "Jerks—in the plural?"

"Yeah. Number one was a star quarterback at UT. She was captain of the cheerleading squad. It was quite the romance until he was drafted by the Philadelphia Eagles. He told her that he had to put his career first for a while. He didn't think he was good marriage material, and he didn't have time for a serious relationship, blah, blah, blah. But it didn't hurt his image at all while he was still at UT to have a piece of eye candy like Macy on his arm."

From outside came the sound of someone leaning on a horn.

"Still pissed," Alan commented. As they exited the house, Cade spotted Macy in the driver's seat of her silver SUV. She didn't glance his way.

"Jerk number two was a wannabe country-and-western star. They were engaged until he got offered a record contract. He left her behind too, with the same excuses that jerk number one gave her. Then you came along."

Cade stuffed his hands in his pockets as they made their way to the street. "Jerk number three?"

Alan shrugged. "If the shoe fits…"

Cade was uncomfortably aware that it did. His predecessors' excuses were pretty much the same ones he'd made to himself every time he'd thought of calling Macy during the last two months. His career *did* come first. He *had* been avoiding any kind of serious relationship for a long time, after seeing up close and personal what a career as a Texas Ranger had done to his parents' marriage. They'd divorced ten years ago.

And his partner, Nate, had been right on target, as usual. What he'd felt for Macy had spooked him. The intensity of their lovemaking, the depth of that connection had triggered feelings that he'd never felt before. So he'd run.

Alan stopped and turned to face Cade when they were still about fifteen yards from the car and pitched his voice so that it wouldn't carry. "I'm sharing all this with you so that before you start thinking of burning up the sheets with her again, you're aware that Macy has already had enough frogs in her life. She's due for a prince."

"I'm not intending—"

Alan raised a hand. "Puh-lease. When I walked into the kitchen a few minutes ago, the temperature was so high that it's a wonder the appliances didn't melt. Anytime the fire's that hot, the moths will return to the flame."

Cade watched as Alan joined Macy in the SUV. But what he was seeing in his mind was a couple of moths being incinerated by a flame.

3

"TWO DOWN and one to go," Alan said as they climbed into Macy's SUV.

After fastening her seat belt, Macy glanced in her rearview mirror and watched Cade moving with that long-legged stride of his toward his black SUV—which was not so coincidentally parked right behind hers. He'd not only followed her to prize-winner number two's place, but he'd also joined the crew members and watched the filming of the segment.

She was sure that Alan saw him too. But he didn't say a word because she'd set up a rule on the ride to the shoot. There was to be no mention of Cade Dillon.

With a frown, Macy shifted her attention back to the street and turned her key in the ignition. "They had to do three takes."

"Not because of you," Alan said. "That young couple was camera-shy. It wasn't until the third take that you warmed them up."

"I forgot to give them the champagne and candles during the first take." The winners of "Brunch in Bed," a cute couple in their early twenties, lived in a third-floor apartment in downtown Austin. They'd filmed on the front stoop of the building, and the segment itself had lasted less than five minutes. All she had to do was unpack each of the three courses and hand them over to the couple while giving instructions on how to store or reheat.

"Director Danny would have reshot it anyway. The two kids were stiff as puppets." Alan patted her hand. "You did great."

She had *not* done great, and the person responsible for that was now sitting behind the wheel of his big black car waiting to follow them. Twice during the filming she'd lost her concentration because she'd felt Cade's presence in the area behind the camera, watching her just as she could feel his eyes on her now. Her skin literally prickled with the sensation. She scowled at the image in the side-view mirror.

"Looks like He Whose Name Must Not Be Mentioned is going to follow us."

"Watch it." Macy infused all the warning she could into her tone.

Alan raised both hands. "I'm following the rule."

"I'm going to ignore him," she said.

"Him?"

She shot him a narrow-eyed look. "Okay, we'll suspend the rule."

"Ignoring Ranger Hunk is going to be a challenge." Alan shifted his sunglasses from the top of his head to his nose as she pulled out into traffic. "Because I don't think he's going to ignore you. Would you pull into that drive-through over there? I'm starved, and you should be too. It's after two."

Taking advantage of a lull in the oncoming traffic, Macy turned left into a drive-through lane. Alan ordered across her at the speaker, adding her usual large fries and cola to his green salad and yogurt. Then she inched the SUV into the pay-and-pick-up line. "He ignored me for two months and I was doing fine."

"Uh-huh."

"I was."

Alan raised both hands, palms up. "Okay. I was just imagining the dark circles under your eyes."

"The only reason he's here is because he wants Elton Leonard in jail. It's a testosterone thing. A Ranger always gets his man."

"Or his woman. For what it's worth, I don't think he's over you."

"Oh, he's over me." The problem was that she wasn't over him. All he'd had to do was brush his finger over her forehead and heat had shot right down to her toes. That hadn't changed. All he had to do was touch her and she wanted. It was just that simple. Just that terrifying.

"I don't think so," Alan said.

"That's because you're so happy with Martin that you see everything through rose-colored glasses."

Alan slipped his sunglasses off and gave them a close inspection. "Nope. My glasses are amber."

"Ranger Dillon thinks I'm in danger. He's just doing his job." She was not going to allow herself to think anything different. She'd let herself hope the last time Cade had walked into her life. Never again.

"He's also worried about you. So am I. I told him about your almost too close an encounter with that taxi on Friday. He doesn't think it was an accident. He believes Leonard was behind it."

"Dammit." Macy rested her head against the steering wheel as her stomach knotted. She didn't want to be reminded of those few terrifying seconds when she'd been teetering on that curb, her arms flailing, while she'd watched that taxi race toward her. Someone *had* pushed her. For three days she'd tried to convince herself that she hadn't felt that hard impact right between her shoulder blades, but she had.

"I believe it was Leonard, too," Alan said.

"Why me? My life is going along just fine—I don't need this. Why did I have to be in that alley at just that precise moment when that billionaire bank robber was changing out of his disguise? Five minutes later or five minutes earlier and I wouldn't have either Leonard or Cade Dillon in my life."

A car behind them beeped its horn.

"If your little pity party is over, we can pick up our food now."

With a sigh, Macy raised her head, inched forward to the take-out window, and dug money out of her purse. Alan reached to take the bags of food while she stored the change carefully in her wallet.

"Here." He passed her the cola he'd ordered for her. "Drink some of this. You'll feel better."

Macy grabbed the paper cup and took a long sip through the straw. Sugar and caffeine always made her feel better— temporarily. Hopefully, the magic combo would clear her head. Then she could decide what to do about Cade Dillon. It was becoming crystal clear to her that she had to have a plan. The ignore-him strategy wasn't working. Try as she might, she could not control her reaction to him. Her mind and body were not in sync where he was concerned. Right now her body was all primed to repeat the experiences of two months ago.

"Here's part two of Dr. Alan's prescription."

Macy took the fry he offered and ate it while she drummed her fingers on the steering wheel. The line to turn out of the fast food restaurant was nearly as long as the one at the pickup window. Cade hadn't placed an order, but he cut in behind her now. The man was sticking to her like glue. Annoyance streamed through her. As she pulled forward to the exit, she saw that the traffic on the street was pretty heavy, and a sudden thought occurred to her.

"I'm going to give him the slip."

"Macy." There was a world of warning in Alan's voice. "You know what usually happens when you give in to one of your impulses."

She shot him a grin. "It's petty and probably childish."

Alan wiggled a fry at her. "May I add dangerous?"

"You may." She snatched the fry. "But it will be worth it just to put a dent in his arrogance. The man thinks he can disappear for two months and then just stride back into my life and throw his Texas Ranger weight around."

Macy concentrated on the traffic. If she judged it right, she just might be able to leave Cade Dillon behind in the dust.

A minute later, an opportunity presented itself. She shot into the center lane and pressed her foot down hard on the accelerator.

Her spur-of-the-moment plan hit its first obstacle when the traffic light one hundred yards ahead of her turned yellow. For a split second as the SUV ate up fifty yards of the distance, she considered flooring the gas pedal. But the cross street boasted six lanes of traffic with a wide grassy median—not the best situation for running an about-to-turn-red light. With a sigh, she pressed her foot on the brake.

The pedal depressed straight to the floor and her SUV hurtled into the intersection.

"Macy!" Her drink and bag of French fries went flying. Alan braced both hands against the dash board.

"No brakes. No brakes." Macy wasn't sure she said the words aloud or if they were just part of the little chant repeating itself over and over in her head. Panic skittered up her spine as her foot futilely pumped up and down on the pedal. In spite of the angry blare of horns, she cleared the first two lanes of traffic. But beyond the median, she could see the cars already moving. If she didn't do something, she was going to hit a sweet little yellow convertible dead-on.

At the last minute, she wrenched the steering wheel to the left and prayed that she could merge into the lane behind the sunny little car. Her tires squealed, searching for traction, then her car went into a spin. She tasted fear as they clipped the fender of the convertible. The collision only added momentum to the spin. Horns blasted, more tires screeched. Metal screamed against metal as she sideswiped a van.

Macy gripped the steering wheel, straining against the pull

of the seat belt. Still, she couldn't prevent the SUV from going into a skid and shooting up onto the median. For one terrifying moment, she was sure the car was going to barrel across into a lane of oncoming traffic. Using all her strength she jerked the steering wheel to the right. The SUV tilted crazily to one side, then settled and leapt forward. Macy swallowed hard.

Her best bet was to keep the car on the grass until it lost momentum. Her SUV mowed down two saplings, a flower bed and a small hedge before finally meeting its match in a concrete planter the size of a hot tub.

Then the air bags inflated and Macy's world went black.

TRAPPED two cars behind the traffic light, Cade could do nothing but watch as Macy's car shot into the intersection and headed on a collision course with three lanes of cars. Fear shot through him as he willed her to turn the wheel.

"Good girl, good girl," he muttered, then swore when her car sideswiped a convertible and went into a spin.

All hell broke loose after that. For Cade, the experience was like watching the end of a car chase in an action movie. Except it was real. Horns blared, tires screamed. Macy's SUV bounced off a minivan and shot onto the median. For one endless second, it teetered wildly. Cade was sure it would topple over and slide into a lane of oncoming traffic. He simply stopped breathing.

Then her vehicle plowed forward on the median. "Good girl," he murmured. Macy Chandler could keep a cool head in a crisis. He spotted the concrete planter just an instant before the SUV slammed into it. Steamed poured out of the engine, and fear iced his veins.

He had to get to her. The light turned green, but with several disabled cars still blocking the intersection, it took Cade several minutes before he could negotiate his car onto the median and follow the path Macy's had taken. The extra time allowed him to imagine several scenarios. Alan got out of the car first, then Macy. It was only then that some of his panic abated.

By the time he finally reached her, she was sitting cross-legged behind the SUV with Alan beside her. Cade noted the handkerchief she held to her nose and the bloodstains on her T-shirt, and his stomach clenched. Squatting down in front of her, he gripped her free hand in his. "You're hurt."

"The air bag gave me a bloody nose. That's all."

Cade shifted his gaze to Alan. "You all right?"

"My nerves are shot, but I fared better in my encounter with the air bag. She's pretty shaky."

Who wasn't? Cade studied Macy's face again. She was alive. And miraculously uninjured. "Reaction is setting in."

"I could go for some caffeine and sugar," Macy said.

"FYI—your drink is presently decorating my slacks. You'll be getting the dry-cleaning bill."

"Don't I always?"

The banter between Alan and Macy did more than their assurances to ease some of Cade's fear and allowed room for a spurt of anger.

"What in hell made you try to run that light?" he asked.

"I didn't."

"She was trying to give you the slip," Alan said.

"Rat fink." She shot a look at Alan, then returned her gaze to Cade. "I didn't try to run the light. I considered it, but it was too risky. So I put on the brakes, and they didn't work. They were fine in the drive-through, then suddenly there was nothing there. I tried pumping them, but it didn't work."

Sirens sounded from a distance, and for the first time, Cade glanced beyond Macy and Alan to the SUV. Steam still rose from the hood. "Do you take care of your car?"

Macy's chin lifted. "My livelihood depends on that car. It's only six months old, and I had it in for service last week."

"Wait here." Cade's anger only increased as he rose and edged his way to the front of the SUV. But this time—if what he suspected was true—he was angry at himself. Just behind the front left tire, he lay down on the grass and slid his head and shoulders beneath the car.

What he suspected was definitely true. Elton Leonard had managed to make another attempt on Macy's life, this time right under Cade's nose. Easing himself out from under the SUV, he took two deep breaths before he rose and strode back to Alan and Macy. The first police cruiser was on the scene. The man driving the yellow convertible was talking to two officers and gesturing in Macy's direction. One of the officers started toward them.

Macy glanced up at him. "He's going to arrest me, right?"

"Not unless you cut your own brake lines," Cade said.

4

HANDS on hips, Macy paced back and forth in her living room. It had taken more than an hour to fill out the accident reports and arrange for her SUV to be towed to a garage. Cade had spent most of that time on his cell phone. However, at one point he'd taken a break, made his way to a nearby convenience store and brought back cold drinks. Hers was a sugar-and-caffeine laden cola and Alan's was an iced green tea.

The gesture had been so sweet. Stopping short, Macy frowned. It simply would not do to dwell on the fact that the tall, tough Ranger Dillon had a softer, sensitive side. Closing her eyes, she pictured a large neon sign reading The Man Dumped You! There. That was what she should be dwelling on.

Satisfied, she resumed pacing. When they were finally allowed to leave the accident scene, Cade had dropped Alan off first—but not before assuring her assistant that he would be spending the night at her house and that a couple of other Rangers would be on surveillance outside.

Alan had been relieved. She hadn't been. The idea that Cade would be spending the night inside her house had set off a whole new mind-over-body struggle inside her. Macy summoned up the image of the neon sign again.

So far Cade had been very professional. When they'd arrived, he'd escorted her into the house and checked out all the rooms. Only then had he left to check in with his partner, Nate Blackhorn, who was parked outside.

She was the one who was having trouble remaining professional. Neither she nor Cade had spoken on the short trip from Alan's place to hers. She hadn't looked at him either, but her entire body had been intensely aware of him. She hadn't been able to breathe without inhaling his scent. And whoever had said that the sense of smell was the most evocative when it came to memories was dead on.

Sitting there beside him, her mind had drifted back to the first night he'd driven her home. It had been the day after she'd chosen Elton Leonard out of a lineup. Cade had picked her up that morning and taken her to his office. They'd spent the entire day—twelve hours plus—going over the testimony she would give at Leonard's trial.

Up until that night, their relationship had been entirely professional—unless you counted the fact that every time she came in contact with him, her whole body had gone into a meltdown.

All day long she'd assumed that he was indifferent, that the intense attraction she was experiencing was one-sided. That assumption had gone up in flames—literally—when he'd parked in her driveway, sworn under his breath and kissed her right there in the front seat of his car. Macy closed her eyes as heat began to build inside her.

In her entire life she'd never experienced a kiss like that. Each little detail was etched indelibly in her mind. The moment his mouth had covered hers, all the longing, all the need that had been building up in her during that endless day had exploded. She'd fisted her hands in his hair to keep his mouth from leaving hers.

His taste—she'd never before experienced a flavor so dark, so rich. His hands—she'd never imagined the kind of sharp-edged pleasure those wide, rough palms could send through her system. Her heart—she'd never before felt it pound that hard. The beat had been primitive.

He'd pulled away at one point to mutter something about going inside, but she'd said, "Right here. Right now."

And he'd obliged her. He'd more than obliged her. Just thinking about it turned her knees to jelly and she had to sit down abruptly on the arm of her sofa. Later, when they'd finally made it into the house, they'd never gotten to the bedroom. They'd made love right here. The images tumbling into her mind had her shooting to her feet and striding across the room.

She had to get a grip. If she continued to stroll down memory lane, she was going to jump Cade Dillon the instant he walked through her front door.

Remember, he dumped you. Remember, he dumped you. Moving into the kitchen, she grabbed another cola from the supply she kept in her refrigerator, snapped the top open and took a long drink. She'd always considered herself a practical, organized woman. There'd been two other men in her life. When they'd dumped her, she might have faltered for a bit, but she'd picked herself up and gone on. Both of those men were history.

Moving to the window, she looked out at the lawn where Cade stood talking to his partner. The problem was, Cade wasn't history. Try as she might she hadn't been able to get him out of her system. She still wanted him. Badly. There. Maybe admitting it was half the battle.

Cade Dillon was different for her. Why was that? She studied the two men talking on her lawn.

She'd met Nate Blackhorn on the same day that she'd first met Cade. The two of them had a lot in common. They were both tall with broad shoulders and narrow hips. They both had that slow way of talking and walking and that slight Texas drawl. Plus, the two of them had that Ranger thing going for them. If you ever got in trouble, you'd want these men on your side. The biggest difference was in their coloring. While Cade's hair was a tawny kind of lion's-mane brown, Nate's dark hair and bronzed skin testified to the fact that he was part Cherokee.

Nate was standing near his car with his back to her while Cade faced the house. She felt it the moment that he glanced at the window and his gaze collided with hers.

What was she going to do about him?

"EARTH to Cade Dillon."

"What?" Cade tore his gaze away from Macy to find his partner grinning at him.

"You wink out on me every time you look at that pretty little woman of yours. It's kind of cute."

"She's not my woman."

"She's your something. You haven't been the same since you met her."

Cade frowned at Nate. "Right now she's a job."

"Uh-huh. That's what she was supposed to be on your first go-around with her. Take it from me, you can't go back once you've crossed that line into intimacy."

"You've been watching *Dr. Phil* again."

Nate laughed. "Look, you've been keeping me out here, going over the same instructions for the last fifteen minutes. I don't need Dr. Phil to tell me you're stalling. Sooner or later, you're going to have to go in there."

Cade sighed and glanced back up at Macy's house. One of the reasons that he and Nate worked so ably together was that they knew each other very well. "The problem is, she should be a job…but she's not. Hell, I don't what she is. I just can't seem to shake loose from her. But right now her life is in danger. That has to be our priority."

Nate's grin faded and he put a hand on Cade's shoulder. "You'll handle that part. We'll have her under surveillance 24/7. If Leonard makes a move on her, we'll have him."

Cade met Nate's eyes. "I don't like the fact that we're using her as bait."

His friend shrugged. "Not out of choice. Leonard is responsible for that part. Can you think of a quicker way of catching him?"

"No." Cade wished he could.

Nate patted his shoulder. "I'll be out here in front. Cal will be circling the block. All you have to do is figure out a way to get through the evening with Ms. Chandler."

Cades sent Nate a glare. "You're getting way too much of a kick out of this." Then he picked up his duffel and the bag of food that Nate had brought and strode toward the house.

"Don't do anything that I wouldn't do," Nate called after him.

BY THE TIME Cade walked into the living room, he had a speech prepared. He'd intended to set Macy's mind at ease by explaining the security measures he'd put in place and to assure her that for the time being, she had nothing to fear from him on a personal level.

But seeing her standing there in the fading light with blood still on her T-shirt and grass stains on her jeans sent the words out of his mind and every detail of the accident flooding in. For those few endless moments when her car had gone into that crazy spin, he'd been sure he was going to lose her. Even now the images triggered emotions he couldn't put a name to. And he couldn't say a word.

"We need to talk," she said.

They were on the same page there. Usually he'd have had no trouble doing just that, but Macy was the one person in the world who seemed to have the power to tie his tongue up in knots.

She waved a hand vaguely and moistened her lips. It was that small gesture that told him she might be feeling just a little of what he was feeling. Some of his tension eased as he lifted the shopping bag.

"Why don't we talk over linguine?"

"You brought linguine?" Surprise was what he read in her eyes as she shifted her gaze to the bag.

"With red sauce. I had Nate order it." Satisfied that he was able to string several words together that time, Cade improved his odds of carrying on a coherent conversation by moving away from her and into the kitchen.

He'd made the decision to keep their relationship professional when he'd seen those cut brake lines. More especially since she'd become the bait they were using to catch Leonard. It was his only rational choice. Neither of them could afford the distraction of renewing their affair while Leonard was on the loose. Besides that, he wanted to give her time—to give himself time—to figure out what they were going to do about what had happened and what was happening again between them.

"Alan told me you'd had a total food intake of one french fry today."

"The rest of my order bit the dust on the floor of my car."

He unpacked the shopping bag, opened the containers and set them on the island countertop. "Where do you keep the silverware?"

"I'll get it."

Cade located wineglasses and opened a bottle while Macy set the places. Within minutes they were seated across from each other digging into the meal.

Macy twirled pasta around her fork. "This was a great idea."

"I have them occasionally." Cade broke off a chunk of garlic bread and handed it to her. "Alan told me you rarely cook for yourself. Why is that?"

She shrugged as she scooped up more pasta. "I need a break from the work."

He sipped his merlot and discovered that he enjoyed watching her dig into the food. "So, what do you eat if you don't cook?"

Her eyes flashed with humor. "Sometimes takeout, but mostly junk food. Alan's always after me to be more careful about what I put into my body. I keep fruit around." She glanced around the kitchen. "Usually. There's probably some yogurt in the fridge. And I have a stash of chocolate for emergencies."

She paused to eat more pasta, then added, "Why are you so interested in my eating habits?"

"Curiosity. There are lots of things I don't know about you."

This time it was wariness that he saw in her eyes. "That's really for the best since our relationship is going to be temporary." After setting down her fork, she began to turn the stem of her wineglass. "We should have that talk now."

"Okay."

"I've been going around and around in my head about this."

"This?"

"Us. What happened between us two months ago was a mistake. Obviously, we both agree on that point. And now we're spending time together again—in close proximity. So I think it would be best if we laid down some ground rules."

"Okay." Cade sipped his wine. Her tone was cool and polite, just as it had been that morning. He wondered why he so much preferred her in spitfire mode.

"What happened then was then." She took a sip of her wine, then folded her hands together. "This is now. Once you catch Leonard, we'll go our separate ways again."

"Why would you think that?"

Her gaze narrowed, and he saw for the first time that she wasn't quite as cool as she wanted him to think.

"Experience. You left without a word, and I haven't heard from you for two months."

"My priority was to track down Leonard. I blamed myself that he skipped town. If I hadn't been so involved with you, I might have prevented that. For the past two months I've been following his trail across most of Texas." It was the truth, and Cade absolutely hated the fact that his tone had become defensive.

"I understand perfectly."

Her smile made him grit his teeth.

"And now you're back because Leonard's back and since I seem to be his target, I realize that you have to stick close to me. I'd be a fool to object to that. I just don't want it to interfere with my personal or professional life."

Cade drew in a deep breath and let it out. "Understood. I'll do my best to see that your business isn't affected. While you were talking to the police, Alan briefed me on your schedule for the next week. Nate and Cal, another man from the office, will be staking out the house and following us in case we need backup. Clearly, Leonard is somehow watching you. I'm hoping that they may spot him at some point. If that happens, we'll move in to take him, and all this will be over."

"Good. I'm also hoping that we can handle the personal side of our relationship in an equally professional manner. Just because we got caught up in something…something very irrational that made us act like greedy, giddy teenagers, doesn't mean we have to allow it to happen again. We're both adults with career obligations, and we can control our…urges."

Annoyance streamed through him. They sure as hell hadn't been able to control their urges two months ago. One of the many places they'd made love was on the kitchen floor just a few feet away from where they were sitting. Cade barely kept himself from mentioning that fact. Instead, he reminded himself that she was only saying what *he'd* intended to say when he'd come in the front door.

So why did he have a sudden *urge* to grab her and kiss her until she was boneless?

"Since I don't have a guest room, you'll have to sleep on the couch. I'll bring down some blankets and towels. You can use the downstairs bathroom."

Cade set his glass down. "Do I get a chance to offer some input here?"

"Sure." She blinked. "Of course."

"On the topic of controlling our—what did you call it?

Oh yes, *urges*—I just want to say that we *are* going to make love again. However, I'm willing to wait until Leonard is behind bars."

Her eyes narrowed. "You're *willing* to wait?"

"That's what I said."

Macy slid off her stool and fisted her hands on her hips. "And you assume that once you've got your man, you'll take up where we left off two months ago?"

Cade raised his wineglass in a little toast. "Works for me."

"Why you—of all the—" She opened her mouth, clamped it shut, then jabbed a finger in his direction and tried again. "Let me tell you—you—"

If looks could kill, Cade figured he'd at least be on the injured list, and since he didn't want to end up wearing linguine, he wisely bit back a grin. How could he have forgotten how cute she looked when her temper was on a roll? Her cheeks had turned a rosy pink and her green eyes were practically shooting out sparks.

He watched with admiration as she drew in a breath and ruthlessly reined that temper in. Lifting her plate, she carried it to the sink and turned the water on. It was only as she flicked the switch on the disposal that he allowed himself a silent sigh of relief.

"You know," she finally said in a much calmer voice, "it's a wonder you don't have back problems considering the size of that ego you carry around with you. Why don't you go in the other room and play with the TV and the remote while I load the dishwasher?"

That would be the wise thing to do. It was actually what he intended to do right after he cleared the island. In his mother's house, everyone helped clear the table.

When he set his plate and the two wineglasses next to the sink, a fork clattered to the floor. They nearly bumped heads when they squatted simultaneously to pick it up.

When she lifted her face, they were eye to eye. Close enough that he saw her eyes darken to the color of a river running fast, and he was on the verge of being swept away by the current. Her scent invaded his system as he dropped his gaze to her mouth. Desire snaked into his gut and curled tight. To hell with the ground rules. He had to have that mouth.

She moistened her lips. "We should…"

"Yeah. We should."

Their lips met and immediately fused together. Heat speared up—Cade wasn't sure if it came from him or her. All that was certain was that it spread with the speed and ferocity of a wildfire as their tongues tangled.

Her taste—wild and erotic—poured into him, shimmering through his blood like a drug. How had he managed to stay away for two months? He had to touch her. Fast and greedy, he ran his hands up and rested them against the sides of her breasts. She rose up on her knees and pressed herself more fully against him.

"More. More." The words came out on ragged, desperate breaths as teeth nipped and scraped and blood thundered. This time when they drew apart to drag in air, Macy said, "I told myself I wasn't going to do this again."

"Ditto," Cade muttered. Then he went very still. "Do you want me to stop?"

"No. Don't you dare." She dragged his mouth back to hers and fisted her hands in that tawny, silky hair. Heat streamed through her. Need, raw and primitive, pummeled her. And all she could think of was she had to have even more.

Frantic now, they grappled with clothes. He tossed aside her T-shirt while she struggled with his. Once he was free, she ran her hands up his back, absorbing the taut hard ridges of muscle, that smooth damp skin. Her own skin trembled as he freed her mouth and began to work on the front closure of her bra. She feasted on the hollow at his throat.

With a groan, he rose, hauling her up with him and pressing her against the end of the island. He pulled at the snap of her jeans. "Every time I'm with you, I want this. I want you."

"I know. It's crazy." She spoke the words against his mouth. "And fabulous." His body was marvelous, but it was his taste that created the perfect aphrodisiac. She simply couldn't get enough of the flavors. Here was the hunger, the desperation that was such a perfect match to her own. She felt herself drowning in sensation with no thought of coming up for air.

Macy nearly cried out when he drew back to hook his thumbs in the waistband of her jeans and shove them down her legs. Then suddenly, he went very still. "Ohhh…" The word came out as a whispered moan.

"What?"

Straightening, he rested his forehead against hers and drew in a ragged breath. "I need a minute here."

Seconds ticked by, and there was only the sound of their breathing.

"You're not wearing any underwear," Cade finally managed.

"I didn't get to the laundry this week."

His laugh was wry and hoarse. "If I'd known, the linguine would have gotten very, very cold."

He ran his hands down her bare skin in one possessive stroke, then dug his fingers into her hips, lifted her and settled her on the island countertop.

"Hurry," she said.

"Need to touch you." He ran his hands up her sides, rubbed the rough pads of his thumbs over her nipples.

She arched back, offering more, and he took. When his mouth closed over her breast, the pleasure was so sharp, her need so urgent that she cried out. Wrapping her legs around him, she ordered, "Now."

Drawing back, he kept his eyes steady on hers as he moved his hands slowly down her sides and hips until those hard wide palms rested on her thighs. Very slowly he slipped his thumbs into the slickness of her folds and drew them down, tormenting, teasing, opening her. Then he withdrew his hands.

"Don't." The word burned her throat.

"Don't what?"

But relief was already streaming through her as she saw that he was dealing with his jeans and a condom.

She tightened her legs around him. "Don't stop."

"This time I won't." He gripped her hips and his eyes stayed intent on hers as he slowly pushed into her. When he finally filled her and she surrounded him, both of them stilled for a moment.

Finally, he said, "Now," and he leaned forward to take her mouth with his. As the kiss deepened, slowly, surely, they both began to move.

5

WHEN THE alarm rang, Macy sat straight up in bed, slapped the buzzer off, then stared at the time. Seven. As she struggled to orient herself, her first clear thought was that she'd overslept. She only used the alarm as a backup. Her inner clock always woke her up at six.

Then she smelled the coffee. When she spotted the tray with a mug and a thermal carafe on her bedside table, she remembered exactly why she'd overslept.

Cade Dillon. Just thinking about him had her heart taking a little bounce. Up—and then down. Not good. She poured herself a cup and took that first bracing swallow of caffeine. Then she sighed and ran her fingers lightly down the carafe. First he'd brought her linguine and now this.

The man was definitely trouble. The pillow beside hers still carried the imprint of his head, and the bedclothes looked as if they'd been tied in knots. Macy's lips curved. Considering what they'd done to each other in bed last night, it wouldn't surprise her if they were.

She drank more coffee. No regrets. She didn't believe in them. Nor did she believe in lying to herself. Life was too short. Besides, how could she possibly regret last night when she knew that she wanted to repeat the experience?

Plan A—the be-professional strategy—had definitely bitten the dust. So…Macy considered while she tapped her fingers on the side of her mug. So what? Climbing out of bed, she headed for the shower. She was a practical woman, wasn't she? She still had options. Twisting the faucets, she turned the water on full-blast. If there was one thing she'd learned in life, it was there was always a plan B. Whatever mistakes you made, whatever dreams of happy endings might be ruined, you could always pick yourself up and start over.

Hadn't her whole life been a testimonial to that? A lot of people had walked away from her and she'd survived. Her dad had left when she was ten. Then her mother had remarried and moved east when Macy had started at UT. She'd been pretty much on her own since then.

Satisfied that the water was hot enough, she stepped in and turned her face up to the spray. The important thing would be to keep a handle on reality. She and Cade were two adults who were very focused on their careers. She poured shampoo into her hand then rubbed it into her hair. Twice now they'd been thrown together, and once Leonard was behind bars, they would each go their separate ways. End of story.

The mistake she'd made the first time around with Ranger Cade Dillon was in thinking that he was different from the two other men she'd become involved with. That had been stupid. Her problem was that she always expected too much. And by and large, people disappointed you.

After shutting the water off, she pulled on a terry robe and toweled off her hair. Her best strategy would be just to enjoy what she and Cade could have together—a very temporary and extremely satisfying affair.

And there she had it—a very viable plan B. While she dressed, Macy ignored the little band of pain that squeezed her heart a little tighter and turned her attention ruthlessly to the day ahead.

TEN MINUTES later, Macy paused just outside the archway to her kitchen. Alan and Cade were sitting at the counter while

Alan scribbled away on a piece of paper. For a moment, she was struck by the differences in the two men.

The contrasts went far beyond the fact that Alan was gay and Cade wasn't. As usual, the always meticulously groomed Alan looked as if he'd just stepped off the cover of a men's fashion magazine. His hair was perfectly arranged, his tan, Macy knew, came from a bottle and boasted an SPF of 45. His brilliantly white shirt and tailored black jeans provided eye-catching drama. Alan worked at attracting attention.

Cade didn't. That glorious mane of tawny hair looked as though he'd finger-combed it after his shower. And his tan hadn't come from a salon or a bottle. So where had it come from? Two months ago, the man had seemed to be chained to his desk at Ranger headquarters. Obviously, he must do something outdoors on the weekends. She shifted her gaze to the denim shirt and jeans; both were faded from many washings.

Nope. Cade Dillon was not going to set a new trend in men's fashion anytime soon. But he didn't have to because of the rangy, toned body the clothes covered.

And it wasn't merely clothes and grooming styles that made the two men so different. Alan was always in perpetual motion. When he talked, he gestured with his hands. And even now, when he was silent, he was tapping his pencil on the list whenever he wasn't actually writing.

On the other hand, Cade looked perfectly relaxed, one elbow resting on the counter, his long legs stretched out in front of him, and his bare feet crossed at the ankles. Just looking at those feet had lust curling in her stomach. She wondered why it was that bare feet were so sexy on a man. Or perhaps it was just Cade's bare feet that she found sexy. Whatever it was, her throat had gone as dry as dust. If Alan hadn't been sitting there at the counter, she would have jumped Cade again.

Macy reminded herself to breathe. Good thing she'd decided to terminate plan A and go with plan B.

"This is her schedule for the next four days," Alan said. "I've marked off the things like the marketing and some of the deliveries that I can do without her."

Macy dragged her gaze away from Cade's feet and narrowed her eyes. *Her schedule?*

They stopped talking the moment she walked into the kitchen. That together with the guilty expressions on their faces told her a lot.

"What about my schedule?"

"Nate brought us breakfast," Cade said. "Have a donut."

"You shouldn't encourage her deplorable eating habits," Alan scolded. "I brought yogurt."

"She stockpiles those in the refrigerator," Cade commented. "From the size of the stash and the number that have passed their expiration dates, I'd say she doesn't eat many of them."

Alan sighed. "Hope springs eternal."

"Okay." Macy circled the island and poured herself another cup of coffee. "I'd appreciate it if you didn't talk about me as if I wasn't in the room. And I want to know what you think you're doing with my schedule. Because if you—"

"Sorry." Cade waved the box of donuts under her nose. "Peace offering."

Since she was not the kind of woman who cut off her nose to spite her face, Macy climbed up on a stool, inspected the contents and made her selection. Chocolate frosted were her favorites. "Thanks," she said around a mouthful, "but no peace until you tell me what you were plotting behind my back."

"Alan gave me a general outline of your schedule yesterday. I just asked him to write out the details," Cade said easily. "It's very regular. You visit the market three days a week at the same time and you go to the same stalls."

Macy licked frosting off her thumb. "Fresh ingredients are the key to good cooking."

"You prepare and take meals to the same three clients on

Mondays and Thursdays. Then you have several other clients who want meals on the weekends."

Macy set down the last quarter of her donut. "We often deliver two or three days of meals at a time. That way, nothing has to be frozen. And I'm not going to stop doing that. Plus, we're adding five new clients."

Cade raised a hand. "I'm not asking you to stop. It's just that the regularity of your schedule makes life very easy for Elton Leonard to get to you. I'm betting that he's memorized your routine and that he even knows what routes you take when you deliver these dinners. You're making it easy for him. I want to make it hard."

Macy felt a little skip of fear shoot up her spine. Last night and this morning she'd been so focused on Cade that she hadn't given much thought to the billionaire bank robber who evidently wanted to put a period to her existence.

"I can do the marketing and deliver the meals by myself," Alan said. "We probably should consider letting me take over some of that permanently now that we're picking up more clients. You're going to have to spend more time meal-planning and cooking."

Macy deliberated while she polished off her donut. "I won't give up the marketing altogether. And I want to stay in contact with our clients."

"I agree." Alan nodded. "But you can do that once a week and let me handle the other two days."

She met his eyes. "I'll consider it." Then she turned to Cade. "What else have you decided?"

"Leonard has been keeping you under surveillance. If, as I suspect, he was the one who pushed you into the street last Friday, it's very possible that he didn't want to kill you—that day."

Macy set down the second donut she'd selected without tasting it. "He just wanted to scare me?"

"That, too. But Elton Leonard likes attention. We've known ever since he became our prime suspect in the 'Clyde' bank robberies that he doesn't do it for the money. He does it for the thrill of outsmarting the authorities. Even when he cut your brake lines, he couldn't be sure that you would die."

"So he's toying with me?" Macy asked.

"No, I think he's toying with me," Cade said. Rising, he moved to the coffeemaker, brought the pot back to the island and refilled their cups. "I've been chasing him for a while now. Do you remember the movie, *The Thomas Crown Affair?*"

"The Pierce Brosnan or the Steve McQueen version?" Alan asked.

"Either one. Thomas Crown stole that painting to prove to everyone—the museum security, the insurance agent, the police—that he could outsmart them. I think Elton Leonard fancies himself another Thomas Crown. He needs to prove to everyone that he can rob banks and get away with it. And now that he's decided to commit premeditated murder, he wants the police and me to know that he can get away with that too. He's been sending me cryptic e-mails for two months. The one he sent last week said, 'When push comes to shove…' Yesterday's said, 'Buckle up.'"

"He's taunting you by giving you hints of what he's going to do," Alan said.

"Exactly. But not enough of a hint that I can do anything."

Macy's hands had grown so cold that she wrapped them around the mug to warm them.

Cade reached over and closed his hand around her wrist. "He's not going to get away with it. So far he's been one step ahead of us, but that's going to stop right now. I'm going to be with you 24/7. Leonard is a meticulous planner, so we're going to change your routine a bit and try to throw him off stride. When you don't go to the market and you don't make the delivery tonight with Alan, he'll have to improvise, and we hope he'll make a mistake. That's what we want."

Macy swallowed hard. "You're not making me feel any better."

Cade squeezed her wrist. "Whenever you do go out, I'll be with you, and Nate and another Ranger will be following you. We're going to get him."

For a moment, as she met Cade's eyes, Macy let herself believe that. After all, Cade *was* a Texas Ranger.

"Well…" Alan cleared his throat as he rose. "If you two will excuse me, I'll just get my list and do the marketing."

Macy slid off her stool. "I haven't printed it out yet."

"While you're doing that, I'll check in with Nate," Cade said.

The moment that the front door closed behind Cade, Alan joined Macy at her desk. "Tell me everything. When I got here, Ranger Hunk answered the door in his bare feet and told me you were still sleeping. You're always up at least an hour before I get here. Plus, there was no evidence the couch had been slept on. I want details."

"There aren't a lot. I just decided to have another temporary affair with Cade."

"Temporary?"

She tapped keys and the printer whirred. "Yes. I've decided that I'm a temporary kind of woman. Men find me very easy to say good-bye to. My big mistake in the past was that I've always hoped for more. This time I'm going to be satisfied with what I can have—a very enjoyable time with Cade."

Alan studied her. "You've discussed this with him?"

"No, but I'm sure we're on the same page. Once he gets Elton Leonard behind bars, we'll both go our separate ways. End of story." She handed him the printout.

Alan folded it and tucked it into the pocket of his jeans. "That's what you want?"

She beamed a smile at him. "That's exactly what I want."

Saying nothing, Alan turned and walked away. But he turned back when he reached the doorway. "Liar."

6

FOR AT LEAST the fifth time in an hour, Cade glanced up from his file on Elton Leonard to check on Macy. She was still seated at the island in her kitchen, staring at her laptop while she fiddled with a button on her sweater. She rarely sat perfectly still.

He'd moved her away from the desk because it sat in front of a window. Nothing in Leonard's file indicated that he had sniper abilities, but Cade wasn't taking any chances.

They hadn't spoken more than a few words to each other since Alan had left for the market. That had surprised Cade. He'd fully expected that once they were alone, Macy would want to lay down some new ground rules and organize their relationship. He'd spent some time thinking about a few rules himself. But when he'd reentered the house with the files Nate had brought him, he'd found her busy at her laptop, planning the "Sexy Supper," the final and grand prize in the Valentine's Day contest.

So he'd followed her example. For a while at least. There'd been a new e-mail with the usual cryptic message—Smoke gets in your eyes. He should be concentrating on figuring that out. Instead, he was sitting here like a schoolboy, staring at a woman he wanted. A woman whom, try as he might, he couldn't stop wanting. No other woman had ever affected him in quite this way. Right now, he wanted to go to her, snatch her up off that stool, and make love to her again on that counter.

Disgusted with himself, Cade shifted his gaze back to the information he'd accumulated on Elton Leonard. At least with Leonard he had a better idea of what his next step should be. If Cade didn't miss his guess, Leonard would make his final move on Macy at some point during the shooting of her last TV show. Nothing would please the man more than having his work captured on film and run on the twenty-four-hour news channels.

The problem was figuring out what kind of a move Leonard would make. And when. Even though the man was a master of disguise, it would be safer to make his play when Macy was delivering the dinner to the lucky winner. But Leonard didn't always play it safe—he'd run quite a risk cutting those brake lines yesterday. Cade had been standing no more than fifty yards from Macy's car. The problem had been that he'd been watching Macy.

Just as he was watching her now. No woman had ever affected his concentration this way. And he didn't like it. In the two months that he'd stayed away from her, he hadn't been able to stop thinking of her. He'd pictured her in his office. He'd pictured her in his car. He'd pictured the way she looked when she was lying beneath him and he was inside her.

But he'd never once imagined the way she might be at work. She worked hard. In the three hours since Alan had left, she hadn't taken a break, not even to drink one of her colas.

A whirring sound had Cade stiffening. Macy slid off the stool, grabbed papers from the printer, and moved back to the island. Not once did she shift her gaze to him. Clearly, she was having an easier time concentrating than he was.

For a moment, as annoyance streamed through him, he toyed with the idea of breaking her focus. He knew her weaknesses and he knew how to exploit them. He'd already risen and started to close the distance between them when, suddenly, she tossed the paper down, fisted her hands on her hips and began to pace.

"Problem?"

She turned and blinked. "What?"

"You were a million miles away."

"Yes."

And clearly on an entirely different wave length. Cade straddled one of the stools. "Maybe it would help to talk it through. That's what I do with Nate sometimes."

She studied him for a moment. "Promise you won't laugh."

He raised his right hand. "I swear."

"I don't have a sexy enough idea for my Sexy Supper. It was Alan's idea to run a theme of aphrodisiacs through the three shows."

Cade smiled. "Yeah. I got that. It's very effective. Watching you play with the asparagus gave me a hard-on." Of course, he had one now, and there wasn't a stalk of asparagus in sight. But the worry in her eyes had him keeping that thought to himself. "What's on the printout?"

"Everything you ever wanted to know about chocolate."

Cade pulled it toward him and skimmed it. "The Aztecs called it 'Nourishment of the Gods.' And it's thought to have cancer-preventing enzymes. And it's not strictly speaking an aphrodisiac."

Macy threw up her hands. "But you can't have a Valentine's Day Sexy Supper without chocolate. So I have to think of something sort of erotic to do with it."

"Like what?"

Macy tapped her fingers on the counter. "The best I've been able to come up with is to feed your lover bits of rich dark chocolate between sips of red wine."

He grinned at her. "I could go for that."

She frowned. "I need something better."

"Could you use chocolate syrup?"

"I suppose." Then she narrowed her gaze. "Are you thinking what I'm thinking?"

"I'm thinking dribble it on certain body parts and lick it off. I'd be happy to demonstrate if you've got some syrup."

It pleased him to no end when the color rose in her cheeks.

Then her eyes brightened. "I've got an even better idea. Chocolate tattoos."

He winced. "The kind with needles?"

"No. Fake ones. I could even provide little cut-out stencils—hearts, flowers and a page with the alphabet so you could write your initials in the hearts. Then you paint chocolate into the stencil, let it dry and lick it off. Thanks for the idea."

The smile she beamed at him had something fluttering right beneath his heart. Had she ever looked at him in quite that way before?

"The offer to demonstrate still goes."

"I'll have to give you a rain check. Right now I have to see if I can get the chocolate to the right consistency." She grabbed a bag of chocolate pieces out of a cupboard and poured them into a glass bowl. Then she filled a pan with water and set it on a burner. "You can't melt chocolate directly over heat."

When she turned the gas burner on, there was a loud whooshing noise. Heat and fire shot everywhere. Flames streaked across the surface of the stove and leapt upward to the ceiling. Fire bit greedily into the kitchen curtain over the sink, but all Cade saw was the flame licking its way up Macy's sleeve. He vaulted over the island and ripped the sweater off her.

"Where's your fire extinguisher?"

She pointed at the wall near the sink. "Right there."

The wall was empty.

"It's always right there!" she insisted.

Smoke billowed into thickening black clouds. He pulled her out of the kitchen. "C'mon!"

"My laptop!"

"I'll get it." Releasing her arm, he moved back to snatch it off the island. "Pick up the file I left on the sofa and get out to Nate's car."

Cade cast one last glance at the fire that had now spread over half the kitchen. There wasn't a doubt in his mind that Leonard had set it. *Smoke gets in your eyes.* His eyes were stinging with it when he caught up to Macy at the front door. "Stay close to me. Leonard will be out there somewhere, and I don't want any more surprises."

They were both sitting in Nate's car when the first fire engine arrived.

"MY RANCH isn't much farther," Cade said as he turned onto a narrow dusty road. "I promise you, you'll be safe there. You don't have to worry."

Macy was worried all right. But it wasn't just about her safety. So many things had happened in the past few hours that she was still trying to absorb them all. And at the top of the list—she just couldn't get her mind around the fact that Cade was taking her to his ranch. It was located a mere twenty minutes from downtown Austin, and tomorrow she was going to be filming the Sexy Supper segment there.

She glanced at his face, then at his hands gripping the steering wheel. From the first time they'd met, she'd sensed that he was a man who was highly skilled at his job. And he was equally skilled as a lover. This was a man she'd been intimate with, yet there were so many things she was still discovering about him. First there was the ranch. He'd never mentioned it. Then there was the car they were in. It wasn't the Ranger issue SUV he'd been following her around in. It was a sleek black convertible. Sporty with an air of recklessness about it, it revealed a side to Cade that she'd never seen before.

Another discovery was that he was an absolute rock. Sitting in Nate's car, watching her kitchen burn, she'd nearly fallen apart. But Cade had been so calm, so cool. And he'd handled everything. He'd contacted Alan and he'd even talked to Danny at the TV station to arrange the change in the shooting location.

"The fire inspector isn't certain yet, but he believes some kind of odorless and colorless accelerant was used."

Macy nodded. The inspector had spoken with her briefly. The good news was the fire had been contained in the kitchen. The bad news was that the damage was fairly extensive and she couldn't safely move back into her house until it had been repaired.

She and Alan had prepared the clients' dinners at his apartment. Shortly after Alan had left to make deliveries, Cade had smuggled her out a rear exit of the apartment building, and his convertible had been parked in the alley. Just to make sure they weren't followed, Cade had executed some fancy evasive driving maneuvers before they left Austin.

Now they were on the way to Cade's ranch. The knots in her stomach tightened. She would be foolish to read too much into the fact that he was taking her to his home. He had to keep her safe. He was just doing his job.

"If you want to talk about it, I'm a good listener," Cade said.

Macy swallowed hard. The truth was they still hadn't discussed their relationship. "Yes, I think we should talk about it. We should set down some ground rules."

He frowned. "Ground rules? I thought we dispensed with all of that last night."

"We did—which means that we need some new ones."

He shot her a look. "Are you going to tell me that you don't want to make love again?"

"No. I do want to make love again...I mean, if you do?"

"I definitely do. So if we're in agreement, why do we need more rules?"

"I just think we should both be clear that this is a temporary arrangement. There's no reason why we can't enjoy each other, but we shouldn't expect more out of it than…that. Once Leonard is behind bars, we'll go our separate ways. No harm. No foul."

For ten charged seconds there was silence in the car. Then Cade said, "I'll agree to your rules on one condition. Once Leonard is behind bars, I reserve the right to renegotiate them. And now we should talk about Leonard."

Relief. That's what she was feeling. Not disappointment.

"First of all, I owe you an apology," Cade said. "I did a lousy job of protecting you at your house."

She glanced at him, and for the first time noticed that he looked as tired as she felt. "You did a great job. You got that sweater off me before I was burned. And you made sure that Alan and I were able to service our clients. You're not to blame for what some obsessed criminal has done."

"He's not finished." The look Cade shot her was grim. "My gut instinct tells me that he's going to make his final move on you tomorrow."

"Something to look forward to."

He took her hand and linked their fingers. "When I told your director about the fire, he immediately offered to film the segment in a kitchen at the studio. I think that may have been what Leonard wanted. That may be why he burned your kitchen. Odds are he has an inside person who works at the TV station. The way he knows the shooting schedule, who the prize winners are…he may have even gotten himself a low-profile job there, perhaps as a janitor. We figured out that's what he did at each bank he robbed. He always knew things that only an insider would know. Nate's checking out employees right now."

"Originally, Danny and I talked about filming the cooking segments at the studio, but he liked the idea of doing it in my kitchen."

"So that's why he agreed so quickly to switch the location to my place."

"Why did you want to do it at the ranch?"

"So far Leonard has been having it all his way. I wanted to throw a monkey wrench into his master scenario. If his plan was to have the last segment filmed at the studio, now he has to improvise, and he may make a mistake." Cade pulled to a stop. "Here we are. There's no way he can trace you here."

Macy had been so intent on their conversation that she hadn't noticed where they were headed. Now she simply stared at the ranch house. She wasn't sure what she'd expected, but certainly not this graceful sprawling structure of glass, stone and wood. Flowers bloomed in neat beds and spilled out of terra cotta pots. Shifting her gaze to the outbuildings, she noted what looked to be a stable and acres of fenced-in fields. The whole place shouted money.

When he opened her door, she swallowed hard. "It's lovely."

He took her arm and led her up a flagstone path. "Better than that—it's safe. Only my family and Nate know that I bought the place. There's no record of it at headquarters."

The inside of the house was even more impressive than the outside. Beyond a spacious foyer was a cavernous room with high vaulted ceilings. A huge stone fireplace dominated the far wall, and clustered around it in a U were three comfortable-looking leather sofas. Early-evening sunlight spilled through tall windows and gleamed off wide-planked, cherry-stained floors.

"My family calls this place Cade's Folly."

"Why?"

"Because they can't understand why I bought it. They know how important my job is to me, and running a ranch is a lot of work."

"Why *did* you buy it?"

He moved to one of the windows and Macy followed the direction of his gaze. She saw the stable and fields bordered by neat fences. Beyond that the land stretched for miles. After a moment, he turned back to face her. "When I was a kid, I always had this dream of running a ranch. But I also wanted to follow in my dad's footsteps and become a Texas Ranger. A year ago I was driving around—I do that sometimes when I'm thinking about a case—and I saw the For Sale sign. The owner gave me a tour. There was something about the place that pulled at me, so I bought it. I just knew that it was right. Crazy, huh?"

The fact that he looked a little embarrassed softened something inside of her. "No. I don't think it's crazy at all. Where's the rule that you can only follow one dream?"

For a moment, neither one of them spoke. Then Cade gestured toward an archway. "You'd better check out the kitchen."

When she stepped through the arch, her breath caught in her throat. There were acres of granite countertops, a set of copper pots hung from hooks, and a zero-degree refrigerator nestled snugly against a commercial eight-burner stove. Unable to stop herself, she moved forward and ran her fingers along the refrigerator door. In a moment she was going to drool over that stove. Someday, she promised herself.

"What do you think?"

When she turned to face him, nerves danced in her stomach. "You're rich. What do you have—a few oil wells on the side?"

"Actually, my great-grandfather had them. I've only had this place for a little over a year. I started with a hundred head of cattle, but I'm going to double that in the spring."

At the pride in his voice, Macy studied him more closely. "How do you juggle being a Ranger and running a ranch?"

"I hired a retired cowboy, Dix Hatcher. He hires on hands when he needs them and runs the place when I'm away. He lives in a flat over the stables and takes care of the horses."

"You have horses?"

"Three." He narrowed his eyes. "Do you ride?"

"I haven't since I was in college."

There was a moment of silence as they studied each other.

"There's a lot we don't know about each other," Cade finally said.

But Macy knew one thing for sure. Ranger Cade Dillon was way out of her league.

"Are you bothered by the fact that I have money?"

The man saw way too much. "I just never—" she made a sweeping gesture with her hand "—expected this." It occurred to her then that whatever decision she'd made in her head about a temporary relationship with Cade, there'd been a part of her heart that had held on to a hope that she and Cade would continue to explore their relationship even after Leonard was in jail.

She glanced around the kitchen. This little reality check was exactly what she needed. "My grandfather worked on an oil rig once, I think. But my male ancestors all had wanderlust. My mother believed they had gypsy blood. I'm really a descendant of a long line of waitresses." Now she was babbling. Clamping her lips shut, she reached overhead for one of the copper pots and tested its weight in her hand. "These are beautiful. I had no idea you cooked."

Cade shrugged. "I don't. My specialty is burning frozen pizza, but in a pinch, I can manage scrambled eggs and charred toast."

She was staring at him as if he'd suddenly grown a second head. She'd been nervous on the ride out, but that had obviously increased tenfold since she'd entered the house. No other woman had ever made him so unsure of what his next move should be. He'd agreed to her damn ground rules, hoping to ease some of her tension. Besides, weren't they the rules he'd always used with other women?

But Macy was different. What shocked him was there had been a moment in the car when he'd very nearly told her to shove her damn rules.

"If you don't cook, then why did you buy all these marvelous pots?"

"They came with the house. The man who sold me the place built the kitchen for his wife. He claimed she was a great cook. When she died, he couldn't bear living here anymore."

Macy ran her hand along the side of the copper pot. "He must have loved her very much."

Cade couldn't have said exactly what it was—her tone or the way she looked standing there with the early-evening sun pouring over her. But he knew in that moment that this was why he'd brought her here. He wanted Macy here in his kitchen and in his house. And not just for a few days.

The realization left him shaken. It left him aching. This was what had made him run scared from the beginning with her. This was why he hadn't contacted her for two months.

There was a part of him that wanted to tell her, but the words weren't going to get past the lump of pure fear in his throat. He wasn't ready to say them. And she wasn't ready to hear them.

So he did what he'd been wanting to do all day. He closed the distance between them, yanked her against him and claimed her mouth with his.

OH, YES. Yes, Macy thought. This is what she'd been wanting all day. They might be as different as night and day, but this need was something they had in common. One taste of him had skyrockets exploding in her head and fire shooting through her veins. She couldn't breathe. Didn't want to.

The copper pot dropped to the floor. She barely heard the clatter above the pounding of her heart. There was another noise from further away, but she couldn't make it out. Not when desperation had her rising on her toes and digging her fingers into Cade's shoulders. She had to get closer.

"Cade, you're home. On a Monday. I never expected—oh!" The excited voice trailed off.

Thankfully, the counter was at her back or Macy might have slid to the floor as Cade drew back and she focused her gaze on the tall, beautiful woman who was standing on the other side of the kitchen.

7

"MACY, meet my sister Lonnie," Cade said.

"I am *so* sorry for interrupting," Lonnie apologized.

Cade's sister didn't look sorry. She looked as delighted as a cat who'd just swallowed a canary.

"Wait a minute." Lonnie's eyes narrowed. "You're Macy Chandler—the chef everyone is talking about. Mom caught your first show on the *News at Noon* and we've been watching the segments ever since. You're wonderful."

"Thanks," Macy said.

Lonnie glanced at her brother, then back at Macy. "And you run that personal chef business, Some Like It Hot. Is that how the two of you met? Cade's an abominable cook."

"Thanks, sis." Cade's tone was dry.

"He's protecting me," Macy said.

"Really? What happened?"

"It's a long story," Cade said discouragingly.

Lonnie turned to her brother. "The reason I dropped by is that I have curtains for your guest bedroom. Why don't you go out to my car and get them while Macy fills me in." She flashed him a mile-wide smile. "In fact, you can even take them upstairs and hang them while we chat."

There was a resigned look on Cade's face as he left the room.

Lonnie climbed up on one of the stools at the counter. "Tell me everything."

That's exactly what Macy did. Then Lonnie had questions.

Fifteen minutes later, when she'd finished answering all of them, Lonnie sighed. "I really am sorry I interrupted. But I'm happy to have met you."

"Same here." Macy liked Cade's sister, and she'd learned a lot about his family. His parents had divorced when he was in high school, and after that he'd taken on the role of looking after his two younger sisters. Lonnie was three years younger than Macy and ran a small interior decorating firm, and Lissa was in her last year of college.

"He's never brought a woman here before," Lonnie said. "It's about time."

Macy felt heat rise in her cheeks.

Lonnie leaned close and pitched her voice low. "And my sister and I would know. There'd be evidence."

Macy's eyes widened. "You spy on him?"

Lonnie grinned. "Payback for all those years he spied on us. Believe me, Big Brother was always watching."

"You shouldn't get the wrong idea. The only reason he brought me here is to keep me safe."

Lonnie shook her head. "I don't think so. Cade is a straight-and-narrow, follow-the-rules kind of guy. And I'm sure there's some big rule against getting involved with a material witness. Besides, if all he wanted was to protect you, he could have stashed you in a safe house. The Texas Rangers have a number of them in Austin. You'd be assigned to a couple of his men and he'd be back at his office working. He's a bit of a worka-holic, you know."

Macy smiled. "I've noticed."

"The curtains are hung, Lonnie," Cade said as he strolled into the kitchen. "And if you're through talking about me..."

"That's my exit line." Lonnie winked at Macy, then slid from the stool and walked over to hug her brother. In the archway to the foyer, she turned back. "Have fun, you two."

Cade waited for the sound of the outer door closing before he said, "Did she fill you in on all the family secrets?"

Macy arched her brows. "I don't know. How many are there?"

"Knowing Lonnie, you've probably learned the lion's share of them. She's on her cell phone right now catching Lissa and my mother up on what she walked in on. All three of them will find an excuse to drop by now that they know you're here."

He loves them, Macy thought. She could hear it in his voice, see it in his eyes, and she felt something soften inside of her.

"On the topic of what we were doing when she walked in..." He moved toward her, took her hands and pulled her close. "I like to finish what I start."

Macy grinned at him. "I think we were about to use the counter—and not for cooking."

"Ah, yes." He brushed his lips over hers, then took them on a journey down her throat. "I need you, Macy."

It wasn't just the words, it was the intensity of his tone that sent her heart into a free fall.

He brought his mouth back to hers, and whispered against her lips. "I've been thinking of doing this ever since I left your bed this morning." Then he began that delicious journey down her neck again.

"You seemed to be totally focused on work."

"I was trying." In a smooth movement, he lifted her into his arms and with a few long strides, they were climbing the stairs. She was sure her heart stuttered.

"This is what I was thinking of doing as soon as Alan left this morning. You, on the other hand, were hunched over your laptop as if the world hung in the balance."

She fisted her hands in his hair and brought his mouth to hers. "I was thinking of this, too."

"Great minds think alike," Cade murmured as he settled her

on his bed. Sitting beside her, he pulled her T-shirt off and dropped it on the floor.

When she reached for the snap on his jeans, he captured her hands and set them back on the bed. "We always seem to be in such a hurry. Why don't we try something different?"

It already was different for her. The heat in his eyes as he inched the jeans down her legs had her insides melting and her mind starting to fog. He unfastened her bra without taking his gaze from hers. She'd never had a man strip her, look at her in quite that way—as if she were all he wanted to see. Her body trembled.

"Panties today, I see." He ran a finger along the band at the top of her thigh. "I much prefer imagining you without them."

"Then get rid of them."

"We're on the same page again." When they were off, he spread her legs and leaned down to press quick kisses along her inner thigh.

"Cade." She arched upward as heat arrowed through her.

He settled on top of her then, stilling her movements and linking her hands with his.

"You have all your clothes on," she objected.

"I'll get to them. But first I want to do this." He explored her mouth, slowly, thoroughly, until she was drowning in his flavor.

The gentle movement of his lips, the weight of his body trapping hers was an erotic torment she'd never experienced before.

"And this." His lips were so soft, a featherlike brush as he moved over her cheek, then down her throat.

"And this." He sampled the skin on the swell of each breast, then lingered over each nipple as if there was some flavor there he couldn't get enough of.

Her heart pounded, her vision blurred as he took that clever mouth and tongue on a slow, patient journey down her torso, only to linger at the tops of her thighs.

He'd released her hands, but what he was doing to her had turned her muscles to water. "Please. Cade, I want you. Now."

"You'll have me. I promise. But first I need more of you." He shifted until he could cover her mouth with his again. She was so generous, so responsive. So captivating. He felt the heat that she always ignited begin to build, but he kept it banked. More than anything, he wanted to draw out the pleasure—for her, for him. Finally, with great reluctance, he moved away from her mouth again, only to be equally enchanted with the curve of her cheek and the pulse that thudded at the base of her throat. As he absorbed the knowledge that it was beating for him, he felt the desire move through him and clamped it down.

He wanted to go slowly, to savor each taste, each flavor. Seeing her in his kitchen, watching her talk with his sister had opened a well of tenderness inside him that he'd never tapped into before. Even now, steeped in her scent and in the silken texture of her skin, he needed to cherish her. What he hadn't expected was to drown in a whole new world of sensations, and to have his own excitement build in a way it never had before.

As his mouth once more roamed lower over her thudding heart and the damp, trembling skin on her stomach, he felt his own blood begin to pound and his own need escalate.

"Cade, now. Please."

The desperation in her voice was nearly his undoing, but he fought for control. Spreading her legs apart, he began to sample the one flavor that he hadn't yet indulged in. Using teeth and tongue, he drove her higher and higher, absorbing each separate sensation—the catch of her breath, the tightening of her muscles, the helpless arch of her body. Finally, there was the hoarse cry of his name as she reached the peak.

A feeling of power shot through him, along with a need to give her even more. Rising, he watched her as he rid himself of clothes and put on a condom. Then he covered her body with his and framed her face with his hands. "Macy, look at me."

She opened her eyes.

"I'm going to take you again."

"Yes. Now." She wrapped her arms and legs around him.

With his blood pounding in his ears and burning through his veins, he kept the rhythm slow and easy—until his control finally slipped and he surrendered everything.

"MORE wine?"

Macy shook her head. The moonlight picnic on the living-room floor had been her idea. She'd taken one look at the frozen pizza he'd managed to overcook and announced that it needed a good bottle of wine and some ambience. He'd provided a nice merlot, and she'd lit candles in the fireplace and spread a cloth on the floor in front of the hearth.

Now Macy sat there wearing one of his shirts and nothing else. That was ambience enough for him. Cade studied her in the moonlight. He couldn't seem to get enough of her. He wondered if it would always be that way. Setting his wine-glass down, he said, "I have a favor to ask."

There was just a touch of wickedness in her eyes. "If what you want is another chocolate tattoo, I'd be happy to oblige. The recipe isn't quite right yet. I really need to test it again."

"It worked for me."

Her eyes narrowed. "The rule was to wait until I licked the tattoo completely off. You broke it."

Unrepentant, Cade chuckled. "I got distracted." And he certainly had. "I think it was a placement problem." She'd brushed it onto his stomach, then straddled him and started fanning it to help it harden. But the chocolate wasn't the only thing that had hardened. Somehow in the process of brushing the tattoo onto him she managed to trap his erection in very nearly the right place. How he'd managed to wait until she'd licked off half the chocolate, he didn't know. But one torturous moment longer and he might not have gotten the condom on.

Macy pointed a finger at him. "This time we stick to the rules."

He took her hand and pressed a kiss into her palm. "Deal. But another chocolate tattoo isn't the favor I had in mind. Will you go horseback-riding with me tomorrow morning?"

He watched the play of emotions on her face—surprise, pleasure and finally wariness. The last had his temper flaring.

"Why?" she asked.

He could read her like an open book. She was reminding herself of her ground rules and pulling back. He wasn't going to let that happen. He reached for her hand and raised it to his lips. "Please come with me. I'd like to show you the ranch."

More than that, he wanted to see the ranch with her at his side. The realization sent fear sprinting through him again. He was almost getting used to the sensation.

"Okay. Sure." She reached for their plates and wine glasses as she rose. "It'll be fun. I haven't been riding in years."

Patience was a virtue he'd had to hone as a Ranger. And all he needed was a little more of it, he told himself as he followed her to the kitchen. How could he fault her for wanting to keep a little distance when he was still hesitating to tell her how he felt?

She poured chocolate bits into a bowl and placed it over a pan of simmering water. He'd let her draw away for now. She was under enough pressure, what with her final TV show to film and a crazy man trying to kill her. For the time being he'd let her believe that he was still playing by her ground rules.

MACY WAS careful to keep her back to Cade as she stirred chocolate and adjusted the heat. She heard the rattle of silverware as he placed it in the dishwasher. The silence was companionable. Almost.

He'd asked her to go riding with him. Surprise and pleasure had been her first reaction. But it wouldn't do to read too much into it. He simply wanted her to see the ranch. But why? The question was dancing at the back of her mind, but she couldn't afford to let herself explore the possible answers. She was not going to waste a moment of the time she had with Cade wishing for something she couldn't have.

"There. It's ready." She poured melted chocolate into a small bowl, then nearly jumped when she turned to find Cade standing right behind her.

"This time it's my turn to be the tattoo artist," he said.

"Okay." She barely kept her hand from trembling as she handed over the chocolate.

"I get to choose the body part and the position, right?" He snagged her wrist and drew her with him toward the sofas.

"Yes. But you have to stick to the rules."

He glanced at her as he set the chocolate and the stencil on an end table. "I will unless you change your mind and tell me to break them."

"I won't."

"We'll see."

When she started to unbutton her shirt, he stilled her hands. "You can leave that on for now." Gripping her by the waist, he turned her so that she was facing the arm of one of the sofas. He slipped his hands under her shirt and pushed it up. Then with one hand on her back and the other pressed against her stomach, he lowered her until the upper part of her body was resting against the leather seat of the sofa and her derriere was raised up over the arm.

Perhaps it was the fact that she couldn't see him, or the fact that her feet were dangling several inches above the floor, leaving her feeling exposed and vulnerable, but her blood had already started to pound, and she could feel herself beginning to thaw.

He ran a hand over her right buttock and positioned the stencil low near the top of her thigh. "Perfect." By the time he'd finished brushing the chocolate on, the heat battering her system was brutal. Then he drew her thighs apart, and began to blow on the chocolate.

She tried to raise herself up, but her arms were so weak. "Cade, please."

"Please what?"

This time she felt his breath right at her core. The blast of pleasure that shot through her was so intense she was sure it must have liquefied the chocolate tattoo. His tongue pierced her then, and the instant contraction of her inner muscles told her that her climax was close.

Then suddenly, he withdrew. "I forgot about the rules for a minute. I'm supposed to remove the whole tattoo first, right?"

"Forget the rules."

As if that was all that he was waiting for, Cade rose. She heard him zip down his jeans and the tearing of the wrapper on the condom. Then he was stretching her and filling her at last.

And she was so hot, so tight, so ready for him that Cade very nearly came on that first thrust. She was close too. He could tell by the way she pulsed around him. He gripped her hips to hold her perfectly still, intending to keep them both right there teetering on the brink.

"Now, Cade—right now."

His body betrayed him, moving of its own accord, thrusting in and pulling out. Each time he seemed to thrust deeper; each time she gripped him more tightly, making it harder for him to withdraw. Even when he did, he knew that he was leaving parts of himself behind.

The moment that he felt the first ripple of her climax, his own slammed into him with a force that made his vision gray. All he could do was to cry out her name as he thrust into her one last time and shattered.

8

CADE READ the new e-mail message for the third time: Now you see her…

Now you don't. The rage and frustration he was feeling was exactly what Leonard wanted, so he willed the emotions away. A cool head was essential if he was going to protect Macy. Checking, Cade saw the message had been sent at 8:00 a.m.; he and Macy had been out riding.

Just as they'd gotten back, Nate had arrived with Alan, and Cade had escaped to his office to go over the report Nate had brought. His hunch that Leonard might be working at the TV station hadn't panned out. All current employees had been there for at least ten months. The other possibility was that Leonard had an informant—someone on the inside who was feeding him information.

And that someone would be working as part of the crew today. Cade was betting on it.

"Earth to Cade Dillon."

Cade swiveled his chair around to see Nate standing in the doorway.

"I brought you coffee and company," Nate said as he entered the room.

"I thought you were on kitchen duty." After taking the mug, Cade stretched out his legs.

"It's getting crowded. First Dix arrived. I didn't think that old geezer ever left the stables."

Cade smiled. "He took a shine to Macy. He says she has a 'fine seat' on a horse."

"I see. Your mom and your sisters arrived about fifteen minutes ago, and they've taken a shine to her also."

"Shit." Cade took a long swallow of coffee, then started to rise.

Nate waved him back in the chair. "Everything's fine. Macy invited everyone to sit at the counter and play audience while she and Alan worked. She said it would be like a dress rehearsal. I made my escape when they all started to paint chocolate tattoos on each other. Cal's on guard duty outside the kitchen door, and the TV crew isn't due for another twenty minutes."

Pausing, Nate sipped coffee while he studied Cade. "She's slipping into your life and becoming part of your family."

Cade narrowed his eyes. "If you're going to say 'I told you so…'"

Grinning, Nate held up his free hand in a gesture of surrender. "I value my front teeth too much. Have you told her yet?"

"What? That I'm falling in love with her?"

Nate's grin widened. "You took the fall two months ago. But have you told her?"

"No." Cade scowled. "I agreed to her damn ground rules. We're having a temporary affair until we put Leonard behind bars. And if you could stop grinning like a loon, that's what we should be focusing on." He shifted his gaze back to the computer screen. "I just got a new e-mail message. 'Now you see her…'"

Nate thought for a minute, then shrugged. "You already know that he's going to make his move today."

"Yeah." Cade rose and moved to the window. "He won't make it here at the ranch. We made sure he had no way to know about this place and, therefore, no way to case it. Leonard never moves without a plan. So he'll strike at the prize-winner's house."

"You sound confident," Nate said.

"If we're right and he has someone on the inside at the TV station, he knows who the winner is and has had some time to set up an alternate plan. I'm betting that he'll try to abduct her. 'Now you see her, now you don't.' That way if something goes wrong, he can use her for insurance."

"So he'll make his play when Macy delivers the Sexy Supper, and we'll catch him," Nate said easily. "We've got a surveillance team in place. I walked the space when I sketched it for you." He pulled a paper out of his pocket and laid it on Cade's desk. "It's a small, boxy ranch house on a quiet residential street. There's a yard that runs along the back and one side with a seven-foot privacy fence."

"Gates?"

"Two." Nate pointed to two spots on the sketch. "I spoke with the director, and he plans to shoot the presentation on the front porch. It will be the same crew that's here at the ranch."

"Leonard's accomplice will be on site."

Nate nodded. "True, but there's no way that Leonard can get near Macy without our spotting him. Ditto for anyone on the crew who makes a move."

Cade stared out at the flat stretch of land between his house and the stables, picturing Nate's sketch in his mind. "I've been over and over it in my head, but there's still something that I'm missing." He turned back to Nate. "If you were Leonard and you wanted to personally eliminate Macy and get away with it, how would you do it?"

Nate picked up the sketch and studied it. "If you're right and he plans to abduct her, I'd create a diversion, cause some panic. In the confusion, I'd make my move. And I'd have a getaway car close by."

Cade joined him at the desk.

"This would be the spot for a car." Nate pointed to the street that ran behind the house. "So we should have someone there."

Cade studied the drawing. The street was the obvious spot, but one thing Cade was pretty sure of—Leonard wouldn't go for the obvious. And that wasn't the only problem. "Even with a diversion, I can't figure out how he'll get near enough to snatch her."

"You'll figure it out."

As he continued to study the sketch, Cade wished he felt as confident as Nate sounded.

She was a natural in front of the cameras. Cade stood in the archway to his kitchen, flanked by his mother on one side and his two sisters on the other. Nate and Alan stood on either side of Macy, just out of camera range. Cal stood on the other side of the island behind the lights, keeping his eyes on the crew.

Everyone had their attention totally focused on Macy. There was a natural and engaging energy about the way she talked and smiled at the camera that drew people in.

Since the cameras had started rolling, she hadn't once given any indication that her life was in danger.

"She's amazing," his mother said in a low tone.

Cade couldn't have agreed more.

Macy looked right into the camera and held up three fingers. "To grill a perfect steak, first you need to preheat the grill until it's smokin' hot. Number two, place the meat on the surface."

A cameraman moved in for a close up as she set two steaks on the grill. Steam rose and a sizzling sound filled the kitchen.

"Step number three—don't touch the steaks until it's time to turn them. Four minutes on each side for medium rare, six for medium, and eight if you like your steaks to taste like shoe leather."

Someone on the crew chuckled.

She winked into the camera. "If you're tempted to touch them, find something else to do with your hands until it's time to turn them."

The premise behind her sexy Valentine's Day Supper was to create an easy to prepare menu to make with your lover. Her suggestion that to add a little extra "heat" to the meal, the chefs might try working in nothing but their aprons had the whole crew breaking into laughter.

"I like her," his mother whispered.

"So do I."

"I invited her for dinner next Sunday."

Surprised, Cade shifted his gaze to his mother. "Did she agree to come?"

"She did." She grinned at him. "When I didn't take no for an answer. You can come too if you're free."

Sunday, Cade thought. He had to make sure that Macy was still here on Sunday. What in hell was he missing? What was Elton Leonard's master plan?

And why the e-mails?

Because Leonard wanted him on the scene? Over the last two months, it had become personal—did Leonard want to prove that he could eliminate Macy right under Cade's nose?

In front of him, Macy plated the steaks. But he no longer saw what she was doing. Instead, he was picturing the sketch that Nate had made of the prize-winner's house. Now you see her… How was he going to make Macy disappear in front of a camera crew? Even with a diversion, how would Leonard get close enough to Macy? Cade was confident that Leonard wouldn't let an accomplice handle it. The man had too big an ego. Always before he'd had the advantage of working on the inside, but he wasn't working at the TV station. So how could he…?

Suddenly, Cade had a very good idea of just how Elton Leonard was going to get to Macy. After signaling Nate to follow, he strode back to his office.

Once they were both inside, he said, "Here's how I think it's going to go down."

"SMILE into the camera, Macy."

As Macy followed Danny's direction, she once more searched for Cade beyond the lights. He'd left before they'd finished shooting at the ranch. Nate had assured her that he would be on site for the prize presentation. Cade had just gone on ahead to check everything out.

But for the life of her she couldn't spot Cade anywhere in the group that had gathered on the front lawn of the Killian residence. And she missed him. Of course, that was ridiculous. But there was no other explanation for the ache deep inside of her. It wasn't because she was afraid. In spite of the fact that Nate and Cade were both convinced that Leonard was going to make his move any minute, she was being well-guarded. Alan stood five feet to her right, and Nate was only a few feet further away to her left. Two other Rangers were mingling with the crew.

If Leonard did succeed in snatching her, Nate had put a wire on her so that she could let them know where she was. Macy was trying very hard not to think about that particular scenario.

"Ready, Mr. Killian?" Danny asked.

Please say yes, Macy prayed.

"Yes, sir," Barry Killian drawled in a deep, gravelly voice. "I'm as ready as I'll ever be."

"One minute." The makeup woman raced up the porch steps to pat Macy's nose.

Macy bit back a sigh. She wanted it over. They'd been here for half an hour already, setting up the shot. In spite of the fact that Danny had walked them through it three times, the grand-prize-winner, Barry Killian, was still a bit nervous.

Barry was a Johnny Cash wannabe. He wore all black from head to toe—jeans, shirt, cowboy boots. Even the Stetson and the sunglasses were black.

"Places," Danny called out.

"Hope I remember what to say," Barry said.

"You'll be fine." Macy shot him a glance. He even sounded like Johnny Cash. But he had a slighter frame and he wasn't as tall, not even in the cowboy boots and Stetson.

"Mr. Killian, you go back inside the house now and wait for Macy's knock," Danny said. As soon as Barry closed the door, Danny said, "Ready in five."

Macy took a deep breath.

"One…two…three…"

If Cade was right, Leonard would make his move any minute now. But she couldn't think about that.

"Four…five."

Pushing everything else out of her mind, Macy beamed her best smile at the camera. "The grand-prize-winner of our Valentine's Day contest is Barry Killian. I'm about to present him with a very Sexy Supper which he tells me he will be enjoying at midnight so that he can welcome in Valentine's Day with a very special guest. And you all can join him because this Sexy Supper is one that you can very easily assemble and prepare at home." She lifted the basket. "You don't have to be a gourmet chef to make steak and salad and open a bottle of wine. If you tune in tomorrow to *News at Noon,* I'll show you just how easy it is to prepare. The most complicated part of the menu is the chocolate tattoos." She winked into the camera. "And there's really no way to make a mistake with them."

"THEY'VE started filming." Nate's voice came in loud and clear over the small receiver in Cade's ear. "Too bad you're missing it. You wouldn't think Macy had anything on her mind other than charming her TV viewers. She's got a very cool head."

She was going to need it, Cade thought. From his position in a large tree just behind Killian's privacy fence, he couldn't see the front yard. But if Leonard succeeded in snatching

Macy, Cade was banking on the fact that the man wouldn't choose the front of the house as his exit route.

Earlier, when he'd checked out the neighboring houses, he'd found what he suspected would be Leonard's means of escape—a motorcycle that was currently parked behind the next-door neighbor's garage.

But he could be wrong. There could be some angle that he hadn't considered. In his mind, Cade reviewed the scenario that he was betting Leonard would use. If he was right, Leonard would pull her into the house away from the crew surrounding her in the front yard. He might even be inside the house now just waiting to make his move.

He hoped it wouldn't go that far. There was a very good chance that Nate and the two other Rangers who were stationed out front would get Leonard before he could fully implement his plan. But if the man did get his hands on her, Cade was banking on him making his escape through the back or the side doors which would give him easy access to the motorcycle.

"She's finished the intro," Nate said. "She's moving toward the front—"

Nate's last word was blocked by a series of loud explosions. For one endless moment, Cade thought it might be gunshots. Had Leonard shot her? Could he have been that wrong?

It took every ounce of will power he had not to jump from the tree and race into the front yard. That was exactly what Leonard would bank on. If Cade's theory was right, it would be during the mayhem that he would snatch Macy.

Nate coughed in his ear.

"Nate? What's going on?" But Cade could already see black smoke rising over the roof of the house and billowing skyward.

"Smoke bombs," Nate managed between coughs. "Went off like a...string of firecrackers."

More coughing. "Two went off on the porch. I can't... see...Macy."

Cade pushed down on the fear that threatened to erupt. Leonard was making his move right now. But he wouldn't hurt her. Cade was banking on the theory that Leonard would hedge his bets and use Macy as insurance until he was clear of the area.

As more smoke billowed skyward, Cade prayed that he was right.

9

WHEN THE string of explosions went off, someone—a woman—screamed. Macy couldn't see who it was because black smoke billowed everywhere. Tears burned her eyes. She couldn't even spot Alan or Nate.

"Cut. Stop the filming," Danny shouted.

"Macy?"

She recognized Alan's voice but when she opened her mouth to reply, all that came out was a cough. Then a hand closed around her wrist and yanked hard. She stumbled over the threshold as she was pulled into the house. Panic bubbled up as the door closed behind her.

"Are you all right?"

Macy recognized Barry Killian's drawl even before she blinked the stinging tears out of her eyes. "Yes." Relieved, she drew in a deep breath. "I'm fine."

"C'mon." Barry took her arm. "We have to get out of here."

"No, I'm sure they'll have it all under control in a minute." She didn't want to get very far away from Alan and Nate.

Barry tightened his grip on her upper arm and dragged her down a short hallway.

"Wait, you don't understand—" She broke off because suddenly she *did* understand. She had to let Cade know. "You're not going to get away with this, Mr. Leonard."

He stopped and turned to face her. Then he removed the dark sunglasses and tipped up the Stetson. What she saw in his eyes had her backing up. This time when he spoke, there was no trace of the drawl. "Oh, but I will get away with it. You think you're so smart—you and that Ranger. But I'm smarter. I will never go to jail."

His soft confident tone contrasted sharply with the fever she saw in his eyes, and a sliver of icy panic shot up her spine. She couldn't afford to give in to it. Cade was listening. He would know what to do.

He pulled her into the living room. "Once you're out of the picture, the D.A. will have to make a public apology to me in the *Austin Herald* and drop the charges."

"Cade Dillon will stop you."

He laughed, and the sound chilled her to the bone. "Ranger Dillon is no match for me. The men he assigned to protect you are stumbling around in that smoke like the Three Stooges."

They were moving fast now. Too fast. She had to think. If she could keep him talking, maybe she could rattle him.

"Why didn't you just finish me off last Friday when you shoved me into the street?"

"That would have been too easy. And I wanted Ranger Dillon on the scene. You should have seen his face when your car went out of control in that intersection. I wish I'd thought to snap a picture."

Another burst of panic shot through her. He'd been watching. The man had to be mad. She forced herself to take a deep breath. Talk. Just keep him talking. "Where's the real Barry Killian? Have you hurt him?"

"No. In here." Leonard shoved her into a small, glass-walled sunroom and took a moment to scan the yard through the floor-to-ceiling windows.

Macy let her gaze follow his. There was no sign of Cade. But she had to believe that he was out there somewhere. "Who set off the explosions for you?"

"I have a friend who works at the TV station."

So Cade had been right about that. Leonard started to move again, pulling her with him. Somehow she had to slow him down. Five feet short of a louvered glass door, she stumbled.

He pulled out a gun and poked it into her ribs. "Do that again, and I'll shoot you on the spot."

Macy swallowed hard and willed the fear away.

"Open the door."

Her hand was shaking so badly that she didn't have to fake fumbling with the latch. What if Cade was waiting at the back door? "Why are we using the side door?"

"Hurry." Leonard poked the muzzle of the gun into her ribs again.

She closed her hand over the knob and twisted it, taking as much time as she dared. The door swung open easily and they stepped onto flagstones. The yard was narrow and there was no place for Cade to hide.

The shouts from the front yard were louder now and in the distance, she heard a siren. They were headed toward a door in the tall privacy fence. *Stall.* That's what she had to do. "You can still give yourself up."

"Open the fence door."

Her palm was so damp that it nearly slid right off the handle. "If you go out this way, the neighbors could see you."

"All they'll see is Barry Killian. I'm wearing his clothes, and this Stetson is covering my face. Open the door, Macy."

Cade would be on the other side. She had to believe that. Gripping the door handle, she pulled it down slowly then pushed. The opening was narrow. They'd have to go through it in single file. Leonard tightened his grip on her arm, and for the first time, he shifted the gun away from her ribs. "Easy now. On the long shot that Ranger Dillon is waiting on the other side, convince him to back off or I'll shoot him first."

Macy fought off the fear that threatened to paralyze her and stepped through the opening. She glimpsed Cade out of the corner of her eye one instant before his fist shot out and smashed into Elton Leonard's face. The gun went off. The explosion nearly deafened her, and pain sang through her body as she hit the ground and Elton Leonard landed on top of her.

"Macy? Are you all right?"

She tried to answer but there was no breath left in her lungs.

Cade hauled Leonard off of her, snapped cuffs on his wrists, dropped him back on the ground, then knelt beside Macy. "You're all right? He didn't shoot you?"

She gulped in air. "No. I'm fine. He wanted to shoot you. Is he…?"

"He's out cold. Too bad the man has a glass jaw. I would have liked to hit him a few more times." Cade pulled her to her feet and gathered her close. "You're sure you're all right?"

She was now. Wrapping her arms around him, Macy simply held on. It was only then, when her cheek was pressed against his chest that she noticed the blood on his arm. "You're not all right. He shot you."

"It's only a scratch."

She drew back. "It's a gunshot wound. I'll go get help."

He tightened his arms around her. "It's just a graze.

"Someone should take a look at it."

He pressed her head back against his chest. "Later. Right now I need to hold you."

She needed to hold him too—it was what she'd been wanting all day. This sweetness, this warmth. "I did my best to slow him down."

He brushed a hand over her hair. "I know. You did fine."

He went on talking to her and stroking her hair and Macy wished that the moment could last forever. With a sinking heart, she realized that she'd done what she'd promised herself she wouldn't do. She'd fallen in love with Cade Dillon all over again.

They were still standing there holding each other when Nate appeared in the fence opening.

"Looks like I missed all the fun."

"Did you get his accomplice?" Cade asked.

"Sure did," Nate drawled. "It was that pretty little makeup girl. She still had quite a supply of smoke bombs and explosives in her kit. Pity. I was thinking of asking her out."

"You should be sharing a bottle of celebratory champagne with Ranger Hunk instead of talking to me on the phone," Alan said.

With her cell pressed to her ear, Macy paced back and forth in Cade's bedroom. Though she would never admit it to Alan, he was probably right. She should be feeling relieved. Happy. Elton Leonard was behind bars. And now that he was charged with home invasion, attempted kidnapping and shooting a Texas Ranger in addition to bank robbery and murder, there was no way that his team of lawyers was going to get him out on bail again.

"Let me count your blessings for you," Alan said. "Number one, 'Clyde' is behind bars. Number two, I fielded a phone call from Kate Sinclair, and she says that the number of contest entries after your first TV show went far beyond expectations, and subscriptions for the *Austin Herald* have increased a full five percent. The corporate office of DITH in Houston is very pleased. They want you to write a weekly column on cooking. Three, Director Danny says that the producers of *News at Noon* are interested in having you continue the cooking segments. Their ratings have gone up since they started featuring you. You're going to be a TV chef. I tell you, everything's coming up roses!"

"I know."

"Last but not least—Ranger Hunk took you home with him. I see that as a good sign."

Was it? That was the question that had her pacing in Cade's

room. "He's a kind and generous man, and my house won't be habitable for a couple of weeks."

"Kind my foot. He wants you in his house. It's a basic male instinct that can be traced back to our cavemen ancestors. FYI—when I told him you could stay with Martin and me, he refused the offer."

"Because we have to talk." Macy sank down on the edge of the bed. That's why her stomach was tied in knots. That's why she'd called Alan. She was avoiding the talk. She was afraid of what Cade would say. "He told me that once Leonard was behind bars, he reserved the right to renegotiate our ground rules."

"I assume you're talking about the we'll-have-a-fling-and-go-our-separate-ways ground rules?"

"Yes."

"And ditching that would be a problem because?"

"I…don't want any ground rules." As the realization struck her, every knot in her stomach tightened. "I just want him."

"Finally! She admits it. Picture me doing a happy dance."

"What if he wants out or he's happy with the status quo?"

"Here's Dr. Alan's advice. Tell the poor chump what you want and put him out of his misery. Cheerio."

Macy turned off her cell, wishing that she was half as confident as Alan was. Cade wanted her. That much she knew. She was almost positive that he wasn't going to walk away from her again. At least not yet.

Her biggest fear was that he'd want to extend their current ground rules and just continue to enjoy each other until what they were feeling faded. *Then* they'd go their separate ways. No harm. No foul. Fisting one hand, she rubbed at the little ache right under her heart. She wasn't sure that she could agree to those rules.

She thought about what she'd felt when Cade had simply been holding her earlier—that sweet and steady warmth. That feeling of belonging to someone. She'd wanted that moment to go on and on.

Once Nate had arrived on the scene, Cade had gotten back to work. They'd found the real Barry Killian tied up in the closet of his bedroom. The man had been a terrific sport about the whole thing. He'd not only agreed to testify against Elton Leonard, but he'd even agreed to finish filming the TV segment, although at a later date. Afterward, he'd taken her aside and told her that he'd invited a special lady friend over for Valentine's Day, and he had very specific plans for those chocolate tattoos.

On the ride back to the ranch, Cade had spent most of his time on his cell, tying up loose ends. When they'd arrived, he'd sent her up to shower and change, claiming that he had a few more things to see to. She'd welcomed the reprieve, but one glance at her watch told her it had come to an end. It was close to midnight.

"Macy?"

Her time was definitely up.

"Why don't you come down?"

It wasn't until she reached the top of the stairs that she heard the music. Martina McBride's "Do It Anyway." In the foyer, she caught the scent of food. Steaks? No. Cade couldn't be cooking—at least not anything edible. It had to be the lingering scent of the meal she'd prepared in front of the cameras that morning. But as she entered the kitchen, she spotted two tapers burning on the island.

Then she saw two steaks resting on a platter and a salad in a glass bowl. Cade was pouring wine into two flutes. Her heart went into a freefall even as her throat filled with tears.

CADE'S eyes narrowed as Macy stepped fully into the candlelight. He couldn't quite read her expression, but it didn't look happy. The nerves in his stomach were already stretched as tight as the strings on a fiddle.

"Champagne?" He held out a flute.

She took the glass but didn't drink. "You cooked for me. How—?"

This close she looked so pale. He'd wanted to surprise her, not send her into shock. "It's just the Sexy Supper. You said anyone could do it." No way in hell was he going to admit that he'd spent the last half hour sweating bullets as he reran all of her instructions over and over in his mind.

Now she was looking at the steaks as if she expected one of them to jump off the platter and bite her.

"Where did you get the food? We left the prize with Barry. You didn't have time to shop."

"My mother. I called her on my cell and she had everything waiting here in the refrigerator when we got back."

"But why?"

The questions were beginning to tick him off. "Why do you think?" He glanced at his watch. "In fifteen minutes it will be Valentine's Day. It occurred to me when I finally got you away from that homicidal mental case today that I'd never given you any romance. We've never even gone out on a date. So I—" His sentence trailed off abruptly when tears spilled down her cheeks.

"Damn it." He circled the counter, sat down on one of the stools and pulled her onto his lap. "What did I do wrong? You didn't mention on your show that the Sexy Supper was going to have this effect. Shouldn't there be some kind of warning label?" With his thumbs he gently rubbed away the tears.

"Sorry." She attempted a smile. "You didn't do anything wrong. No one has ever cooked for me before."

"Well, this reaction is enough to make me think twice before I do it again."

Her gurgle of laughter eased some of his tension. Not all. He tilted her chin up and studied her face. "That's not the only thing that's bothering you. What is it?"

She swallowed. "We have to talk."

He'd been hoping to postpone the talking because he was pretty sure he didn't want to hear what she was going to say. He needed time to show her that he was not going to hurt her again. Tonight was just step one of his plan.

"You said that after Leonard was in jail, you'd reserve the right to renegotiate our ground rules."

Icy panic slithered through him. "I've changed my mind."

"Oh."

He didn't think she could look any paler, but she proved him wrong.

Macy swallowed hard. "You're happy with what we agreed on?"

"Hell, no." Because he was very much afraid that she was going to turn and run, he shifted her onto the stool next to his, then rose. "I wanted to postpone this conversation until I had time to show you that things will be different this time."

"What things?"

"Everything." He grabbed her shoulders. "Everything has been different with you from the very beginning, and I didn't know how to handle it. I still don't. I tried to tell myself that we were just having extraordinary sex and it would fade."

Panic spiked inside him again when he saw more tears fill her eyes. Cade drew in a deep breath. He had to make her understand. He had to understand it himself. Dropping his hands, he took a step back. "Remember yesterday when I told you how I felt when I first saw this ranch? I knew that I had to have it because it was…just right. I knew that I had to build a life here."

She nodded, and the fact that the tears hadn't fallen yet helped to settle some of his nerves. "The same thing happened two months ago during those three days that we spent together. I didn't fully understand it then. But it scared me to death. So when Leonard bolted, I ran."

"You said you left because of your job."

"Yeah. Well, that was the truth, but not the whole truth." He gripped her shoulders again and looked into her eyes. "This is the whole truth—as much as I know of it anyway. Two months ago when I walked out on you, I couldn't face the fact that I was falling in love with you. I didn't fully realize that I had until yesterday when I saw you standing in my kitchen. Even then I was afraid to tell you. But I'm telling you now. I love you. And I don't want to get over you. I don't think I could."

She simply stared at him, and his panic spiked again.

He gave her a little shake. "To hell with ground rules. If you insist on laying some down, I'll just break them."

"What do you want?"

He drew in a breath and let it out. "I want you. Here in my home. In my life. And…shit. Now you look more thunder-struck than when you saw the steaks."

Macy pressed a hand to her heart, which was bouncing up and down like a demented basketball. "I need a moment here."

"You look like you could use CPR." He handed her a flute of champagne. "Take a sip. I'm going to shut up before I put you in a coma."

She took a drink and studied him over the rim of the glass. He looked frustrated and afraid, and suddenly she felt perfectly calm. "I guess it's my turn to talk. Maybe you should sit down."

He did, but he met her eyes steadily. "Whatever you have to say, you should know I'm not going to walk away this time."

"Me neither."

"I know that I haven't given you any reason to believe me yet. And if you try walking away—what? What did you say?"

His stunned expression made her smile, and she covered the hand still gripping her shoulder with her own. "I'm not going to walk away either. And I don't want any ground rules. I just want you. I want to explore what we can have together and build a life together. I love you, Cade Dillon."

"Thank God," Cade murmured as he leaned toward her and took her mouth with his.

Before she let herself sink totally into the kiss, she pressed a hand against his chest and drew back. "It's not going to be easy. We both have careers. Danny says the TV station is talking about giving me a regular spot on the *News at Noon*. And the *Austin Herald* has offered me a weekly column on cooking."

"Congratulations." He raised her hand to his lips and kissed it. "Easy would have been if we could have walked away from this. So we'll have to make do with complicated."

"Okay."

"Now for the important question. Do we eat the Sexy Supper before or after we make love?"

Smiling, Macy framed his face with her hands. "I've always thought that cold steak and warm champagne was an extremely sexy supper."

Cade's laughter filled the kitchen as he swept her into his arms and headed toward the stairs. "Happy Valentine's Day, Macy Chandler."

"Same to you, Ranger Dillon."

Epilogue

NUMBERS never lied. Nevertheless, Sophie Cameron took one more look at the results on the Valentine's Day promotions that she and Jarrod Tucker had helped create for DITH's newspapers in Houston, San Antonio and Austin. They'd encouraged the editors of the local "Sex in the Saddle" columns to run contests tied to Valentine's Day. The incentive had been a bonus for the editor and staff whose paper received the most entries.

Sophie had examined the numbers six ways to Sunday, and Kate Sinclair and her staff at the *Austin Herald* were clearly the winners. Not only had their contest entries beat out the other cities by a margin of three to one, but the *Austin Herald*'s circulation had increased by nearly five percent during the contest; those numbers had not only held steady in the two weeks since Valentine's Day, but they'd continued to increase. Kate had done a phenomenal job.

Sophie once more glanced down at the report that had arrived on her desk that morning. The odd feeling right beneath her heart had begun the moment she'd first read the results. She picked up her pencil and drew it through her fingers. No that wasn't strictly true. The odd feeling had started back on New Year's Eve, the moment that she'd made that stupid bet with Jarrod.

It had been her idea to wager the course of their future relationship on which city received the most contest entries in their Valentine's Day promotion. She'd given him Houston and she'd taken San Antonio. If he won, they'd sleep together. If she won, they'd keep their relationship strictly professional.

But they'd left Austin to chance. If the *Austin Herald* won, then they'd accept it as fate that they were meant to be together.

Sophie pressed a hand to her heart and rubbed. Hello? What had she been thinking? Then, disgusted with herself, she tossed down the pencil and swiveled her chair so that she could look out the window. Clearly, she'd been looking for an excuse to give in to her hormones—the ones that had gone into overdrive from the moment that she and Jarrod had begun to work together.

She wanted Jarrod more than she'd wanted any other man in a long time. And the proof? The damn bet. Hadn't she given him great odds?

Turning back to her desk, Sophie glanced at her watch. Four-thirty. She had to call Kate Sinclair and give her the good news. Then she had to tell Jarrod. Her heart did a little bounce.

In the nearly two months since they'd made the bet, Jarrod hadn't once referred to it. Nor had he initiated any kind of a move on her. They'd worked side by side on several projects and their behavior had been strictly professional—if you didn't count the fact that her hormones went haywire whenever he was within arm's reach.

She picked up her pencil and began to tap it on her desk. He had to have known that the report would be in today, but he hadn't dropped in or called to find out the results. Could he have forgotten the bet?

No. The man she knew hadn't forgotten. A better explanation was he was just confident he'd won the bet. After all, he was the one who'd insisted that fate had brought them together. And fate or not, maybe it was time that she stopped struggling against something that she wanted so much.

Sophie drew in a deep breath and reached for her phone. First things first. She'd call Kate Sinclair and give her the good news.

IT WAS nearly six when Sophie stormed into Jarrod's office. He was still there, but if he hadn't been, she would have tracked him down. Her chat with Kate had been very enlightening, and the fact that he was sitting there with a bottle of champagne already on ice had her temper spiking even higher.

Striding to his desk, she slapped her hands flat on the surface and glared at him. "You cheated."

"Cheated?"

"Don't play innocent. I just got off the phone with Kate Sinclair."

"Ah, so the *Austin Herald* won. That's good news. Would you like some champagne?"

She waved the offer away. "Don't play dumb. You knew they'd win all along. All Kate did was rave about the advice you'd given her. She thinks you walk on water."

Jarrod's brows shot up. "Isn't that my job—to give advice to the staff at DITH's various newspapers?"

She pointed a finger at him. "Don't play innocent with me. You called Kate Sinclair right after we made the bet and suggested that she select a personal chef to provide the prize. Next you came up with the idea of offering three prizes instead of one and spacing them so that the publicity generated by each prize winner would increase entries for that final prize. And she told me that you also made a call to an old buddy of yours at the local TV station and arranged for the chef to demonstrate her recipes on the *News at Noon*. Last but not least, Kate thinks that offering the personal chef her own weekly column in the paper was a stroke of quote, 'pure genius', unquote."

"Her column seems to be increasing circulation. What's the problem, Sophie?"

She threw up her hands. "No wonder the Austin paper won. You personally saw to it that they would."

He rose and met her eyes steadily. "Yes, I did. I told you even before we made the bet that I wanted to explore a relationship with you. I don't just want to sleep with you, Sophie. I want us to discover everything we can have together. What do you want?"

Dammit. She wanted that too. It was all she could do not to climb right over the desk to get to him. But she said nothing.

"When I want something, I go after it. And surely you'll admit that nothing I did was really cheating."

She drew in a breath and let it out. "Okay. Maybe not. But what was all that talk about fate bringing us together? We were supposed to leave the Austin paper to chance."

"There are some things that I prefer not to leave to chance. You're one of them."

Dammit. The look in his eyes was melting her bones, and her heart was no longer bouncing. It had just gone into a free fall. She watched him pour champagne into two flutes.

He offered her one. "Drink to our future with me, Sophie?"

She drew in another deep breath, reached for the flute and tapped it against his before she took a sip. Then she walked back to the door and flipped the lock. When she turned to face him, his eyes had darkened and he was once more giving her that look that she could feel right down to her toes. "Why don't we make that future start right now?"

He swallowed, then moved around the desk to meet her. "You're on."

$1.00 OFF

The bestselling Lakeshore Chronicles continue with *Snowfall at Willow Lake*, a story of what comes after a woman survives an unspeakable horror and finds her way home, to healing and redemption and a new chance at happiness.

SUSAN WIGGS

NEW YORK TIMES BESTSELLING AUTHOR

SUSAN WIGGS

"Susan Wiggs's novels are beautiful, tender and wise."
—Luanne Rice

Snowfall at Willow Lake
The Lakeshore Chronicles

On sale February 2008!

SAVE $1.00 off the purchase price of SNOWFALL AT WILLOW LAKE by Susan Wiggs.

Offer valid from February 1, 2008, to April 30, 2008.
Redeemable at participating retail outlets. Limit one coupon per purchase.

5 2 6 0 8 1 6 8

5 65373 00076 2   (8100) 0 11463

® and TM are trademarks owned and used by the trademark owner and/or its licensee.
© 2008 Harlequin Enterprises Limited

MSW2493CPN

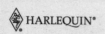

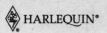

HARLEQUIN *Super Romance*®

Bundles of Joy—
coming next month to Superromance

Experience the romance, excitement and joy with 6 heartwarming titles.

BABY, I'M YOURS #1476 by *Carrie Weaver*

ANOTHER MAN'S BABY
(The Tulanes of Tennessee)
#1477 by *Kay Stockham*

THE MARINE'S BABY (9 Months Later)
#1478 by *Rogenna Brewer*

BE MY BABIES (Twins)
#1479 by *Kathryn Shay*

THE DIAPER DIARIES (Suddenly a Parent)
#1480 by *Abby Gaines*

HAVING JUSTIN'S BABY (A Little Secret)
#1481 by *Pamela Bauer*

Exciting, Emotional and Unexpected!

Look for these Superromance titles in March 2008.
Available wherever books are sold.

nocturne™

Dark, sensual and fierce.
Welcome to the world of the
Bloodrunners, a band of hunters
and protectors, half human,
half Lycan. Caught between two
worlds—yet belonging to neither.

Look for the new miniseries by

RHYANNON
BYRD

LAST WOLF STANDING
(March 2008)

LAST WOLF HUNTING
(April 2008)

LAST WOLF WATCHING
(May 2008)

Available wherever books are sold.

HARLEQUIN®

Blaze™

COMING NEXT MONTH

#381 GETTING LUCKY Joanne Rock
Blush
Sports agent Dex Brantley used to be the luckiest man alive. But since rumors of a family curse floated to the surface, he's been on a losing streak. To reverse that, he hooks up again with sexy psychic Lara Wyland. Before long he's lucky in a whole new way!

#382 SHAKEN AND STIRRED Kathleen O'Reilly
Those Sexy O'Sullivans, Bk. 1
When Gabe O'Sullivan describes his friend Tessa Hart as a work in progress, it gets Tessa to thinking. She's carried a torch for Gabe forever, but maybe now's the time to light the first spark and show him who's really ready to take their sexy flirting to the next level!

#383 OFF LIMITS Jordan Summers
Love happens when you least expect it. Especially on an airplane between Delaney Carter, an undercover ATF agent, and Jack Gordon, a former arms dealer. With their lives on the line, can they find a way to trust each other… once they're out of bed?

#384 BEYOND HIS CONTROL Stephanie Tyler
A reunion rescue mission turns life-threatening just as navy SEAL Justin Brandt realizes he's saving former high school flame Ava Turkowski. Talk about a blast from the past…

#385 WHAT HAPPENED IN VEGAS… Wendy Etherington
For Jacinda Barrett, leaving Las Vegas meant leaving behind her exotic dancer self. Now she's respectable…in every way. Then Gideon Nash—her weekend-she'll-never-forget hottie—shows up. Suddenly she's got the urge to lose the clothes…and the respectability!

#386 COMING SOON Jo Leigh
Do Not Disturb
Concierge Mia Traverse discovers a body in the romantic Hush hotel, which is booked for a movie shoot. Detective Bax Milligan is assigned to investigate and keep Mia under wraps. Hiding out with her in a sexy suite is perfect—except for *who* and *what* is coming next….